SUNDAY OR THE HIGHWAY

OTHER TITLES BY CINDY FAZZI

Domingo the Bounty Hunter series

Danger No Problem

Sunday or the Highway

Stand-Alone

My MacArthur

SUNDAY OR THE HIGHWAY

A NOVEL

DOMINGO THE BOUNTY HUNTER

CINDY FAZZI

THOMAS & MERCER

This is a work of fiction. Names, characters, organizations, places, events, and incidents are either products of the author's imagination or are used fictitiously. Otherwise, any resemblance to actual persons, living or dead, is purely coincidental.

Published by Thomas & Mercer, Seattle

www.apub.com

EU product safety contact:
Amazon Media EU S. à r.l.
38, avenue John F. Kennedy, L-1855 Luxembourg
amazonpublishing-gpsr@amazon.com

ISBN-13: 9781662528545 (paperback)
ISBN-13: 9781662528552 (digital)

Cover design by Ploy Siripant
Cover image: © pigface / Shutterstock; © mdesigner125 / Getty

Printed in the United States of America

I dedicate this book to my editor, Chantelle Aimée Osman, who once described her role as that of a "translator" between the author and the reader. American literature is more robust today because of editors like her who amplify the voices of authors of all colors and perspectives.

CHAPTER 1

What It Means to Be an Alien in America

Tell me what comes to your mind when you hear the word alien*? For me, it's the monster that burst out of Sigourney Weaver's body in the movie* Alien*. Under the US immigration law, however, any noncitizen in the country is an alien—tourists, foreigners traveling for business, foreigners with student visas, foreigners with worker visas, foreigners traveling for medical treatment, foreigners with religious-worker visas, foreigners participating in cultural-exchange programs, undocumented immigrants, asylum seekers, and migrants.*

If you're reading this, most likely you fall under one of those categories. While most Americans and Sigourney Weaver and Alien*-franchise fans won't call you* alien *to your face, Uncle Sam will. The term is stuck in the Immigration and Nationality Act, and for as long as it's in the law, that's what you are!*

You know what that means? You can't be here after your visa expires. And if you don't have a visa to begin with, you shouldn't be here at all. You are as welcome in America as Sigourney's ET nemesis.

If you managed to evade the authorities and you're still here, here's my advice: Consider yourself lucky. The fact that you're in this country without authorization is a technicality. It's the equivalent of a venial sin for Catholics. You're not scot-free, so don't do any dumb shit to make things worse. The moment you cross the line from technicality to criminality, you can bet your sorry ass I won't be giving you any more advice. The bigger the shit you dump, the more likely your case will end up with me.

I'm a bail enforcement agent and a naturalized US citizen. I hunt down vicious undocumented immigrants no land will ever claim. I catch bad-to-the-bone alien fugitives—drug dealers, gun smugglers, thieves, money launderers, human traffickers, and murderers. My mission in life is to help keep the word immigrant *HONORABLE. I'm the best in the business, which means I get the worst cases that have eluded the US Immigration and Customs Enforcement—ICE.*

If you're one of those cases, I will make you regret the day you came to America. If you're a scumbag giving all of us decent immigrants a bad name, I'm going to kick your ass all the way to the hellhole where you came from. I promise you I'll be able to sniff you from a mile away and spot you at first sight. There's no hiding place I haven't uncovered. Consider yourself forewarned, asshole.

◆ ◆ ◆

Domingo read what he'd written in his small notepad. *Not bad.*

"Are you really writing a book?" asked Cheryl Mott, a PI and friend. They sat drinking Perrier at a table on the Bellagio's vast patio. They were waiting for Cheryl's client, Tessa Woodridge, heiress of the Giant Burgers fast-food empire.

The remains of a summer evening had turned from blood orange to deep purple. It could have been Christmas, the way the courtyard glowed with string lights.

Cheryl had gotten Domingo this gig and had flown him to Las Vegas from New York courtesy of her client Tessa. Cheryl had been instrumental in locating the love of Tessa's life, a Mexican migrant named Julian Alondra, who'd once saved her life in the Arizona desert when she was a kid. Uncle Sam had rewarded Julian, the Good Samaritan, by arresting him for crossing into the United States illegally and then deporting him.

Tessa had finally been reunited with Julian like she'd always wanted, but it had taken nineteen years. That was six months ago, and they'd been dating since.

Domingo stuck his pen and notepad in his blazer pocket. "I don't know that I'm writing a book, but yeah, I like to write whenever I can." He took a sip of his sparkling water. "Tell me what to expect from this meeting with Tessa. I mean, this free trip is like a vacation compared to what I normally do, but she could have just talked to me on the phone."

"To be honest, I don't know much." Cheryl shrugged. She was thirty-seven, five years younger than Domingo, but no less competent in her job. Cheryl's clients were mostly white, like her. She handled insurance work, corporate background checks, and people trying to catch a cheating spouse or hoping to rekindle an old flame. "All I know is that she needs to find a couple of undocumented immigrants, and she needs it to happen pronto. I won't recommend anyone but you."

Domingo gave her a smile of gratitude.

"Sunday, I'm so proud of how you brought Amaury Penn down and single-handedly shut down *The Bull Penn*. You did the world a big favor by shutting up the loudest mouthpiece for anti-immigrant, right-wing nuts in this country."

She meant the case of Monica Reed, the most elusive undocumented immigrant he'd ever chased. "It's history now." He leaned back. "Do you think Tessa's job for me has anything to do with her boyfriend?"

Cheryl had discovered that Julian Alondra had reinvented himself as Julian "Jules" Alexander, a successful civil engineer who traveled freely and legally between the US and Mexico despite his deportation in the past.

"*Everything* in Tessa's life right now is about her boyfriend." Cheryl took a gulp of her Perrier. "She's crazy in love with Julian. She's wearing blinders willingly. Get this." She leaned forward in a conspiratorial manner. "Three weeks ago, Tessa and Julian were spending the weekend in Snowbird, a mountain resort in Utah. Tessa felt like someone was following them wherever they went, but Julian didn't think so. Worse, their hotel room was ransacked, and Julian's iPad was stolen. But Julian refused to report it to the hotel manager or the cops. He told Tessa that it was no big deal since the iPad was old and it didn't contain anything important. He didn't want it back."

Domingo tapped his chin with his forefinger. "That's weird."

"Right? So when Tessa found out that Julian was attending a trade show here in the Bellagio this week, she decided to come along. She knows I live in Vegas, so she set up this meeting, with the additional instruction of bringing *you* with me."

"Okay." He folded his arms across his chest. "But did you say we have to pose as business owners? Why?"

"Because she can't meet with us otherwise. She's not staying for the entire trade show, and Julian expects her to be with him while she's here. She doesn't want to worry about sneaking out to meet with us." She picked up her phone, glanced at it, and set it aside. "Tessa is coming with Julian any minute now. She's going to introduce us as entrepreneurs trying to do business with Giant Burgers."

"Entrepreneurs? Why not connoisseurs? How about saboteurs? Does Julian know you're a PI and you've been snooping on him?"

Cheryl jabbed him in the side. "This is serious."

"Okay, okay. Give me the spiel."

"You and I are co-owners of Prime Meats. Our office is just outside the Strip. That's it."

"Is that all?" he scoffed. "Easy peasy."

Cheryl swigged her Perrier. "It took me a long time to locate Julian because he changed his name to Jules Alexander. When I finally found him, I made sure Tessa attended the opening ceremony of a trade show that Julian was attending in San Diego. When she bumped into him after the ceremony, it looked like serendipity. He didn't know it was the result of my hard work, paid for by Tessa. Bottom line—Julian doesn't know who I am or what I do."

Domingo appraised Cheryl's conservative pantsuit and no-nonsense haircut, a bob. He glanced down at his black blazer and khakis. "I guess we could pass as owners of Prime Meats. We can do this." He swept a quick look around him, noticing the Bellagio's solid, kitsch-free architecture and the people around him also clad in suits or business casual attire. Then he caught sight of a young white woman in a short black dress and sky-high stilettos.

She descended the staircase that led into the patio with utmost care, like a princess surveying her kingdom. Or a delicate bird afraid to fall. *Tessa Woodridge. A bona fide knockout.* He'd seen a picture of her on Instagram.

Tessa reached the bottom of the stairs, paused, and tugged at the hem of the dress that clung to her slim figure. She was looking over her shoulder like she was waiting for someone.

Domingo turned to Cheryl. "Our girl is here. She looks like six hundred million bucks. Isn't that what her company is worth?"

Cheryl followed his gaze and nodded. "That's according to *Forbes*. Giant Burgers is privately owned, so there's little information about it."

Tessa flashed a huge smile when a tall young man appeared at the top of the stairs. The guy was handsome—dark eyes, strong jawline, high cheekbones, a perfect tilt to his nose in profile. He was walking down the steps.

"Is that Julian?" asked Domingo. Julian looked white, though there were many light-skinned Mexicans.

"That's him," Cheryl confirmed.

"Okay, quick—tell me what I need to know about him."

"Julian's thirty-three. He's not married, and yes, I checked the Mexican civil registry. After he crossed illegally as a kid, a relative of his took pity and paid for his college education at the University of Arizona in Tucson. He's a civil engineer. Bridges, roads, infrastructure, and such. He lives in Mexico City, so he and Tessa have a long-distance relationship."

The couple held hands as they navigated the rows of tables and knots of boisterous men and women in the courtyard.

Cheryl waved at Tessa, who waved back.

"When did Tessa inherit Giant Burgers?" Domingo asked.

"Last month, on the day she turned twenty-seven. That's also when she took over as the CEO. She's not Paris Hilton, you know. She's a girlboss, a UC Berkeley grad. A no-nonsense, hardworking woman."

"Good for her."

"Members of the Woodridge family own private shares of the company, but only one person controls it. And that's Tessa Woodridge."

"Isn't that unusual?"

Cheryl shook her head. "Not really. It's meant to avoid family bickering. It's like royalty. There's a line of succession, and Tessa was next in line."

The couple stopped before them. "Hi, Cheryl," Tessa piped. A sleek silver bag hung on her shoulder. Everything about her spoke of wealth, from the alabaster skin to the simple but elegant jewelry and the sheen of her reserved demeanor. She eyed Domingo with those big green eyes—a magnet for any red-blooded male, legal or undocumented. "You must be Sunday." She squeezed her boyfriend's hand and said, "This is Julian." She pronounced it "Hoo-lee-yan," the Spanish way.

Domingo rose. "I'm Sunday. I'm Cheryl's business partner. We run Prime Meats." His full name was Domingo Laban, meaning "Sunday Fight" in Tagalog. In his professional life, he went by Sunday. Just like a stage name. No surname, like Bono or Madonna. Only fellow Filipinos called him Domingo.

Cheryl also stood up and introduced herself. They all shook hands with each other. Cheryl told Julian that Prime Meats was hoping to expand to California and do business with Giant Burgers.

"I'll let you guys talk business, but please join me and Tessa afterward on the upper-level terrace." Julian pointed at the stairs leading to the place. His dark hair was slicked back. He was clean shaven. Dark suit, but no tie. A picture of ease, the very definition of cool. "The construction expo is having a party. It's an open bar. I want you to be my guests."

Cheryl and Domingo exchanged glances before she said, "We'll be there."

Julian pecked Tessa's cheek before excusing himself. They all watched him leave.

Domingo couldn't help but notice that Julian not only looked white, but also had zero foreign accent or indeed any hint of foreignness at all. Well, some people assimilated better than others. Julian obviously had done just that after spending four years at the University of Arizona.

"I'm sorry you had to do playacting," Tessa began. She was about five-five, like Domingo, but the shoes made her taller. What he wouldn't give for a few more inches in height.

Domingo waved a dismissive hand. "No problem." He pulled out a chair for her.

They all sat down. The two women flanked Domingo, Tessa on his left.

"I couldn't postpone this meeting, and I really wanted this to be in person," said Tessa. "I need your help."

"Sunday is the best bail enforcement agent you can find," Cheryl chimed in. "He'll locate any undocumented immigrant for you."

Tessa placed her bag on her lap. "What exactly does a bail enforcement agent do?"

Here we go. "I apprehend criminals who violate their bail conditions," he answered.

"Like a bounty hunter?"

"Exactly." He hated the term, which evoked the image of a gunslinger in the Old West or a slave catcher in the antebellum South, but there was no escaping it.

"So you're like Dog the Bounty Hunter," Tessa added.

"Yes and no. I'm a bounty hunter, but I'm not an ex-con like Dog. More like Robert De Niro in *Midnight Run*." He was picky about his pop culture references, thank you.

"Oh." She narrowed her eyes. "Cheryl said you 'specialize' in undocumented immigrants." She made air quotes with her fingers. "Can you elaborate on that?"

"Sure." He sipped his water. *Bounty hunter* never made it to anybody's top-ten-most-trusted-professionals list, so most clients needed reassurance they were not being scammed. Fair enough.

"About ninety-five percent of undocumented immigrants who get arrested don't have the cash to pay bail to the court or the assets to put up as collateral," he explained. "So they go to a bail-bonds agency for an immigration bond. It's a sum of money they'll receive back as long as they show up for all of their immigration hearings. My boss charges them ten percent of the bail amount, regardless of their guilt or innocence. The fact is, some of them disappear as soon as they're bailed out. That's when I enter the picture. I have to catch them, or my boss loses his money. Here's the tricky part about immigration bonds . . ." He paused to catch his breath. "When an immigration judge orders the deportation of undocumented immigrants, my boss won't get the bond back until those people have complied with the order. And that's why I have to make sure they're *actually* deported, or I deport them myself. Either way, they'll never walk on American soil again." Boy, that was long. His cheeks had turned warm—his Filipino accent was making him self-conscious. From his mouth, *bond* came out *band*, and *fact* sounded like *fucked*!

"I see." Tessa nodded a slow affirmation. "Do you speak Spanish?"

"Yes." Spanish was a required subject of study in the Philippines, which had been a Spanish colony for over three hundred years. But Domingo never practiced the language. He'd relearned it in a hurry when he became a bail enforcement agent in America. Unfortunately, he chased a lot of Spanish-speaking bad hombres.

"That's good. You're going to need Spanish to talk to Julian's adoptive parents," continued Tessa. "They're both undocumented. I want you to find them."

"They're missing?"

"No. He's lost touch with them. He doesn't know where they are."

"Is there an arrest warrant for them?"

Tessa seemed taken aback, but she shook her head. "Not that Julian knows of. Will you help me find them?"

"Yes, but on one condition." ICE called undocumented immigrants like Julian's parents *noncrim*, meaning noncriminal. They hadn't committed any crime more serious than entering the country illegally that would merit a warrant of arrest. If they got caught, an immigration judge would likely release them on their own recognizance. This would be an easy case, but he wanted to establish the ground rules just the same.

"What is it?" she asked.

"You'll have to let me do my job my way. It's Sunday or the highway."

"Okay." Tessa extended her hand. "Let's shake on that."

He shook hands with her. "What are their names?"

"Raul and Maria Beltran—Julian didn't take their last name. His adoption was not official; they simply took care of him. Julian remembers the name of the winery they worked for. It's outside of Tucson. They're probably not there anymore, but it's a starting point. I can text or email you the information."

"Here's my number and email address." Domingo pulled out his wallet and handed Tessa his business card. "How come Julian doesn't know where they are?"

"He says it's complicated. In other words, he doesn't want to tell me. But I can see how much he loves them and misses them. I think it will be a nice surprise for him when I find them."

A nice *surprise*? The girl was so rich she would burn cash for something her boyfriend might not even want—otherwise, Julian himself could have found Raul and Maria Beltran. Domingo was willing to bet there was something else going on between Julian and his parents, but he couldn't voice his thoughts. He drank his water instead.

As though Tessa read his mind, she said, "Of course, it will be Julian's choice if he wants to see his parents. At least I can tell him where they are."

"Of course," echoed Domingo. "Julian made such a big leap from being a migrant to an engineer. How did he do it? Also, why did he change his name to Jules Alexander?"

Tessa planted an elbow on the table and propped her chin on her hand. "He changed his name so he could start over. He chose an Anglo name to blend in better at the University of Arizona. That much he's told me. But there are many things I want to find out, like the details about his deportation. Cheryl said you have contacts at ICE. Can you help me?"

"You don't need me or ICE. Just ask Julian."

Tessa's face flushed. "He doesn't like to talk about his past. There are certain things he just won't discuss." She looked away in a pointed manner, and they all fell into silence.

A warm breeze gusted across the patio, blowing her cinnamon brown hair in a cascade of wavy layers on her shoulders. There was something sad about her. If she were a song, she'd be a Taylor Swift pop ballad, a high-pitched wail about a heart's deepest desire.

According to Cheryl, Tessa lost her parents when she was eight. On Thanksgiving Day, Tessa and her parents had visited her older sister who was living in Tucson with their grandma. The following day, they had been ready to go back home to Phoenix when, on a whim, her dad had detoured to Parker Canyon for a leisurely drive. Their car crashed. Against all odds, Tessa had survived the accident that killed her parents. She was saved by Julian. The fortuitous encounter had convinced Girl Boss they were meant for each other.

"Perhaps you're wondering why I'm dating Julian—a guy I found only through a PI. And now I need a bounty hunter to find his parents too." Tessa rooted inside her bag. "Maybe you think I'm some kind of a crazy stalker." She gave up looking for whatever it was she needed and snapped the clasp of her bag closed. She trained those emerald eyes on Domingo. "Julian isn't just any guy. He's everything to me." Her eyes grew moist, but she blinked back her tears.

Domingo stole a glance at Cheryl, who kept a neutral expression.

"Did Cheryl tell you how I met Julian?" asked Tessa.

"Yeah. Your dad hit a deer and crashed. You wandered in the desert, where Julian found you."

She bit her bottom lip. "I was face to face with a coyote. Every fiber of my body urged me to run, but I stood there frozen. I was going to be eaten alive, and there was nothing I could do about it. Then a sharp whistle pierced the air—Julian came out of nowhere. He shooed the coyote away, but it stood its ground." A small gasp escaped from her. "Julian picked up a fallen tree limb and confronted the coyote. Boy versus beast. It took my breath away. And the coyote pounced on him, feral as hell, but he was fearless! He struck the animal again and again until it scrambled away." She paused, breathless, and then heaved a great big sigh. "He saved me, and in return, the sheriff's deputies arrested him. I will never forget the sight of Julian in handcuffs. I grew up with an unspeakable guilt. Do you have any idea how that feels?"

The image of a little girl crying herself to sleep every night ripened in his mind. She'd probably questioned why she but not her parents had been spared death. And the wound of injustice that had befallen a Good Samaritan like Julian must have cut her deep. Tessa had been mourning not just her dead parents, but Julian's deportation.

A sense of pity swept over Domingo. "I'll find Raul and Maria Beltran for you."

"I would love to meet them," Tessa said.

"Is there anything else we can do for you? Other than drink free chardonnay at the construction expo party, that is." Cheryl smiled in a teasing manner.

Tessa's eyes widened as though remembering something. "The man who was following us in Utah is here. I think it's the same person." Tess smacked her palm against her forehead. "I almost forgot."

"Right here in the Bellagio?" asked Cheryl.

"Yes, this morning! I told Julian about it, but he just brushed it aside." Tessa glanced at Cheryl and Domingo, pinning them both with her wide-eyed gaze. "Can you help me? Can you find out who this person is and why he's following us?"

Domingo's heart rate quickened. He turned to Cheryl, whose dark eyes shone with eagerness. She gave him a confirmation nod. Yes, they would help the heiress. Tessa was young and madly in love with a stranger who had crawled inside her head a long time ago, so deep she wouldn't want him out. Not even when everything about Julian—the deportation he wouldn't talk about, his undocumented parents whose whereabouts he didn't know, the hotel ransacking, and the mysterious tail he refused to deal with—was like a giant signpost pointing to disaster.

"Tell us everything you can remember about the guy." Domingo counted off on his fingers. "One: What does he look like? Two: Where and when did you see him? Three: Was he alone or did he have company?"

And just like that, a new case had begun. Inside him, a bolt of confidence sprang up, like it always did in the face of a new challenge and in pursuit of a new perp still unknown.

CHAPTER 2

Domingo, Cheryl, and Tessa proceeded to the upper-level terrace after their meeting. A banner proclaimed, **WELCOME AMERICAN CONSTRUCTION EXPO GUESTS!**

Julian met Tessa with a hug and a kiss on the lips. He introduced Tessa, Domingo, and Cheryl to his friends and fellow engineers: three men who were about his age and equally good looking. They were Americans; they all called him Jules. One David McCoy, communications director of the American Chamber of Commerce in Mexico City, also called him *El Genio*, or "genius."

It struck Domingo that Cheryl and he, standing beside Tessa and Julian's fashionable friends, could be mistaken for a chaperone and bodyguard, respectively. They simply didn't belong here.

The waiters bustled around with trays of wineglasses. Partygoers stood at high-top tables and sipped their drinks. A bouncy tune by Drake played in the background, but nobody was dancing.

Julian chose a big table for them. Domingo and Cheryl, with their glasses of bubbly, sat across from Julian and Tessa, listening to the guys praise Julian for a successful project that had helped a Mexican company dig a silver mine in Zacatecas using Julian's special method of "geological prospecting and mapping" for more accurate and safer tunneling. Whatever that meant.

Domingo sipped his drink as he scanned the room. He knew Cheryl was conducting situational awareness, just like he was. They'd worked well together in the past; they were attuned to each other's methods.

Behind Domingo, some gray-haired men huddled together talking business instead of socializing. To the far right, a group of unescorted women sipped their drinks. A classic scenario of safety in numbers. Nobody wanted to be seen as a wallflower.

"How did you two meet?" one of Julian's buddies asked Julian and Tessa.

The question pulled Domingo's attention back to their table.

"When I first met Tessa, she was this tall." Julian held his hand out to indicate the level of his chest. The top of his dress shirt had been unbuttoned, and his smooth chest peeked out. "I'd never seen such green eyes before. Plus, she was the smartest little girl I'd ever met. She was eight, and I was fourteen. I called her *niñita*, a term of endearment." He draped his arm around Tessa's shoulders and trained his gaze on her like a floodlight, like they were the only two people in the room. "And now, look at you . . . you're beautiful. I was completely gobsmacked to bump into you after all these years. To have you in my life today is nothing short of a miracle."

Domingo nodded, impressed. Very suave. Julian didn't mention that he'd saved Tessa's life in the desert. His unabashed admiration for Tessa silenced everyone at the table. It diverted all attention to her beauty and away from the fact that Julian had met Tessa only because he happened to be crossing to the United States illegally.

"Do you believe in fate?" Julian made eye contact with everyone at the table. He raised his glass in a toast. "I certainly do. I believe fate brought me and Tessa together, then and now."

"Hear, hear," David McCoy boomed.

They all touched wineglasses.

The way Domingo saw it, fate was like the wind that blew Julian and Tessa and all the tumbleweeds together in the desert. It happened once, and it could have ended there. But Julian must know it was now up to him, not destiny, to make sure the heiress remained in his life. Julian would be a fool not to marry Tessa. In his head, Domingo summarized Julian's life in a headline: Former Migrant Wins Dating Jackpot, Marries Heiress, and Lives Happily Ever After.

It was time to line up at the buffet. Domingo and Cheryl stayed behind to make sure nobody took their table. The aroma of grilled meats and cheesy pasta wafted through the air.

"You see anyone who looks like Jeff Bridges in *The Big Lebowski*?" Domingo asked Cheryl.

She shook her head. They went over their conversation with Tessa, including her description of the guy she thought had been following them. White male, possibly early fifties. He had long shaggy hair. About six feet tall, not fat but too flabby around the girth to be an athlete or a regular gym member.

The perp wasn't around. No middle-aged man in the room had long hair.

When Tessa, Julian, and his friends returned to their table with their plates and drinks, Domingo and Cheryl rose and lined up to get food.

"Who do you think is being followed—Julian or Tessa?" Cheryl whispered to Domingo.

"I'm guessing it's Julian." Domingo scooped up some potato salad. "Tessa only noticed a tail whenever she was with him. Also, she said it never happened *before* she dated Julian."

"True," agreed Cheryl. "I don't understand why Julian seems unconcerned. Does he not believe Tessa?"

Domingo used tongs to pick grilled tri-tip steak, crab cakes, and shrimp cocktail. "Maybe it's machismo. He probably doesn't want to appear like a coward."

"That's stupid, but I know what you mean." Cheryl spooned up three kinds of green salads, and no meat or carbs. She must be on a diet, though she didn't need it.

Back at their table, two women from Seattle had joined them. Tessa and Julian, two of his buddies, and the new women were busy chatting. It left David McCoy no choice but to stick with Domingo and Cheryl.

Domingo turned toward David. "You're with the chamber of commerce, right? You know anybody in Mexico City who needs a meat supplier?"

"I might. Is your meat organic?" asked David.

"One hundred percent USDA-certified organic." Domingo gestured *a-okay*, bringing his forefinger to his thumb to make a circle.

"We practiced sustainable farming long before it became politically correct," added Cheryl.

Nice touch with the sustainable-meat schtick, which ought to please environmentalists. Cheryl and he asked David about potential meat buyers in Mexico City, and the man talked about a government program that matched Mexican businessmen with their American counterparts.

"How long have you known Jules?" Domingo asked David.

"Two years. That's how long I've worked at the AmCham in Mexico City." David sat deeper into his chair. "Jules is a great guy, a very talented engineer."

In the periphery of Domingo's vision, he caught Julian brushing the hair from Tessa's forehead with his fingers. A sweet, intimate gesture. Girl Boss reclined her head closer to his shoulder, and he enclosed his arm around her. Tessa rested her head on the crook of Julian's neck while he whispered to her.

It was easy to assume Julian, or any man, would be interested in Tessa Woodridge's wealth. But nobody could deny the unfettered attraction the couple had for each other. Julian seemed genuinely crazy for Girl Boss. And why wouldn't he be? She was like a beautifully wrapped gift that was his for the taking.

"Jules is a great resource for us. He's like a middleman, a mediator, or whatever we need him to be." David took a slug of his wine. "He's very well connected. He saves us from trouble."

Domingo's ears perked upon hearing *well connected* and *trouble*. "Like what trouble?" he asked.

"Oh, all sorts of things."

"Like what?" he persisted.

"Well, last year . . . there was an American businessman who wanted to open a shuttle service in Dolorosa—you know, to cater to tourists who cross the border for day trips. The guy picked Dolorosa because he thought it was a quiet little town. AmCham was helping him connect with local companies. Lucky I called Jules." He threw a glance at his friend. He grinned at the sight of Julian and Tessa's physical nearness. "*El Genio* is in love."

"Tell us about Dolorosa," urged Cheryl. "What happened?"

"The gringo businessman ditched Dolorosa, thanks to Lover Boy over there." David's eyes lingered on his friend. "Jules told me that a drug cartel executed a crusading journalist who wrote about crimes in Dolorosa. After that, nobody reported anything bad about that town anymore. Not the newspapers, not the TV stations or radio stations. Dolorosa isn't a perfect little town. It's just that nobody's stupid enough to talk about it in public. From then on, we always call Jules *first* if we need information."

Domingo met Cheryl's eyes. He couldn't read her expression. So Julian was well informed. Nothing wrong with that. Good for him.

The overhead lights dimmed. Huge candles in hurricane glasses glowed atop pedestals. Halsey's sexy love song drifted through the room. In an instant, the ambience turned from business networking to a playground. Hookup time. The wallflowers laughed a little too loudly, and men milled around, flicking their eyes at them.

When Julian rose, all three of them turned toward the couple. Julian held Tessa's hand and led her to the dance floor. She looped her arms around his neck, and they slow danced.

Domingo moved his chair closer to David to make himself heard above the music, and said, "Why do you call Julian *El Genio*?"

"His prospecting and mapping technique is brilliant. It allows companies to go way, way deeper underground in boring, digging, and tunneling projects. A silver mine in Zacatecas all but gave up. They didn't think they could dig any deeper safely. Until Julian came along and showed them how to do it." David finished his wine and raised his glass to flag a waiter. "Tomorrow, I'm going to introduce him to the founder of a start-up that's developing the smallest and most powerful TBM—that's a tunnel boring machine."

A waiter came to replace David's empty glass with a full one. The Seattle ladies and Julian's buddies got up to socialize with some people at a standing table.

Domingo just nursed his wineglass. He didn't like to drink on the job. "Why would an engineer like Jules be interested in TBM technology?" he asked David.

"Like I said, Jules is a genius. He has new ideas on TBM that will make tunneling exponentially safer, faster, and deeper than what's possible today. And he knows some potential investors for the start-up."

"What's the name of the start-up?" asked Cheryl.

Domingo had just noticed that Tessa and Julian were no longer dancing. Tessa had joined the Seattle ladies at the standing table, while Julian was walking toward the stairs.

Domingo lifted his glass slightly to catch Cheryl's attention. He tilted his head toward the stairs to indicate that he would follow Julian. She nodded even as she continued chatting with David.

Domingo slinked away from the table. Where was Julian going? He was bounding down the stairs. Upon reaching the patio, he veered to the right, in the direction of one of the multiple swimming pools in the hotel.

The pool area resembled an Italian courtyard with tall topiaries and a garden. Several people were swimming and hanging out, but many poolside chairs and all the cabanas were empty. From Domingo's vantage point behind a cabana, he could see Julian plopping on a lounge chair. He seemed to be reading a text. Then he made a call.

After a few minutes, he got up. From Julian's right, a man in a polo shirt, jeans, and sneakers appeared. Long shaggy hair! This must've been the guy Tessa had seen. Given the right cardigan sweater and a glass of White Russian, this man absolutely could replace the Dude in *The Big Lebowski*.

Domingo eased out from behind the cabana and moved closer to the duo for a better look. The Dude's shaggy hair was graying on top. He was at least twenty years Julian's senior, maybe even older than Domingo. He was unlikely to be a conference buddy or he'd be schmoozing at the party. He snapped a couple of pictures of the man with his cell phone before returning to his spot behind the cabana.

So Julian knew the guy. This wasn't a random stranger asking for directions. They were talking as they inched back toward the patio.

Domingo shadowed them from behind one cypress tree and another. The two men stopped walking. They were face to face, the stranger doing most of the talking while Julian nodded.

Domingo's phone pinged. But Julian and the Dude hadn't heard it. Domingo took it out of his pants pocket. It was Cheryl, wondering where he was. He texted her quickly to apprise her.

When Domingo glanced up from his phone, Julian was loping away toward the stairs leading back to the party. The Jeff Bridges lookalike was scurrying in the opposite direction.

Shit. Should Domingo follow the stranger? Hell yeah.

He followed the guy at a brisk pace. The Dude glanced back, forcing Domingo to stop walking and pretend to check his phone for a few precious moments. Then he continued to follow, but when the guy glanced back a second time, he had to turn around and veer off from the man's sight line.

After a minute, Domingo did an about-face to resume tailing the stranger, who had just entered the poolside bar, where a crowd had promptly swallowed him. Domingo went in, looked around, but didn't see the man. He checked the restrooms. Not there. At least he'd taken pictures.

He left the bar, craving a real drink—bourbon, neat—not the half glass of lukewarm bubbly at the party. But first, it was time to rejoin Cheryl and regroup. He also needed to report to Tessa the first chance he got.

CHAPTER 3

Swimming in the Rio Grande

The proximity of Mexico to the United States means we get a lot of migrants from that country, so much so that within the circle of law enforcement pros, there's such a thing as OTM—Other Than Mexican. In effect, the eleven million undocumented immigrants in this country are categorized simply as Mexicans and non-Mexicans. Unfair, for sure.

It doesn't help that the White House amplifies the prevailing anti-Mexican sentiment. For the top dog to describe ALL Mexicans as "criminals, drug dealers, and rapists" is the height of stupidity and irresponsibility.

There's another term for undocumented Mexicans: wetback. *In Spanish, it's* espaldas mojadas—mojadas *or* mojados *for short. The term supposedly describes migrants who swim in the Rio Grande into the United States.*

Here's my beef with wetback. *It's not only mean, but also a misnomer. When I finally got a chance to see a part of the famous Rio Grande in El Paso, Texas, I couldn't help but snicker. You know why? The murky water was ankle-deep! Yes, the once mighty Rio Grande is drying up, thanks to climate change. In times of drought, any fool can stroll across the parched riverbed. Sure, there's barbed-wire fencing there, too, but migrants can climb, jump, run, or do whatever they need to do to cross into the Land of Damn Opportunity.*

◆ ◆ ◆

Domingo was sitting on a bench at the Bellagio's conservatory and botanical garden, writing on a little notepad. He checked his watch. It was time to meet with Tessa to talk about the *one* Mexican who mattered in her life. Cheryl couldn't join them because of an appointment with a new client.

He crossed the conservatory to get to the café at the Bellagio. Sunlight streamed through the glass ceiling, bouncing off the giant sculptures of seahorses and turtles made of plants and flowers. Lanterns in the shape of oversize jellyfish hung from the ceiling. The massive floral exhibit featured begonias, azaleas, lilies, and other flowers he couldn't identify.

In the café, he picked a table overlooking the garden and ordered coffee.

After snooping on Julian last night, he'd returned to the party, but he couldn't pull the heiress from Julian's company to inform her about the Jeff Bridges lookalike. Indeed, Julian and Tessa had left the party ahead of everyone at their table to go "somewhere quiet." Bottom line: It was a date night for them, and they needed to be alone. Their long-distance relationship meant they saw each other in person about twice a month, and the rest of the time via FaceTime or Zoom.

At least Domingo and Cheryl had had a chance to discuss their new case. She'd gotten more information from David McCoy about the start-up, Terra Firma, and its quest for angel investors. According to David, it was the reason Julian had come to the construction expo. Julian was bent on playing matchmaker between Terra Firma and a group of Mexican investors for a big referral fee.

Between last night and this morning, Domingo had laid the groundwork for his search for Julian's parents, making phone calls and booking a flight to Tucson. Locating people in hiding like the Beltrans, with neither immigration documentation nor a deportation order, was like looking for ghosts. Technically, they didn't exist. That made Domingo a Ghostbuster of sorts but without the advantage of a fancy proton pack, just an inherent doggedness and a keen sense of observation.

Julian and Tessa arrived before the coffee. Domingo had hoped Tessa would come alone, but he wasn't surprised. Girl Boss and Lover Boy, as David had called Julian last night, were inseparable.

Julian, Tessa, and Domingo exchanged a "Good morning."

Julian clapped Domingo's shoulder. "Did you say you own Prime Meats?"

"Well, Cheryl's the top dog. I'm a partner." He handed Julian a phony Prime Meats business card. Thank goodness for Cheryl's foresight. Last night, she'd given Domingo the card. "Cheryl has another meeting. She sends her apologies."

Julian studied the card, but before he could say anything, Domingo caught sight of the floral sculptures outside, and he blurted out, "Maybe it's just me, but it feels like I took the wrong turn and now I'm in Disneyland."

A smile crossed Tessa's face, luminous like the summer morning. "You mean the under-the-sea theme? Yes, it's begging for a little mermaid." She'd arrived wrapped up in happiness. Requited love did that. Good for her.

Julian stared at the phony business card for what seemed like eternity, but his thoughts were left unsaid because a waitress served Domingo's coffee, and they all sat down and ordered breakfast.

After the waitress left, Julian asked Domingo, *"Hablas Español?"*

He sat across the table from the couple. *"Si. He aprendido por necesidad."*

Julian, a dubious look on his face, inquired why it was necessary for a meat supplier to learn Spanish. Tessa narrowed her eyes at Domingo, perhaps a tad worried they might get busted.

He added cream and sugar to his coffee, buying a precious minute. "I learned Spanish because there are many people like you who mistake me for a Puerto Rican or Mexican, though I'm Filipino. When that happens, I simply say, *'Ahora que sabes no soy Hispano, perdona mi Español.'*"

Julian laughed. Tessa looked bewildered.

"I was just telling Julian that many people mistake me for a Hispanic even though I'm Filipino. But now that he knows I'm a fake Hispanic, he can at least forgive my butchered Spanish." Domingo owed not only his Spanish but his career to Joe Medina, an ex-cop from Manila and owner of Immigrants Bail Bonds Agency in Brooklyn. Like a good entrepreneur, Joe invested in training, whether it was Spanish or self-defense and learning how to fire a gun.

If not for Joe, Domingo would never have found his calling. He loved *Midnight Run* and *The Hunter*, but he never imagined he could be a bounty hunter, like Robert De Niro or Steve McQueen in those movies. Joe had shown him the ropes and invested in polishing up Domingo's fighting skills. "You fight like a hoodlum," Joe had teased him once. "I can see you're capable of kicking ass, but I want you to become a professional, like a soldier or a cop. You need proper training."

In Manila, Domingo learned how to fight courtesy of Mando, the only brother of Domingo's late father, whom he called *tito*, meaning "uncle." Tito Mando had trained him in his own brand of fighting style that mixed the Filipino martial art of *escrima* with boxing, wrestling, karate, kung fu, and whatever it took to kick ass. In other words, hoodlum fighting.

Julian wrapped his arm around Tessa's shoulders and looked into her face. "Sorry, babe. I'll speak English from now on."

Tessa's response was a demure smile.

Julian's body language, the way he held Tessa all the time and let his gaze linger over her, smacked of proprietorship, if not arrogance, as though he owned her. Maybe it was just machismo or a strong sense of self-assurance. And Tessa positively reveled in his presence. Maybe it was true love. None of his business. What mattered was

Domingo had succeeded in breaking the ice, and Julian didn't seem suspicious.

They chatted about the previous night's party and the sessions Julian planned to attend at the construction expo today. No mention of his scheduled meeting with Terra Firma. Not that Domingo expected him to broadcast all his plans for the day.

Their food arrived. Two plates of pancake breakfast for Domingo and Julian. For Tessa, a vegetable omelet.

"If you guys have to talk business, just don't mind me. I eat pretty fast. I'll be out of your hair soon," said Julian in between mouthfuls of pancake smothered in syrup.

Domingo chewed his food while composing his spiel mentally. He had to invent bullshit to make it seem like he was a meat supplier. "Actually, I was about to ask Tessa which companies supply beef to Giant Burgers."

"Cargill is our top supplier." Tessa was picking at her omelet. "Meat storage is very crucial for us because it prevents food contamination, and Cargill has state-of-the-art facilities."

Julian's cell phone rang. He pulled it out of his suit-jacket pocket.

"With all due respect to Cargill . . ." Domingo observed Julian from the corner of his eye. "The company's an institution, yes, but its meats department is in Kansas. Prime Meats is closer to California. We can save you millions of dollars in transportation costs. I'll email you the estimated cost savings if you like."

Julian was probably reading a text, his expression clouding over with confusion or maybe concern. After a moment, he stuck the phone back in his pocket without glancing at Domingo or Tessa. He resumed eating, twice as fast.

When the waitress returned with more coffee, Julian declined and requested the check instead. "I'm afraid I have to run. I need to make a phone call before the conference starts in twenty minutes." He guzzled his coffee.

The waitress handed the receipt to Julian. Tessa tried to wrest the check from her boyfriend, arguing that it was a business expense.

Julian set the bill aside, took Tessa's hand with both of his, and kissed it. Very sweet, very suave indeed.

"Okay, fine," she yielded, her cheeks a bright pink.

Julian gave the waitress his credit card.

While waiting for the woman to return, the couple bantered as though they'd been together for years. Tessa teased Julian about not washing Amigo, his pet Labrador when he was a boy. Apparently the dog had been cream, but it'd been so dirty it might as well have been brown.

Julian suddenly turned his gaze on Domingo. "Amigo died a heroic death. He saved me from wolves. He lived for a couple of days, and then he died. Too many bites."

"Sorry to hear that." Domingo sipped his coffee. "You said wolves? Where did this happen?"

"In Nogales."

"Nogales, Sonora? Or Nogales, Arizona?"

"Sonora, Mexico, near the Arizona border. I grew up there." Julian shook his head. "I can't have another dog. Amigo was the best."

After a moment of sadness, Julian moved on to another topic that somehow sent him and Tessa giggling, an inside joke only the two of them understood. Theirs was a sizzling chemistry common in great film couples. Leo DiCaprio and Kate Winslet. Ryan Gosling and Emma Stone. Adam Sandler and Drew Barrymore. Girl Boss and Lover Boy could give those couples a run for their box office money. The question was whether their love story would prove to be as ephemeral as a two-hour flick.

The waitress came back with Julian's credit card. He replaced it in his wallet, kissed Tessa's cheek, and rose. "Good luck," he told Domingo. "I hope you and Cheryl get Tessa's business."

Domingo thanked him.

He and Tessa watched Lover Boy squeeze through a group of people streaming into the café.

Tessa pushed away her plate of half-eaten omelet. "What did you find out last night?"

"I saw the guy who was tailing you." Domingo took out his phone and showed her the picture.

"Yes, that's him! Where did you take this picture?"

"Poolside. Where the cabanas are." He forked a piece of sausage. "Swipe right on the screen. There's another photo you need to see."

She did. Her jaw slackened. "Is this Julian . . . with the guy?"

"Yep."

She made a face and handed him the phone.

"So that's the reason why Julian isn't worried about being followed," Domingo surmised. "He knows the man. And yet, unlike his other buddies, he hasn't introduced this person to you. Also, he seemed secretive about the whole thing. He left the party to make a phone call and talk to the man." Domingo snarfed down the rest of his breakfast.

She clutched her cup with both hands, just nursing it. When the heiress sat still like this, her green eyes ablaze, she looked like a doll. She gave off an air of vulnerability that touched Domingo. Perhaps it was her delicate features, plus her youth, plus the fact that she was an orphan. Everything about her evoked his sense of protectiveness.

Julian was clearly a mysterious guy, but Domingo didn't want to judge him without all the necessary facts. He didn't want to think of him as a "perp" but as a subject. He wanted to play the devil's advocate. "Tessa, has Julian mentioned a start-up company called Terra Firma?" he asked.

She shook her head.

"David says it's the reason Julian is attending the construction expo. He wants to reach out to Terra Firma because he has some ideas for a tunnel boring machine that would make digging exponentially faster, safer, and deeper. Julian wants to connect the company with some Mexican investors."

She set down her cup. "He's never mentioned anything about it."

"Exactly." Domingo had finished his breakfast. He wiped the grease off his mouth with the napkin. "Terra Firma and the guy following you belong to the same bucket in Julian's life. These are things he doesn't want to share with you. Maybe that's all there is to it."

She knitted her eyebrows together. "I don't care about Terra Firma. I'm sure there are many companies he wants to approach and investors he wants to work with. He's a go-getter, and I like that about him. But the *Big Lebowski* doppelgänger bugs me. Who is he? Is he even attending the trade show? How come he was in Utah too?"

"If it's bothering you, then just ask Julian who the man is. But if you do, you'll have to confess that I saw him, and he's not going to believe that I saw him by accident. Or—" He raised his forefinger. "Don't ask him at all. And just accept the fact that there are things he doesn't want to share with you."

"There are *many* things he refuses to share with me." She shifted her gaze away from him, disappointment etched on her face. "In the past six months, he's visited me at home and stayed with me in my house once a month. But he's never invited me to his house, although I've asked him several times." She had a faraway look, as though she was just thinking aloud. "He always has an excuse. One time he had to replace his carpeting, so he took me to Valle de Guadalupe instead. Another time, he took me golfing in Puerto Vallarta because his house had plumbing problems. Last night, I asked him again. He didn't bother to make an excuse; he just said he had a better idea—we could go to Los Cabos instead. I don't want a tour of Mexican resorts. I want him to let me into his life! I think he's hiding something. At first, I was afraid he's married, but Cheryl already looked into it, and he's definitely not married."

Domingo didn't know what to say. He drank his coffee. He kicked the asses of criminals, never babysat clients the way Cheryl had been doing with Tessa.

In the past two decades, he'd hunted down some of the most dangerous men in America, undocumented criminals who had eluded the federal government for years. He always caught the bad guys. He nurtured his reputation as the best in the business. The Immigration and Customs Enforcement, ICE for short, even sought his help in special cases.

The thought of criminal fugitives reminded him that Mexico was notorious for kidnappings. Maybe Julian was afraid to bring home his rich girlfriend for that reason. There was also the possibility that although Julian was *unmarried*, he wasn't single. There could be another woman or women in Mexico City. Who knew?

Well, he wasn't about to broach *that* to the heiress. He cleared his throat. "I've been to Mexico City a couple of times. This is what I know—the State Department's standing travel advisory for the city is to exercise extreme caution because of its high crime rate. So if Julian doesn't want you to visit him there, it's probably for the best."

"Yeah, I guess." She folded her hands on her lap, her gaze cast down.

Julian's flair could blind any girl, especially this one. Domingo wanted to open her eyes. Short of just blurting out *Please make your life easier and find another guy to date*, he had no advice for her.

And then it hit him. The "nice surprise" of locating Julian's parents might be the key to understanding the man's past and his mysterious, complicated present. It might ultimately open Tessa's eyes. And if she still loved Julian afterward, at least it would be an informed choice.

Domingo swigged down his water. "I got your email about Raul and Maria Beltran. Is there anything else you want me to do in addition to locating them?"

"I want you to find out the details of Julian's deportation. How long was he detained? How did he get out?" She sipped her coffee. "I signed an SOW with Immigrants Bail Bonds last night. Your retainer is retroactive to yesterday. All your expenses will be reimbursed."

She meant *statement of work*, a contract defining the terms of Domingo's gig. "Thanks. The border patrol, not ICE, is likely to have the information we want. I'm going to pay a visit to a contact at the border patrol in Tucson. The winery where the Beltrans worked when they first crossed to Arizona is about thirty miles from Tucson, so I'll check it out while I'm there."

"When are you leaving?" she asked.

"As soon as we finish here. I'm on standby for a flight to Tucson."

"I brought my laptop so I can do some work today," she said. "Julian's staying here for two more days, but I'm going home to California tomorrow. Call me if you need anything," she said.

With that, they both rose and left.

Outside the café, more people had arrived for the botanical exhibition. Domingo hated crowds; he wanted to flee but couldn't, seeing Tessa's despondent expression, as though she was trying not to cry.

He peered into her face. "Are you okay?"

She shook her head. "There are so many things I want to know about Julian, but I don't want to keep asking or I'll scare him away. My connection with him has been so precarious. I always feel like I could lose him at any moment. I feel terrible about snooping on him."

There again. It was the scared orphan girl speaking, so vulnerable. He shifted on his feet. "You know, in the Philippines, we say, *Ang taong mulat, hindi nagugulat.*"

She pursed her lips. "What does it mean?"

"She who's aware never gets startled. Or hoodwinked," he translated.

"Is it a Filipino proverb?"

"Exactly." *Nope.* He just made it up. But if a fake proverb could help her, why not? "It's like the saying 'A danger foreseen is half avoided.'" He stuck his hands in his pants pockets. "Tessa, the boy who saved you in the desert was *Hoo-lee-yan Alondra.* The guy you're dating right now is *Jules Alexander*. You have every right to learn more about him, snooping and all."

"Thank you." A soft closemouthed smile crossed her face.

CHAPTER 4

One if by Land, Two if by Sea, but What About by Air?

If Paul Revere were to warn us of undocumented immigrants today, his signal would have never worked because he would have never guessed that more than half of them arrive by air—legally. They're the tourists, students, professionals attending international Rotary or Lions Club conferences, and software programmers on limited workers' visas who stay forever. US embassies throughout the world considered those visitors worthy of a visa and entry to America. There's no way to predict beforehand who's going to abuse such hospitality.

Like your rich relative who invites only other rich relatives and never invites you to his Christmas parties, Uncle Sam plays favorites. There's a group of select countries whose citizens don't even need a visa to come to America for ninety days or less. The government calls it the Visa Waiver Program (VWP). I call it Very Wrong Prejudice.

But I digress. What I'm trying to say is, this country has been consumed by the southern border for no good reason. Most undocumented immigrants didn't even cross the Mexican border. Paranoid bigots ought to obsess over airports instead of building a wall. Better yet, they ought to look at themselves and ask why they hold such hatred for their fellow human beings. Get a life!

◆ ◆ ◆

Domingo was waiting at Las Vegas airport. Naturally, his writing focused on airports. He'd been writing snippets to compile everything he knew about undocumented immigrants.

He'd started writing two years ago, while looking for Monica Reed for the third time in almost two decades. Back in 1998, Monica had traveled from the Philippines to America on a tourist visa to find her white father, a four-star air force general who had promptly hired Domingo to facilitate the deportation of his illegitimate daughter with a Filipina. Domingo had caught Monica in less than twenty-four hours, but he'd let her escape in the end.

The general's family had hired Domingo two more times to find Monica, not for deportation but for other reasons. His unresolved feelings for her had prompted him to continue writing. Maybe his book would serve as an underground self-help manual of sort for undocumented immigrants and would-be immigrants. If nothing else, his writing would serve as a warning about the serious hazards of the American dream.

He stuck his notepad and pen in his backpack. If he got lucky, he would be able to take the next flight to Tucson in about three hours if a passenger canceled or failed to show up. If not, he would have to wait much longer to fly this evening.

In the meantime, he would meet with Cheryl, whom he'd spoken with briefly this morning. He'd apprised her about his conversation with Tessa and asked her to review her research on Julian's college days in Tucson for any helpful contacts there.

He scanned his surroundings—Cheryl was bustling across the airport lobby. She wore yet another pantsuit and carried a briefcase in addition to the leather bag hanging on her shoulder. She met with clients more than Domingo would ever do, hence the business attire.

He waved at Cheryl, who nodded in acknowledgment. He removed his backpack from the bench and set it on his lap so she could sit beside him. As a bail enforcement agent, he was prepared to go anywhere at a moment's notice. *Travel light* was a way of living for him. *No attachments* was his mantra. It meant optimum efficiency. He always carried just one bag so he didn't have to check in any luggage.

She sat down. "Are you really going to Tucson today?"

"Hopefully in a few hours. Do you have anything for me?"

"Yes, a name." She was panting, her face harried. "Kevin Godfrey, Julian's college buddy. He still lives in Tucson. I'll send you his contact information." She took her phone from her pocket and was already texting.

"Give me some background on Tessa's family."

"The Woodridge family is super close knit. After the girls' parents died, the grandmother, Alicia Woodridge, raised Tessa and her sister, Alice. They call her Grammy. Alice is named after her. Alice, who's ten years older than Tessa, has a mild form of cerebral palsy. Today she and Grammy live together in Folsom while Tessa lives on her own five miles away from them. As CEO of Giant Burgers, Tessa ought to live in San Francisco, where the company's based, but she can't bear to be away from her grammy and Alice, so she works in the Sacramento office and commutes to the headquarters once a month."

He imagined Tessa's sister as an older version of her—brown hair, green eyes, and all. But what did Alice's cerebral palsy look like? His limited knowledge of the condition came from the Daniel Day-Lewis movie *My Left Foot*, about a man with cerebral palsy so serious that the only body part he could control was his left foot. "Have you met Alice or Grammy?" he asked.

"Never met them." Cheryl stacked her purse atop the briefcase on her lap. "Tessa emphasized that Alice is smart and doesn't have intellectual disability. It took Alice, however, longer to learn how to read and write even with special tutors. She speaks and walks with difficulty and has a full-time caregiver."

They were momentarily silenced by the stream of people. A little girl towed her pink roller bag noisily, followed by a couple, presumably her parents. The family lugged suitcases. A group of young men ran past the family, probably late for their flight.

Domingo glanced at Cheryl's things on her lap. Ordinary people would let their bags drop at their feet. Not the two of them. What if someone took off with their stuff? Their professions required them to always be vigilant.

Growing up in Manila had taught Domingo to never let his defenses down. He'd juggled two jobs to pay for college. He'd worked with Tito Mando as a stevedore at the pier three days a week. His uncle had considered loading and unloading sacks of rice or sugar the best kind of workout to keep Domingo's body strong.

On weekends, Domingo had sold bootlegged Betamax tapes outside Quiapo Church. He'd had to hawk the illegal merchandise at lightning speed. One moment he would be standing on a corner with a duffel bag brimming with B movies from Hong Kong and Seoul. The next moment he'd be running away from a cop demanding his cut, or he'd be chasing a swindler who'd refused to pay the full price for a tape. Bottom line: Moxie and speed were great qualities to have, but without vigilance, he would have ended up in jail for either bootlegging or brawling.

"Tessa told me Julian doesn't seem inclined to invite her to Mexico City," said Domingo. "It's possible there's another woman there, you know. I won't be surprised if Girl Boss asks you to tail Lover Boy south of the border."

"Don't give her the idea." Cheryl swatted his arm. "I can barely say *hola* and *adios* . . . you, my friend, are more suited for that gig."

"As smart as Tessa is . . . she's also perplexing. Why can't she find a boyfriend who will open up to her? Someone who doesn't live in another country. I don't understand her."

"Julian's her knight in shining armor. What's there to understand? Besides, the physical distance between them makes the relationship more exciting. They only see each other every couple of weeks, so every time they meet, they're on a honeymoon."

"Every couple of weeks?" He rolled his eyes. "So they must be on their best behaviors when they're together. They're not seeing each other's true colors." He could just imagine Girl Boss and Lover Boy entrenched in the sweet honeymoon cocoon. Did they even talk to each other? How were they supposed to really know each other? Their bodies probably did all the talking in bed. Never mind that Lover Boy could be a psycho or a narco or a cuckoo.

Cheryl nudged him with her elbow. "Tell me what you *really* think of Tessa Woodridge."

"She's naive." He sighed. "Okay, what are her weaknesses?" Most of the time, Domingo located undocumented immigrants to make sure they showed up for court hearings. He needed to research only the subjects to do his job well. But the Beltrans' case was unusual; he needed to understand not only the subjects but also the client. The more he understood Tessa, the better his investigation would be.

"Other than Julian?" asked Cheryl.

He smiled. "Other than Lover Boy, yes."

"Definitely Alice and Grammy. Tessa would do anything for them."

Knowing Tessa's weaknesses was like an expanded and deeper situational awareness. Domingo wasn't only taking note of his physical surroundings at any given time but also of anything that could potentially affect his client during his investigation. What if the Beltrans turned out to be dangerous criminals and locating them opened a Pandora's box of unwanted consequences?

The very mention of Grammy, an old lady, and Alice, a young woman with a disability, made him realize Tessa's vulnerabilities. He could think of so many ways to harm them. *Kidnapping one of them or both. Robbing them at gunpoint. Home invasion. Carjacking.* How awful. But if he could think of those things, then any scumbag could too.

Cheryl blew out a breath. "Listen, you're right about Tessa. Between the trauma of witnessing her parents die in a car accident at eight years old and being responsible for a multimillion-dollar business at twenty-seven, she's *different*. But she's also Girl Boss, who's used to getting results, even if it means hiring a PI and a bounty hunter. She *wants* him, can't you see?"

"Clear as day."

"Ladies and gentlemen," boomed a recorded announcement. "Please don't leave your luggage unattended. Any unattended luggage will be confiscated . . ."

He got up and heaved on his backpack. "I need to check if American Airlines found a seat for me on the plane."

They ambled toward the ticket counters.

"Does the Woodridge family have bodyguards?" he asked.

"No way. They're rich, but they're low key."

"Now I know why Tessa wants me to dig up Julian's past and find his parents."

"Why?"

"For security reasons."

"Care to explain it?"

"Girl Boss has no bodyguards because she's not that kind of person, so she's investing in information instead. She just wants to protect Alice, Grammy, and the Woodridge family."

Cheryl frowned. "What's that got to do with Julian?"

"Tessa wants to make sure he's trustworthy."

Cheryl gave him a mock side-eye. "You still think she's naive?"

"No. *Vulnerable* might be the better word. And we're the only ones she's got by way of security detail. We gotta look out for her."

CHAPTER 5

A long line of people snaked at the American Airlines check-in counters. Domingo was one of them, waiting patiently, his thumbs under the straps of his backpack. Cheryl had left already.

An airline employee pushing a wheelchair carrying an old woman cut the line, eliciting scowls and grunts. Airports harbored the grumpiest people on earth.

Domingo was parched. He had no bottled water since it was banned beyond the checkpoint, but at the rate this line was going, he would get dehydrated before he could find out if he was getting on a flight anytime soon.

He glanced behind him. A young guy wearing a Kappa Sigma T-shirt and jersey shorts was staring at his phone. "Bro, can you save my spot? I'm just gonna go find water or something to drink."

"Sure. Stick with water and skip the slot machines," joked the frat boy.

Indeed, only Nevada airports could claim to be gaming centers. Domingo weaved through the lines and clusters of people, and about ten feet away, he spotted someone familiar. The poor man's Jeff Bridges, with his singular *Big Lebowski* shaggy hair and sloppy clothes. Yes, it was Julian's secret friend or maybe foe or who knew what.

The guy was engaged in a somber conversation with a woman. If he was a construction expo attendee like Julian, then why was he at the airport instead of the Bellagio? All of a sudden, the guy walked away, waved goodbye to the woman without breaking his gait.

What to do? Domingo glanced at his watch. He had over two hours to be on standby. He'd lost the guy last night. Well, not this time.

He broke into a half run to keep up with the guy.

The guy glanced back. Without meaning to, Domingo caught his gaze. *Shit, shit, shit.* The guy accelerated his pace. Maybe he suspected Domingo. The eye contact was a big mistake. Domingo had been too close, so he slowed down to let the man gain a head start and relax a little.

The guy stopped, looked around, and entered the restroom. Domingo hung back. His phone rang. It was his office. It could wait. He pulled the phone out of his pocket and put it on vibrate mode.

The man emerged from the men's room. Domingo was on his heels.

When the man glanced over his shoulder, Domingo avoided eye contact this time. And yet he suddenly made a beeline for the escalator.

Damn it. The guy knew he was being stalked. At that point, Domingo had nothing to lose, so he tailed him all the way down to the baggage-claim area. Physical chase always invigorated him.

He doubted this guy was picking up a suitcase, so he must be trying to shake Domingo off, a sure sign that he was hiding something or afraid of someone. Otherwise, he could have confronted Domingo and asked him, man to man, what he wanted. At least, Domingo would have done so if the situation had been reversed.

But no, the Jeff Bridges doppelgänger was zigzagging through the crowd. He glanced back at Domingo time and again as his strides got bigger and his movement faster. What was he afraid of?

At the end of the vast hall, there were doors for airport employees only. The guy was now jogging toward one of those doors, right next to a baggage carousel teeming with people picking up their luggage. He pulled something from his jeans pocket, an ID of some kind.

Domingo's pulse raced at the thought of losing the guy again. He shouldered past several people, his backpack hitting someone, as he stumbled after the man, who swiped the ID card on the door. In one seamless movement, the door opened, and the man stepped inside.

The door slammed in Domingo's face. *No shit.* The guy was an airport employee? Now what? He backed away, looking for an alternative door that might be open.

He ought to give up this chase. He had a flight to stand by for. Perhaps the guy was just a buddy of Julian's who happened to work here. But why had he been to Utah too? More than anything, *that* compelled Domingo to pursue the man.

He was pacing up and down the hall, hoping against hope that an employee would come out from one of those secured doors. He would simply jump in.

But not a single door opened. He glanced at the carousel where he'd been, still packed with harried travelers picking up their bags. The next carousel was empty. It was a conveyor made of stainless steel, gleaming under the bright overhead lights. It was stopped at the moment—and it was connected to a gaping hole in the wall where suitcases would come out once activated.

Without another thought, he secured his backpack tighter, hopped onto the carousel, and slid on his butt like a bowling ball rolling down a lane. Instead of hitting pins, he fell into a chute that took him into a restricted area that looked like a warehouse. He got up. All around, multilevel conveyor belts were moving suitcases, bags, and boxes through x-ray machines.

He crawled and hid behind a tall pile of boxes. Employees were transporting luggage with hand trucks and dollies. *One Mississippi, two Mississippi, three Mississippi.* He couldn't duck forever. He came out of hiding and blended with the workers, scanning his surroundings for the man.

Not more than twenty feet away, the man was on his cell phone, his back toward Domingo. *Aha!* He increased his pace without running as he rehearsed in his mind what he would say. He could pretend to be a

PI screening Julian for a subcontracting job in a dam project or some shit like that. Maybe he'd get new information from this man.

The guy glanced over his shoulder, his gaze landing squarely on Domingo. He ran.

Damn it. Domingo leaped over some boxes and gave the man a chase. "I just want to talk!"

"Hey, what are you doing?" someone called out. "This is a restricted area!"

Nothing could stop him now, not when he was catching up fast. Domingo grabbed the Dude by the shoulder and jumped him. He crashed on top of the man and pinned him face down.

"Sunday, get off me," croaked the guy.

The sound of his name surprised him. "You don't know me, man. And you don't get to order me around when you're underneath." He straddled the guy's back. "What's your business with Julian?"

"Stop it!" Someone yanked Domingo's arm. "Call security!"

Two men grabbed Domingo from behind and pulled him off the stranger. A small crowd surrounded them, several people talking at once. "This is off limits—"

"Who are these guys? Anybody know these clowns?"

"Get Eileen right now!"

The Dude got up with great effort. The guy could use a weekly Zumba class to lose the flab.

"It's okay. Let him go. Everything's okay." The man flashed his ID card. "SJI Task Force. I'm allowed to be here, and he's with me."

The *what* task force? The guy was law enforcement?

The two men let go of Domingo. A woman twice his size barreled her way into the crowd. "Lou, what's going on?" Then she addressed the employees. "Everyone, back to work! The show's over."

She was clearly the boss. The men scattered back to their posts.

"Sorry, Eileen." The man called Lou pressed his hands together, fingers pointing up, like saying a prayer. "We're getting out of here. It won't happen again, I promise."

She gave Domingo an annihilating stare. “You two know each other?”

Domingo shrugged, but Lou interjected. “It’s a misunderstanding. He’s on our side.” He extended his hand to Domingo. “I’m DEA Special Agent Lou Harold with the Special Joint Interagency Task Force.”

Whaaat? His thoughts jumbled together. *Drugs. Drug trafficking. Drug cartel. Money laundering.* Was Julian involved in one of those? All of those? Could it be that Julian was law enforcement too?

Eileen continued to glare. No choice but to shake hands with Lou and introduce himself.

Lou thanked Eileen. To Domingo, he motioned toward the door. “Let’s get out of here.”

“Wait a minute—I’m not going anywhere with you. We can talk right here.” He had a million questions to ask.

But Eileen fixed her scowl at him until he was forced to move his ass out of her territory. He followed Lou out the door, hoping this trail of breadcrumbs would lead to answers about the mystery called Julian Alondra.

CHAPTER 6

Domingo was twice as thirsty after chasing Lou Harold. He wanted to sit down with the DEA agent in a coffee shop to get things squared away. What was Lou's connection with Julian? How the hell did Lou know Domingo's name?

"I could use iced coffee right now." Domingo was walking beside Lou in the airport lobby. "You wanna sit someplace where we can talk?"

"Sorry, I don't have time for coffee. I'm catching a flight back home." Lou slipped on the lanyard with his task force ID around his neck. He wore baggy dad jeans and the kind of polo shirt you'd find on a clearance rack.

"Man, I'm dying of thirst," complained Domingo.

Lou pointed at the water fountain outside the restrooms. "Problem solved."

Domingo cut away and slurped cool water from the fountain until it dribbled down his chest.

Lou gave him an amused look. They continued walking.

"Where's home?" Domingo asked.

"San Diego. I'm flying Southwest." He ticked his chin at the escalator.

Domingo let the agent lead the way. "How do you know my name? What's your business with Julian?"

"I saw you and your pal Cheryl with Tessa Woodridge yesterday. I did a quick background check on both of you. You're a bounty hunter, while Cheryl's a PI. I'm guessing the Giant Burgers heiress hired the two of you."

Lou stepped onto the ascending escalator, Domingo right behind him.

"Yes, Tessa hired us to find out if she and Julian are being followed. She thinks it happened in Snowbird, Utah, and it happened again at the Bellagio yesterday. Last night, I tailed Julian, and I saw him having a secret powwow with *you*. What's your business with Julian?"

Lou looked over his shoulder with a smile. "I could use someone like you. We could work together. Have you ever thought of working for the DEA?"

"No. I like my job. You haven't answered my question."

Lou nodded. "Let's just say that I'm just as interested as you are in Julian."

"Is Julian involved in a crime?"

"Not yet."

"What does that mean?"

"It's highly confidential."

"Then why am I here with you?"

"Frankly, I didn't expect you to be here. But now that you are . . . Well, I have a proposition for Tessa Woodridge. I want you to relay my message to her."

"It depends."

"On what?"

"On the message."

They'd reached the second floor and got off the escalator. They walked side by side, but because Lou was taller, Domingo was craning his neck to hear him better.

"Listen, Sunday. What I'm about to tell you is strictly for you and Tessa only. It's confidential, okay?"

"Okay."

"Yes, I've been following Julian. We believe he's designing a secret high-tech tunnel in the Sonoran Desert for the Malverde Cartel. I've been trying to convince him to give me information in exchange for immunity from federal prosecution. I offered him a deal in Utah last month. I offered it to him once again last night. He denied any knowledge. I'm hoping Tessa would help me out."

The Malverde Cartel was a Mexican narco organization trying to fill the void left by El Chapo's imprisonment. *Julian. That bastard.* Domingo was momentarily stumped. He had so many questions, he didn't know where to begin. Getting through the crowd streaming to and from various arrival and departure gates didn't help. It was like swimming against the tide of harassed humanity.

Domingo kept in lockstep with the DEA agent. "Did you ransack Julian and Tessa's hotel room in Utah?"

Lou only smirked.

"That was you." Domingo wagged his finger. "All you found was Julian's old iPad."

Lou laughed the way someone did when something was *not* funny. It was all the confirmation Domingo needed. "How on earth did Julian get involved with the Malverdes?" asked Domingo. "He's a civil engineer, not a drug dealer."

"Precisely. He's a very talented civil engineer who can build a cutting-edge hidden tunnel for a very important client," said Lou.

El Genio. Now Lover Boy's prospecting and mapping expertise, his interest in a start-up developing the smallest and most powerful tunnel boring machine, made sense.

When they reached the TSA checkpoint, Lou Harold cut in the precheck line and showed his ID to an agent while Domingo hung back.

"He's with me." Lou waved Domingo in.

No shit. It made him feel like a VIP. Nobody checked Domingo's backpack. They breezed through the body scanner.

"You just go into airports flashing your badge? That's your job?" teased Domingo.

"My turf is anywhere drugs can be smuggled in—airports, borders, docks, and piers." The man didn't even crack a smile. "Sunday, I want you to tell Tessa Woodridge that her boyfriend could be in big trouble unless he cooperates with me. If she loves him, she'll do everything in her power to convince him to work with me."

"She's not going to believe me, okay? I can hardly believe it myself. You haven't told me how Julian got involved with a cartel."

Lou slumped in a chair in the waiting area. He patted the empty spot beside him.

Domingo sat down with his backpack on his lap. The electronic display board showed that the San Diego flight wasn't due for another forty-eight minutes. No wonder there were only a few people at this gate.

"I'm not really after Julian but Tio," explained the agent. "I've been tracking Tio's movement for twelve months now. Julian entered the picture only seven months ago."

"Who's Tio?"

"Santiago Sepulveda de Santiago, a.k.a. Santiago Santiago, a.k.a. Tio." The agent pulled out a small plastic box of mints from his jeans pocket and offered it to Domingo, who declined.

"So Julian's uncle, then?"

Lou shoved a handful of white mints in his mouth. "Maybe. I don't know. Everyone calls him Tio. I've told you a lot already. Now it's your turn. Why did Tessa hire you?"

Domingo leaned sideways, closer to Lou. "She wants me to look for Julian's adoptive parents. They're undocumented."

"Julian's adopted? That's news to me." The agent shook his head, chewing the mints. He probably traveled so much, he used mints instead of a toothbrush for oral health care. He certainly didn't look like he owned a comb, judging by his unkempt hair.

Domingo was still trying to process all the new information about Julian. *Cartel, tunnel, and Tio.* All of them bad news for the heiress. It reminded him of *The Firm*, the movie starring Tom Cruise as a newbie attorney named Mitch McDeere, who unwittingly became a mob lawyer. In Julian's case, a young civil engineer was working for the cartel. But was Julian like Mitch McDeere, who had been tricked into working for the cartel? Or had he willingly aligned himself with the bad guys? That was the big question—without an answer at this point. He scratched his temple as his thoughts went round and round. "Why don't you go after Tio? How do you even know that Julian is part of the build-a-tunnel plan?"

"You see, Tio is a tough one," said Lou. "He owns a construction company. He's a respectable contractor and upstanding citizen with no criminal record. He never leaves Mexico or travels stateside, and I can't jump him outside of my jurisdiction. Tio and Julian have worked on projects together. I need Julian to get to Tio, who has a direct hotline to the Malverdes."

Domingo let out a tsk-tsk sound. He couldn't imagine breaking this kind of news to Girl Boss, who would shatter like a delicate teacup at the thought of her beloved Julian's dealings with a drug cartel. "Why don't you go straight to the Malverdes? How do you even know Tio has the hotline to those guys?"

"Those *guys*?" Lou perked up, agitated all of a sudden. "They're not just *guys*. They're a vicious, faceless transnational organization. We don't know who they are. Ever since El Chapo's arrest, there are more little cartel factions in Mexico than candy in a piñata. The Malverde Cartel is an incorporation of all these groups. It's a different kind of beast from old-school cartels that carry the family names of drug lords, like the Arellano Félix Organization for the Arellano brothers. We knew right away who ran the show. The Sinaloa Cartel was named after El Chapo's home state. Easy enough to identify him as the president and CEO of that organization. You know how the Malverdes got their name?"

Domingo shook his head. He chased small-time mules and dealers, not drug lords.

"Jesús Malverde is the patron saint of narco traffickers." Lou had pronounced it "Hay-sus." "Not a real saint, by the way, but more like Robin Hood—a bandit who became a legend. Drug smugglers love him." The agent leaned back in his chair.

Domingo sighed. This wasn't the type of case he dealt with, nor was the DEA his kind of feds. He'd only worked with ICE agents, and before 9/11, he'd cooperated with INS.

"How do you know Tio is linked to those—" He bit his tongue before he said *guys* again. "The cartel."

"We apprehended a drug courier with seventy pounds of heroin. Worth almost two million dollars on the street. He smuggled the drugs through a secret tunnel built by Tio. That's all I can tell you about that."

Lou pressed his lips together for emphasis. His eyes, the same color as his faded jeans, scanned their surroundings as though he was on the lookout.

They grew quiet for a while. Lou chewed more mints while Domingo watched a new wave of travelers arriving for the next flight on Southwest. Boarding would probably start soon, and he had to check his own flight.

Lou scooted closer to him. "How about just get me a meeting with Tessa?" The agent was so near he blew a heavy, minty breath on Domingo's face. "Just thirty minutes of her time, wherever she wants—in Folsom or Sacramento or San Francisco. I understand you don't want to get involved. Just get me face time with her."

Domingo let out another exasperated sigh. "What's in it for me? You said we could work together. How?"

"Quid pro quo. Fair enough." Lou nodded. "If and when you need me and my resources, hit me up. How about that?"

"A rain check."

"In your line of work, you're bound to need me at some point." The agent was looking around again. Typical of the law enforcement type. Always aware of his surroundings.

"Okay, you got yourself a deal," said Domingo.

Lou stood up, towering over Domingo, and pulled a business card from his wallet.

They exchanged cards. Domingo guessed they were done. Just in time, too, because a man announced over the intercom that boarding for the Southwest flight to San Diego would begin in ten minutes.

Domingo got up and hoisted his bag on his back. "When do you want to talk to Tessa?"

"ASAP." Lou pointed his chin toward the numbered columns where passengers waited according to their boarding numbers.

They walked toward column A. Of course, nothing less than VIP boarding for the DEA special agent with his powerful task force badge. Domingo would kill for this kind of clout. He could use the man on his side for the long haul.

"Can I ask you something?" said Domingo.

"Shoot." Lou thrust his hands in the pockets of his jeans, his lanyard ID swaying a bit.

If Domingo didn't know better, he would have guessed he was talking to an autoworker or a bricklayer—a blue-collar worker, not a federal agent. "Why did you run away from me?"

At last, Lou cracked a grin. "Because you were chasing me? And you look like you can karate chop me to death?"

"No, seriously. You have authority from your super-duper task force. So why didn't you just talk to me?"

"I'm a DEA special agent, not Batman. I have the fight-or-flight instinct like everyone else, with the flight part stronger than usual after spending twenty-five years on the job and packing on twenty extra pounds on my belly. I haven't been chased by anyone or chased anybody myself in . . . I don't know, fifteen years. There!" He shrugged, both palms up. "I'm just a tired middle-aged agent who would like to retire alive. Okay?"

"Okay." This time, Domingo was the one who grinned. "By the way, a karate chop won't kill anyone. You'll only break your fist if you don't know what the hell you're doing. You're better off with a solid elbow to the face. An elbow is harder than the fist."

Lou shot him an amused look. "I'll try to remember that."

Domingo extended his hand.

Lou shook it with vigor. "I'll be waiting for your call. You won't regret aligning with me, I can promise you that."

Domingo nodded and waved goodbye as he walked away. He liked Lou Harold. He liked a man honest enough to acknowledge his fear and humble enough to recognize that Domingo could indeed injure him seriously. *Karate chop to death.* It made him smile. Yep, he could topple the agent—or any man, for that matter—with the right move at the right time.

CHAPTER 7

The border patrol "holding facility" for undocumented immigrants just outside Tucson was essentially a prison—dusty grounds, chain-link fence topped with razor wire, and warehouse-like buildings. It was not quite eight in the morning. Domingo was in the parking lot, waiting in his rental car for his appointment with a Border Patrol contact. There were many cars but not visitors.

He'd arrived in Tucson yesterday afternoon, a few hours after his unexpected meeting with DEA Special Agent Lou Harold. He'd spent most of yesterday at a vineyard in the area, gathering information about Raul and Maria Beltran.

The manager, a Mexican American old-timer, had been most helpful. The man had started working at the vineyard with the likes of the Beltrans two decades ago. He remembered Raul, whose wife had joined him a year later as a harvest worker. While the old-timer had risen through the ranks to become manager, the Beltrans had lost their jobs and had since moved to California. A Catholic church in the Napa Valley area had helped the Beltrans and a few others who'd lost their jobs. Domingo had gotten the name of the church.

Domingo couldn't stand idling with the car's AC on. He turned it off, rolled down his window, and killed the engine. He'd tolerate the desert heat for a bit instead of wasting gas. Even after living in America for over two decades, he'd never outgrown his "immigrant mentality." He never wasted a penny, always finished the crust of a pizza slice, and washed and reused all ziplock bags. He lived by the Filipino proverb "*Kung may isinuksok, may madudukot.*" You reap what you save.

He pulled his phone from his pocket and called Tessa Woodridge.

"Where are you?" she answered.

"At the border patrol. I have a meeting with a BP agent this morning," he said.

He wasn't about to reveal the existence of Lou Harold. Not yet. He needed to get his ducks in a row first. However, he updated her about his trip to the vineyard and the information he got from the Mexican American manager. He told her he would continue his search for the Beltrans in California. "Are you with Julian right now?" he asked.

"No. He's attending the trade show. I'm on my way to the airport to catch a flight to Sacramento."

"Has Julian ever talked about any of his relatives? Maybe an aunt or uncle?"

"He mentioned Tio."

"What do you know about him?"

"He paid for Julian's college education. Julian's very fond of Tio. That's all I know, actually." Tessa's voice had dropped into a mumble. "If you can find out more about Tio and about Julian's biological parents and his adoptive parents, that would be great."

The quiet tenor of her voice made Domingo wonder if the heiress still felt guilty about snooping on her boyfriend. Or had Lover Boy done something to make her so sad? "Tessa, are you okay?" he asked.

"I don't know."

"If you don't feel safe being with Julian . . ."

"He's *always* made me feel safe—that's the problem. I feel like I'm eight years old again. I'm afraid he'll leave me."

"Leave you?"

"That something will happen, and he'll be taken away from me again."

"You mean . . . the way the sheriff's deputies arrested him and took him away from you."

"I guess." After a bump of silence, she continued. "Julian has a tattoo."

"Come again?" He shifted the cell phone from his right hand to the left.

"Two black parallel bars. Like a barcode—that is, if there were more lines."

"Where's his tattoo . . . Which part of his body?"

"It's on his left forearm."

Domingo himself had no tattoos. He didn't find them cool or attractive, but he knew gang members branded themselves out of loyalty and pride. The Sureño gang's symbol was the rock star of all gang tattoos. It consisted of two horizontal lines and three dots representing the number thirteen in Aztec or Mayan or whatever.

"Were there any dots?" he asked.

"No dots."

"Good. At least he's not a Sureño gang member." He meant to tease her, but she'd grown quiet again. "Hello?"

"I've asked him about his tattoo before, but it was only last night that he finally talked about it. He said it was meant to cover the scar from a knife wound."

"How did he get wounded?"

"Several months before we met in the desert, he got into a knife fight with a gang member who wanted to kill him. He stabbed the guy, but apparently he didn't get arrested at all. Is that normal in Mexico? You can just stab anybody without any consequences?"

Ding, ding, ding! His internal alarm went off at the very mention of *gang member*. "Tell me the gangbanger survived and he's happily retired now."

"Yeah, the guy lived and left Julian alone after that."

"Do you know what started the fight?"

"No. He clams up when I ask questions."

Domingo's mind raced. What did it mean for a teenage Julian to scare off a gang member who'd intended to kill him? Whatever caused the fight was irrelevant. What mattered was Julian Alondra had intimidated the hell out of the bad hombre. The fact that Julian was an engineer today, who traveled to the United States legally, meant that he had no criminal record from the stabbing. Perhaps the gang member hadn't reported the incident to the cops. Or maybe Julian served time for the stabbing but got out and managed to reinvent himself as a law-abiding citizen. The mystery surrounding Lover Boy grew every day. The picture of Julian in his mind changed as often too.

"Don't worry about the tattoo, okay? It doesn't mean anything," he assured Tessa. *You should worry about the implications of the knife fight,* he wanted to add. He grappled with the idea of a fourteen-year-old boy winning a knife fight against a gangbanger. It implied a kind of viciousness he hadn't expected from a Good Samaritan like Julian. Worse, it meant he moved in the same circles as gang members.

Tessa had reached the airport, so they ended the call.

He glanced at the time on his phone. Another ten minutes before his appointment. His mission: to dig for information about Julian's deportation almost two decades ago. He drummed his fingers on the steering wheel. No breeze. He felt the prickle of summer heat at his hairline.

He'd hoped to get the facts from Joe Medina's contact at ICE in Phoenix, but the man hadn't found anything in their records. Domingo had drawn two possible scenarios as to why Julian Alondra's name wasn't in the system.

First, Julian's arrest and deportation in 2000 predated ICE. The Department of Homeland Security was created in 2003 in the aftermath of the terrorist attacks at the World Trade Center in New York and the Pentagon in Washington, DC. Homeland Security created ICE that same year to replace the old department of Immigration and Naturalization Service. Who knew what happened to INS records? Had everything been digitized, or was it languishing in a warehouse?

Second, a kid without a criminal record like Julian couldn't have been a priority for ICE compared with adult undocumented immigrants, especially criminal fugitives. In all likelihood, the sheriff's deputies who'd arrested Julian had transferred him to Border Patrol, which had detained him. Domingo was willing to bet that Julian's case had never reached ICE.

He glanced at the time on his phone again. Time to go. His pulse quickened with anticipation. What happened after Julian's illegal desert crossing two decades ago? Today he intended to find out. It could help solve the mystery that was Julian Alondra, a.k.a. Jules Alexander, a.k.a. Lover Boy.

CHAPTER 8

At the reception area of the border patrol facility, Domingo met a young BP agent named Birdy Jenkins, who was all swagger and cocksureness. A contact at ICE had referred him to Birdy. His buddy had assured him Birdy would help, as long as Domingo refrained from calling the guy by his first name: Bartholomew.

Birdy wore an olive green uniform similar to military fatigues, which had replaced the brown police-style uniform of old. A telltale sign of the changing role of BP from guard to warrior. *This is the immigration war zone,* the uniform seemed to say.

"How much does a bounty hunter make?" Birdy began.

As blunt as it was, the question didn't surprise Domingo. It matched the guy's haughty personality.

"More than a rookie government employee like you." Domingo shook his hand, though he wanted to slap him. Birdy didn't get the sarcasm, because he launched into a job hunter's spiel.

"If you need help in my neck of the woods, I'm interested. I've got two solid years of law enforcement experience and fifty-eight hours of BP academy training. I can get references. You won't regret hiring me."

So this was the reason Birdy had agreed to help him. "Duly noted. I'll ask my boss when I get back to New York if he's hiring. Can we talk about my case?"

"Sure. Let's chat while I work. I believe in multitasking." Birdy handed Domingo a visitor's ID. "I'm going to take your cell phone, bro. We've gotten such bad press. We can't allow any photos."

He meant the viral videos and pictures of undocumented children wallowing in squalor at detention centers after they'd been separated from their parents, thanks to the government's zero tolerance for illegal immigration. Under this policy, all undocumented adults were subject to criminal prosecution, but children couldn't be held criminal, and so they were forcibly separated from their families. The White House used family separation as a tactic to discourage migrants from seeking safe haven in the United States. The public outcry had put a stop to the practice for now.

There was a time when Lady Liberty wanted the poor, the tired, and huddled masses yearning to breathe free. Today the White House called those same people "losers" and would like to kick their asses back to their "shithole countries," as the president had described African countries, Haiti, and other poverty-stricken nations whose citizens were once granted temporary protective status in this country.

Domingo handed his phone to Birdy and clipped the ID to the flap of his shirt pocket. They proceeded to the holding area. Birdy carried no gun, but the other agents in the room were armed. Why? Could starving migrants really pose such a threat?

The stench of humanity smacked Domingo. Filthy men were crammed in cells divided by chain-link walls. There were about forty bodies packed in every cell meant for thirty, tops. No beds, just sleeping mats. One toilet stall and sink for every cell.

Domingo wouldn't be surprised if many of these men had been deported before. He called them *multo,* meaning "ghost" in Tagalog. Undocumented immigrants were as invisible as Bruce Willis in *The Sixth Sense* and as unwelcome as the creepy twins in *The Shining*.

Sometimes he thought of them as "desperate hopefuls." Ordinary hope was the New Year's resolution of losing weight, the kind that fizzled out after one month. Desperate hope was the lifelong dream of living in America even if it meant crossing the murderous Sonoran Desert on foot or sailing across the treacherous Gulf of Mexico on a dilapidated boat. Desperate hopefuls try again and again.

"*Mi* cages, *su* cages," said Birdy with a wry grin.

Easy for a white man like Birdy to joke about it. Meanwhile, Domingo's stomach dipped from both the smell and his indignation. "This is wrong. I've seen nicer chicken coops than this. Tell me it's just temporary."

"I wish I could." Birdy took out a packet of chewing gum and offered it to Domingo, but he declined. "We're not supposed to hold these guys for more than seventy-two hours, but ICE is inundated and can't take them. We have to keep them here." He shoved a piece of gum into his mouth and chewed noisily.

What a mess. In theory, the Customs and Border Protection conducted inspections at ports of entry, while Border Patrol apprehended migrants within one hundred miles of land and coastal borders. CBP was like a gung ho K9 police officer, while BP was the killer dog whose sole purpose was to stop foreigners from illegally crossing America's borders. In this scenario, ICE, which was responsible for enforcement of immigration laws in the country, was the lawyer in the cozy office who would then prosecute the migrants caught by BP and CBP. In reality, the alphabet soup of immigration agencies overlapped. All three were short staffed, overworked, unappreciated by Americans, and reviled by legal and undocumented immigrants alike.

Domingo himself maintained neutrality toward the agencies, since he worked with them by necessity. One thing was for sure: He would never want to trade places with Birdy.

The vents blew weak air from an air conditioner that was working hard in a densely occupied space. He wiped his damp forehead with the back of his hand. He could see through cage after cage because there were no real walls. No privacy either.

"You caught these men crossing the border?" he asked.

Birdy shook his head. "These guys willingly surrendered to us."

"Where are they from?"

"The usual—Mexico and Central America. Lots of Guatemalans and Hondurans."

"How many people have you apprehended so far this year?"

"I've lost track of the total. I do know our southwest sector alone caught over one hundred thousand people last month. It broke the record for one month." He waved at another young man in uniform. "Hang tight. I need to check this morning's intake."

Birdy and his colleague huddled over a clipboard.

At nine in the morning, some of the desperate hopefuls munched on crackers, while others lined up with their paper cups at the lone watercooler. *Breakfast of champions.* Dozens slept—fetal position—on the mats. They could be sick or dying or dead and nobody here would care.

The migrants threw furtive glances at Domingo, as though afraid of eye contact. Most of them stared at nothing. They all wore a washed-out expression, their shoulders slumped. A few exchanged whispers in Spanish. For a building overflowing with people, it was eerily quiet, as though their tongues had been cut out along with their dignity.

Birdy swaggered back to his side. "Everything's cool. No new arrivals, so the head count remains the same. Big day today—these hombres will get to shower."

Domingo dared not ask how long ago it had been since their last shower, or where the women and children were detained. *Focus,* he reminded himself. "I need to know how Julian Alondra left BP detention and whether the INS processed him."

"Ah, yes, your perp." Birdy gestured toward the door, and they exited the area. "I haven't eyeballed his paperwork because we don't keep anything older than ten years in our system. I need to check the archives."

They entered a hopping office—phones ringing, a group of agents meeting in a small circle, the TV on the wall blasting.

Birdy reached up to turn off the TV and proceeded to a desk. He dropped on a chair and checked his computer, typing on the keyboard. Then he scribbled something on a Post-it note. Domingo stood to wait since there were no empty chairs around.

Birdy handed him the piece of paper.

He read it. *Ramon Alvarado, 113 Dakota Drive, Tucson AZ.* "Who's this?" he asked.

"That's the sheriff's deputy who arrested Julian Alondra back in November 2000. He's retired now, but I found his home address for your convenience. I figured you could pay him a little visit while I dig into Julian's paperwork."

Domingo couldn't help but smile in gratitude. Birdy had done the legwork that would have taken an out-of-towner like him several days to accomplish. "Appreciate it, man."

"No problem." Birdy rose.

They walked out of the room, back to the reception area. The agent continued to chew the gum like an overgrown kid. "You think you could use someone like me? I'm a hard worker, and I have good contacts within the Border Patrol, plus ICE, CBP, and sheriff's offices throughout Arizona. *This* is where the immigration shit is going to hit the fan, and when it happens, I'm right here for you."

"I'll see what I can do." Domingo handed him the visitor's ID in exchange for his cell phone. "The news about that Facebook group—you know, those BP agents posting racist memes and jokes?"

"I'm not one of those assholes!" Birdy's face turned red. "I don't do social media. I hate it."

"Good to know." Domingo looked out through the glass doors, at Old Glory billowing atop a flagpole and the green Border Patrol flag swaying from a stand. Nothing like those official flags to remind him about the official US policy of closing the door on undocumented immigrants. They were "the other"—the tired, poor, huddled scapegoats doomed to suffer just because they looked and sounded different.

"Sunday."

He turned to Birdy, still chewing and chewing. A nervous tick. Perhaps he considered this meeting a job interview.

"You can see why I wanna bust outta here, right? I didn't sign up to be a prison guard."

"Why did you become a BP agent?" asked Domingo.

"I really enjoy four-wheeling along the border. Plus I get to carry a gun. It was all very cool at first, but not anymore. Being in the middle of this shit is depressing, man. I didn't even show you half of what I have to get through every fucking day. You think I like putting little kids in cages? The way I see it, *I'm* in the same cage as they are. Congress is investigating us for just about everything. The whole country hates us."

Welcome to my world, he almost said. *Mi misery, su misery.* White men like Birdy occupied the top of the pecking order in the US of A. They ruled the day, every day. It was refreshing to see someone like Birdy experience the same brand of pain that most immigrants lived with. They shared that, at least.

"Hang in there, man. I'll ask around about a job for you." He shook hands with him again before leaving.

CHAPTER 9

The sign on one side of the food truck announced, **HOME-MADE TACOS SERVED ON FRESH TORTILLAS**. On the other side, it said, **BEAT THE HEAT WITH REFRESHING RASPADO**.

The truck occupied two spots in the parking lot of a recreation center that boasted an outdoor swimming pool and a summer day camp.

Domingo helped Ramon Alvarado, retired deputy sheriff, unfold some lounge chairs and a patio table with an umbrella. He'd met Ramon in his driveway, just as he was leaving with his grandson, Bobby, for work. They ran a taco truck, and Ramon had invited Domingo to tag along.

"What time do you start making tacos?" asked Domingo.

"Around noon. The swim-team kids and their moms are our top customers. On Tuesdays, we cater only to the summer day camp. This is Bobby's business. I'm just the help." Ramon tossed an affectionate glance at his grandson. "This is the beauty of retirement. I can do whatever I wanna do."

Bobby, a somber young man, was making a raspado, a Mexican-style shaved ice drink in bright colors. At half past ten, a couple of women lined up at the truck.

"By lunchtime, we'll get swarmed. You better ask me your questions now." Ramon perched on a chair. "Have a seat."

The deputy looked younger and fitter than any retiree he'd ever met. He probably worked out regularly.

Domingo sat across from him. "Do you remember a young migrant named Julian Alondra? You nabbed him back in November 2000."

Ramon nodded. "One day after Thanksgiving. I'll never forget."

"Why is that?"

"Because the boy showed me the way to the bodies of Henry and Theresa Woodridge, the owners of Giant Burgers. Everyone here knows the Woodridge family. They donated cruisers to the sheriff's department."

"The family used to live here?"

"Henry's parents lived here for many years, though Henry and his family lived in Phoenix. They were going back home after a Thanksgiving Day visit when the accident happened. Giant Burgers used to be based in Phoenix, but after the tragedy, the company moved to San Francisco. The family upped and left Arizona. Can't blame them."

"Do you remember Tessa Woodridge?"

Ramon answered with a smile. "Green eyes, cute as a button, smart as a whip. I personally drove her to her grandmother's house after we picked up her and the Mexican boy from the desert. Did you say Tessa hired you? What's this all about? How's she doing?"

"She's doing great. She's now the CEO of Giant Burgers."

Ramon let out a low whistle. "I'm impressed."

"Tessa and Julian Alondra got together recently. That's why I'm investigating him."

"Got together? You mean . . . like boyfriend and girlfriend?"

"Exactly."

"Really?" Ramon pulled a pair of sunglasses from his shirt pocket and wiped them with the hem of his shirt. "Well, I could tell Tessa and Julian had a special bond. He called her *niñita*, 'little girl.' They'd spent only twenty-four hours together in the desert and he had a nickname for her." Ramon put on his shades. "But why are you investigating Julian?"

The sun glared, making Domingo grateful for the umbrella. The trees blew in the dry breeze. He might as well have been inside an oven. He brushed the straying hair off his eyes. "Giant Burgers is worth six hundred million bucks. Tessa Woodridge is not just any girl, so I'm here to find out as much as I can about her new boyfriend."

"Is that how rich people date? You're screening Julian?" Ramon chuckled.

"Exactly. Tell me what you remember about him."

"Good-looking boy, light skinned. Didn't speak much. I thought maybe he didn't speak English, but that can't be, because he obviously had no problem communicating with Tessa. I felt sorry for him." Ramon shook his head. "After all, he saved the little girl's life. But the law is the law, so I arrested him. He was lucky to be alive. Most of the time, we don't arrest. We pick up bodies of undocumented crossers who die of dehydration or exposure to the elements. The desert is brutal."

Bobby had finished serving the women. Now he wiped the surfaces of the truck, a rag in his right hand and Windex in the left. Wax on, wax off. Like the Karate Kid.

Ramon continued to talk about Julian, who had crossed from Sonora all alone. Domingo had guessed correctly that Border Patrol had detained the boy but he'd been released before he could be transferred to ICE's jurisdiction.

"Do you know why the border patrol released Julian?"

"They had no choice. A relative came for him."

"You know that for sure? Because I can't get any information from BP. At least not yet."

"Oh, I'm sure. Julian's uncle came looking for him at the sheriff's department, so I took the guy to the border patrol's holding facility, where I'd dropped off Julian only a few days before."

It was Tio! Domingo's heart lurched. *Now we're talking.* He pulled his phone from his pocket and tapped the note-taking app. He started typing. "You remember the man's name? Is it Santiago Sepulveda de Santiago, a.k.a. Santiago Santiago?"

"Unfortunately, I don't remember. It was a long time ago."

"But you're sure he was a relative?"

"Why else would he be searching for the kid? Anyhow, Julian called him *tio*. I have no reason to doubt the man was his uncle."

"Was Julian a runaway?"

"He claimed he wasn't, but I've never met a migrant who was fetched by a relative, you know? Also, he was a kid all alone in the desert. I suspected he ran away, yes."

"Do you remember anything about the uncle?"

"Well . . . he was a businessman who crossed the border on a business visa. Also, there was one thing, yeah. One of his legs was shorter than the other—polio. Can't remember if it was the left or the right leg, but at first glance, it was as though he limped. On closer look, it was worse than a limp."

"So the border patrol didn't deport Julian?"

"No. He was picked up by kin, so it was considered self-deportation."

Domingo saved his notes. A group of boisterous kids emerged from the recreation center and lined up at the truck. It wasn't lunchtime yet—more raspado customers. The noise distracted him and Ramon for a moment.

When Ramon turned back to him, he said, "How old is Tessa now? And Julian?"

"Tessa is twenty-seven and Julian is thirty-three. He's a civil engineer who works as a consultant in Mexico City."

"I'm glad he's not here in the US illegally. How on earth did he find his way to Tessa's life?"

"It's quite a story." Domingo was putting together the little pieces of information he had, imagined the teenage Julian hiking from the desert to the highway and flagging down the first car he saw. That led to Deputy Alvarado rescuing Tessa, recovering her parents' bodies, and apprehending Julian. Then Tio fetched the boy and took him back to Mexico. And then what? Domingo was far from understanding Lover Boy's backstory. "Does the name Jules Alexander ring a bell?"

"No," said Ramon. "Who is he?"

"Julian Alondra changed his name to Jules Alexander when he came back here legally as an engineering student at the University of Arizona."

Ramon removed his sunglasses. "I'm really quite amazed. It's not common for a boy like him to turn around his life like that. Most migrants hide forever and do odd jobs, or they end up in prison, or get killed."

"I agree. Julian's something else." No need to share the information about the stabbing and all. "If you've never heard of the name Jules Alexander, then I take it he didn't do anything too crazy in college that would make his name stand out." He tucked his phone back in his pocket.

Ramon was tapping his chin with his sunglasses, his gaze far away.

"Care to share your thoughts?" asked Domingo.

"I wrote a report about Julian, which I then sent to the border patrol. It was SOP, you see. I might be able to ask someone at the sheriff's office to look it up for me."

"That would be great."

"What do you want to know exactly?"

"Whatever you can share with me."

"Copy that." He nodded, a glimmer in his eyes. "You're getting me real curious about this boy. I'm too nosy. Once a deputy, always a deputy."

They exchanged phone numbers.

Domingo thrust his chin at the food truck. "I can't leave without trying Bobby's raspado."

"Try the mango with sweet milk. It's the best in all of Arizona."

They both got up and walked toward the truck for Domingo's treat. Already he was thinking of his next target, thanks to information from Cheryl: Kevin Godfrey, Julian's college buddy.

CHAPTER 10

America Suffers from Serious Wall Envy

I was ten years old living in Manila when President Ronald Reagan urged Soviet leader Mikhail Gorbachev to "tear down this wall." Reagan was talking about the Berlin Wall, which came toppling down two years after his speech. His words, in support of democracy in oppressive East Germany, echoed throughout the globe. At the time, the world heralded America as a hero.

Not anymore. Today the indelible words of Reagan have been replaced with "Build the wall!" The world no longer sees America as a destroyer of divisive walls but a builder of one. Forget about America the beautiful—more like America the bully now.

I wouldn't be surprised if this country slapped never-ending tariffs on China until it's forced to export the Great Wall, because let's face it, Uncle Sam has serious wall envy. People buy into the myth that a "big beautiful wall" in our southern border will stop illegal immigration and drug smuggling. The truth is walls have been built for thousands of years to keep people out to no avail.

America's wall will never stop the migrant trafficking and drug smuggling. Wall supporters know it, but they just want to be seen carrying that big stick to discourage ALL people they don't like from entering this country. The bigots don't want any dialogue and won't listen to any realistic solution to the immigration problem. Their eyes are shut tight. I can think of only one thing that might open their eyes to reason. How about shoving that mighty stick they're carrying up their asses?

◆ ◆ ◆

Domingo heard the receptionist call out his name. Too many *walls* in what he'd written and no time to rewrite it. He tucked the little notepad and pen in one of the many pockets of his cargo pants.

At last, Kevin Godfrey was ready to see him. Domingo had been waiting while the man attended a meeting. Kevin worked for a multilevel marketing company that sold dietary supplements, one of those organizations that bordered on a pyramid scheme. Even the company's name, Honesty, sounded dubious.

It was lunchtime. Employees from various companies in the building were streaming out. Domingo stood in the lobby, a visitor's ID hanging from a lanyard around his neck like a bull's-eye. Even a stranger like Kevin could spot him. Kevin was Caucasian, about six feet tall, probably Julian's age.

They shook hands. Domingo lied about being a PI checking Jules Alexander's academic background as part of an employment screening. Domingo was looking up the whole time. Being the same height since the sixth grade sucked. In the Philippines, Domingo's five-five was average, but not in America, where even Tom Cruise's five-seven was considered short. Tito Mando, who was Domingo's height, had a solution. "You can be short but still be strong and kick ass. If you have the right skills, you can beat your opponent even if he's bigger and taller," he'd said.

In *escrima*, boxing, and martial arts, the right moves and speed were a great equalizer. Bruce Lee had been as short as Domingo. Muhammad Ali had stood over six feet tall, but his power had come from the speed of his jabs and footwork, not his height. And that was why Domingo had taken up martial arts. He'd learned everything he could from Tito Mando, practiced his skills in Manila's rough-and-tumble streets, and sharpened his fighting style in America with the help of training paid for by Joe Medina.

Yeah, he took comfort in the knowledge that he could knock down the Kevins of the world despite their height advantage. Not that there was a need for it. Kevin was gracious enough to meet with him.

Julian's college buddy showed Domingo the way to a patio, which turned out to be a smokers' haven. The employees didn't use the space for eating lunch but for gabbing while smoking.

"Sorry to keep you waiting. I was in a kaizen." Kevin pulled out a chair at a wrought iron table.

Domingo did the same, and they sat down at the same time. "What's a kaizen?" asked Domingo.

"It's Japanese for 'continuous improvement.'" Kevin made air quotes with his fingers. "But in my company, it means a marathon waste of time talking about crap."

Wow, he'd never met anyone so jaded. "Sorry to hear." Kevin wasn't an engineer, like Julian, but a philosophy graduate now working in marketing. He'd changed jobs twice in two years, according to Cheryl, who'd gotten all of this on LinkedIn alone.

Kevin shrugged. "It's just a job." His sleek eyes reminded Domingo of an alligator. "What position is Jules applying for?"

"A consulting job for a big project, a dam in a reservoir."

"Here in Arizona?"

"In the US." Domingo leaned back. "I can't tell you anything more than that because this screening is confidential. I'd really appreciate it if you don't tell Jules about this conversation."

"Oh, no worries. I understand. Besides, I haven't talked to him in a while."

A woman at a table behind Kevin puffed away, the smoke from her cigarette curling high.

"Did you know that your friend's real name is Julian Alondra?" asked Domingo.

"Yes. He sometimes goes by Julian."

Kevin had pronounced it "Joo-lee-yan," the Anglo way. Lover Boy had just scored one point for not hiding his real name. Domingo nodded. "Are you guys close? When was the last time you talked to him?"

"I wouldn't say we're besties, but we keep in touch. The last time I spoke to him, he just got engaged."

That just about knocked Domingo out. "Really. When was that?"

"Oh, back in January. I asked him what his New Year's resolution was, and he said, 'To settle down.' Then he asked me the secret for wedded bliss." Kevin chuckled as though remembering a joke. "Jules was just messing with me. I'm divorced. I'm the least qualified person to talk about marriage."

The conversation between the two men had taken place seven months ago. An engagement could span a few months or years. Could Julian be getting married soon? Was Girl Boss just a distraction before he got married? Was his engagement the reason why he never invited Tessa to his home in Mexico City? He'd been dating Tessa for six months now. He must be very good at juggling women. *Son of a bitch.*

"Who's the lucky girl? You know when the wedding is?" said Domingo.

"He didn't mention any date." Kevin stroked his chin. "You said you want to know about his academic background?"

"Who's the girl?" he repeated.

"It's Dulce, his longtime girlfriend."

Domingo held his breath, waiting for Dulce's last name.

Kevin narrowed his reptilian eyes. "I thought you wanted to know about his education."

"Of course." The guy was getting suspicious. "Any problems of cheating or plagiarizing? What kind of student was he?"

"An excellent one." Kevin folded his hands on his lap and said no more.

The smoke fest was in full swing. Domingo could almost feel cancer growing in his lungs from the secondhand smoke. "Julian's family background is also important in vetting him. Anything you know about his family back in Mexico would be helpful."

"So you mentioned a dam. Like a federal or state project?"

Domingo nodded. Shit, the guy's suspicion hovered above his head, thicker than cigarette smoke.

"Why would a government agency hire a Mexican citizen?" Kevin crossed his legs, right ankle over his left knee. "Shouldn't taxpayers' money be used to hire US citizens?"

"The Government Accountability Office allows foreign companies to bid on projects as long as they're based in one of the fifty-seven countries that maintain international trade agreements with us. Mexico is one of them. Jules is perfectly eligible for a subcontracting job."

"Ha! I didn't know that."

Domingo didn't think so. Joe Medina's rule number four: If you're going to lie, it better be damn good. Know your shit. Domingo wanted to be the driver, not the passenger, of this conversation. He pivoted back to what really mattered. "Have you ever met Dulce?"

Kevin shook his head.

His alligator eyes seemed to say *No mas about Dulce.* Damn it. Meanwhile, Domingo's lung cancer was growing by the second. He needed to get something out of this visit. "You know anything about Julian's family? His parents? Any siblings? Uncles or aunts?"

"No." Kevin glanced at his wristwatch. "I need to go back to my kaizen. We have catered lunch—all part of the exercise in futility. Sorry, I'm not very helpful."

"It's all good, man. Can you vouch for Jules Alexander's character? Can you say he's an upstanding engineer who can be trusted with an important project?"

"A dam funded by the government." Kevin enunciated each word with care, like he was talking to an imbecile.

"That's right." *Fuck.* The guy would probably speed-dial Julian the moment Domingo left. "Before I go . . . How can I buy your products? I've been trying to get my hands on Honesty vitamins. I jog, run, plus I work out in the gym. I could really use some energy boost. I want natural ingredients. None of the synthetic chemical shit. Are you in sales?"

"No, I'm not. But I can refer you to one of our best sales guys. His name is Dennis Yang." Kevin pulled out a business card from his wallet and handed it to Domingo. "This is me, by the way. And, if you like, we can talk to Dennis right now and see what he can do for you."

Kevin was all smiles now. He rose and stood amid the pall of smoke like he was about to perform a miracle, or about to receive a referral fee if his buddy sold some crap to Domingo.

Domingo got up as well. "You have the time? I thought you needed to go back to your kaizen."

"It's not a problem," said Kevin. "It would take all of five minutes."

They strode back inside the building. Kevin began a litany of all the benefits of his company's products.

So Julian was *not* married, and that was why no marriage license existed with his name on it. But he was *about* to get married. *Dulce.* Who the hell was she?

He needed to talk to Girl Boss ASAP. The information from Lou Harold and Kevin Godfrey combined was a game changer. Did Tessa really want to continue dating a guy who was being tailed by the DEA because of his cartel connections? A guy who was engaged to be married?

Maybe there was no longer a need to locate Raul and Maria Beltran. This investigation might end before the day was over. All good, as far as he was concerned. Julian Alondra's mysterious background had not been so hard to discover. It hadn't turned out to be on a par with Domingo's skills, after all.

CHAPTER 11

Back in Domingo's hotel room, he called Birdy at Border Patrol, but the guy hadn't been able to find Julian's old paperwork. It was either misplaced or tossed out accidentally or deliberately; nobody knew. Bottom line: Birdy couldn't find the file.

The weight of Julian's secrets settled onto Domingo's shoulders. As if the DEA's interest in Julian wasn't bad enough, there had to be another woman—Dulce, whose name reverberated in his head like a bad rhyme. *Dulce, Dulce, Dulce. You're a bigger mystery than your fiancé.*

He remembered how the heiress had basked in her lover's adoration as he recounted their first meeting, when he'd called her *niñita.* What was Julian's pet name for Dulce? Domingo didn't even want to think of Lou Harold's "proposition" for Tessa or he would sink into dejection. Doctors, nurses, and psychiatrists probably felt like this, like a sponge absorbing other people's issues.

He needed to get out. He walked around the hotel complex despite the seething weather. He strolled a few blocks to a Mexican restaurant and ate a heaping plate of beef burrito for lunch. Instead of going back to his room, he hopped into the rental car and stopped at the first Starbucks he saw, to drink iced coffee.

After a drowsy hour in the summer heat with too much food and coffee, he finally returned to his hotel room.

He called Ramon Alvarado and was startled when the retired sheriff's deputy picked up his call after one ring. "It's me, Sunday—"

"I was about to call you!"

"It must be ESP because—"

"I can confirm the name of Julian's uncle. It's Santiago Sepulveda de Santiago. He's Julian's guardian."

Domingo grabbed the hotel notepad and pen on the desk. "Really? Any mention of Julian's parents in the report?"

"Nothing about that. In case you're interested, Julian was detained for a total of five days. He had no identification whatsoever. Not even an address."

Domingo jotted everything down as fast as he could. "Five days in detention . . . that's terrible."

"It's a vacation. For a migrant, five days in Arizona with three free squares is nothing."

"Julian was fourteen years old."

"Boys even younger than him marinate in their own piss and shit in detention for five or six months before they get deported," the deputy scoffed.

"So Tio saved Julian."

"That makes the uncle not just the kid's guardian, but his guardian *angel*."

Domingo thanked Ramon and ended their call. How had this Tio character with the longest name become Julian's guardian? Were Raul and Maria Beltran already working illegally in the States then? And if they were, why had they left their son behind?

And now for the hard part. How to report to Girl Boss all this bad news. He checked his wristwatch. He guessed she'd already arrived in California. He texted her to be sure.

He couldn't imagine Tessa would still want to date Julian or indeed find his parents after what Domingo was about to tell her. He started packing the few things he'd brought. He would check the next flight to New York on his phone. Maybe he would just drive to the airport and book a flight there. He only needed to endure Tessa's sadness for a little longer. He would be so relieved to close this case and go home and sleep in his own bed.

His phone pinged. Tessa's response to his text confirmed she was in Sacramento.

He texted back. Will contact you via Zoom in 10.

He hated using his phone's tiny screen for a video call with a client. He got out of his room and ran downstairs to the business center. There were four PCs, all free. The room was empty. Nowadays, everyone brought a laptop or iPad, except him. He preferred to travel light.

Ten minutes later, he was on Zoom with the webcam on. "Hi, Tessa."

"Hi. What's going on?"

She was in her office. Black-and-white photos of the original Giant Burgers restaurant decked the wall behind her. According to Wikipedia, Great-Grandpa Woodridge had founded the business after World War II. He'd sold humongous hamburgers for twenty-five cents apiece. He hadn't made money at first, but his hamburger had attracted a cultlike loyalty among customers that continued to this day.

"I met with four people who gave me information about Julian in addition to the manager at the vineyard," began Domingo. "I'll start with the person who had the most crucial information. His name is DEA Special Agent Lou Harold. He was the guy who tailed you and Julian in Utah and Las Vegas."

Tessa tilted her head ever so slightly but said nothing. Those green eyes, wide and bright, were as clear as though she was in the room, in the flesh, with him.

Once Domingo got started, the words spilled out of him nonstop. "This agent knows a lot of things about Julian and Tio. And I believed him when he said Julian's in deep shit. Your boyfriend's going to drag you down with him unless you do two things."

One side of her mouth pinched. "And what, may I ask, are those two things?"

"First, talk to Lou Harold. He'll meet with you anywhere, anytime. At least listen to what he has to say."

She pressed her lips together. Her eyes watered.

"Second, you gotta break up with Julian. I know this is none of my business, but he's bad news. He's no longer the boy who saved you in the desert. He's a drug-cartel engineer. He's like—"

"Stop it." She lifted her chin and straightened her back like a noblewoman sitting in a king's court. "I don't believe Lou Harold, whoever he is. I'm *not* going to talk to him, and I'm not going to tell Julian about this. That's my answer. My loyalty to Julian is nonnegotiable."

Part of Domingo knew this would happen. Tessa, blinded by an idealized image of Julian the Savior, would stand by her man. Part of him still hoped he'd be able to convince her of the folly of her relationship.

"You said 'Julian is like'—what?" Tessa arched an eyebrow. "What were you about to say when I cut you off?"

"Julian's like Mitch McDeere. You've heard of the name?"

"I'm not a Tom Cruise fan, so I didn't see the movie, but I like John Grisham, and I love *The Firm*."

"Oh, good. So you know what I mean, then."

"Mitch McDeere is an attorney who unwittingly becomes a lawyer for the mob. Why on earth would you compare Julian to him?"

"Just change *attorney* to *engineer* and *mob* to *cartel*."

"Julian is *not* Mitch McDeere."

"Okay. Forget about it. My bad." He waved dismissively. "Do you want to hear the rest of my report?"

"Go on." She leaned back in her chair.

He discussed his meeting with retired Deputy Sheriff Alvarado and Birdy, the Border Patrol agent.

Tessa said nothing about Birdy, but asked how Ramon was doing. "I'll never forget him. He was very kind. He drove me back to Grammy's house after he picked me up from the desert. Okay, what else?"

Domingo had saved the worst for last. The DEA factor hadn't shaken Tessa's faith in Julian, but Domingo's next news might. He braced himself like someone about to let the racehorse out of the gates. "I met a college buddy of Julian's. His name is Kevin Godfrey."

"What did he say?"

"Listen, Tessa." Domingo scratched his eyebrows and then his forehead. "Kevin Godfrey told me Julian is engaged to his longtime girlfriend. A woman named Dulce. I don't have her last name."

She flinched.

A vacuum cleaner started next door. He glanced at the clock on the PC—1:53 p.m. The deadness of the afternoon made it perfect for cleaning. And the worst time for breaking a girl's heart.

"You believe this guy?" Sorrow spread over her pretty face the way red wine had once spilled on his carpet. The stain lasted forever.

"Yes. Kevin Godfrey has no reason to lie. He doesn't know anything about you. He thought I was screening Julian for a contracting job."

She nodded and looked up at the ceiling. Her anguish came at once, tears rolling down her cheeks. "Now I know why he refuses to take me to Mexico City."

The heiress was willing to put up with the possibility of Julian's involvement with a drug cartel but not the idea that he might be in love with someone else. Although both things were deal-breakers, the former was more urgent and serious, as in federal-offense serious that merited twenty years in prison. But not to a girl hopelessly in love. It didn't make sense, but what did he really know about women?

"Why don't you talk to Julian? It's time for a real conversation," he said.

She scrubbed her tears with both knuckles. "You mean tell him how I hired Cheryl and you to track him down and snoop on him?"

"If he loves you, it shouldn't matter."

She looked straight at the camera, her cheeks glistening. "I have *thirteen* journals all addressed to Julian. I began writing to him the day after I saw him handcuffed by Deputy Alvarado." She sniffled. "When I got up this morning, I wrote in my diary, *Dearest Julian . . . some girls dream of becoming an astronaut or a doctor or a lawyer. Me? I only dreamed of finding you.*" Her voice cracked. She covered her face with both hands.

Domingo looked away and focused on the generic painting of flowers on the beige wall, the kind artists probably sold by the dozen to hotels and medical offices. He didn't care for Julian Alondra and the way he kept Tessa guessing about his past. But he understood and respected her feelings for the man.

Domingo, of all people, knew that the heart wanted what it wanted. Desire, love, hope sometimes remained outside the realm of reason. He'd been a few years younger than Tessa when he'd met Monica Reed. He'd had no right to fall for a subject. He'd rationalized it then as a harmless crush, a stupid fantasy. But here he was at forty-two, still occasionally ambushed by memories of her.

He cleared his throat. "Listen, Tessa. You were just a little girl when you met Julian. Your parents' death traumatized you." He paused, though he wanted to add, *You don't really love him. You just feel guilty that you survived the accident.* Instead, he said, "It's different now. You're both grown up, and he's engaged, and he lied to you."

She grabbed something beyond her computer. A tissue. She wiped her tears and blew her nose. "I guess this concludes your investigation."

"Yeah, I know." He ran his fingers through his hair. "I'm taking the next flight back to New York. Are you gonna be okay?"

Her lips curled into a sad smile. "I'll be fine."

"Can you do me a favor?" he asked.

"What is it?"

"Will you please call me or text me after you talk to Julian about Dulce? Just let me know you're okay."

"All right."

And that was pretty much it. What else was there to say? He ought to thank the mysterious Dulce for succeeding where the DEA had failed to break up Girl Boss and Lover Boy. This was the equivalent of getting Al Capone for tax evasion after the feds failed to ensnare him for murder, extortion, and bootlegging. Anyone who'd seen *The Untouchables* knew that. The end truly justifies the means.

He sat there staring at the computer. He could still see Tessa's face, still hear the hurt in her voice. Only a few hours ago, she'd told him she might lose Julian again. How right she'd been. Except there was no sheriff's deputy arresting or deporting Julian. This time, she would do the leaving. She would get to walk away from the philandering bastard.

CHAPTER 12

One Week Later

Domingo had been following the white Nissan Altima with a New York license plate for the last forty minutes. He cranked up the car's AC as an antidote to the summer heat and humidity. Nothing to see on Route 9 in New Jersey on a Friday afternoon except sprawling auto malls and tired-looking diners.

A fire engine raced by, forcing him and the other cars to wait on the shoulder until the emergency vehicle was gone. He was two cars behind the Nissan. For a change, he wasn't chasing a criminal undocumented immigrant. This man owed fifty thousand dollars in child support. A family court had hired Joe Medina's bail-bonds agency to serve legal papers. Domingo's task this afternoon was to serve a subpoena, not apprehend. *Easy peasy.*

After the end of his investigation of Julian Alondra, Domingo had been serving subpoenas, while also monitoring an undocumented Pakistani who was due in court in a money laundering case. If the guy skipped town, he'd chase him.

At last, the Nissan pulled into the parking lot of a motel. Yep, the guy was a sales rep for a solar company and meeting with clients in the area for a couple of days.

Domingo parked his black Pontiac GTO behind the Nissan. The perp was taking his sweet time getting out of the car. He glanced at the envelope to double-check the guy's first name. Calling out his name would buy Domingo several seconds because the person would try to figure out where they'd met before.

The man got out of the Nissan, stretched his arms, then opened the car trunk. Domingo waited. The guy took out a roller suitcase and shut the trunk door. Still, Domingo waited.

When the guy ambled toward the motel's entrance, suitcase in tow, Domingo hopped out of his car. "Glenn! Yo, Glenn!"

The perp stopped to appraise Domingo; it was long enough for Domingo to close the short distance between them in three long strides. "Special delivery for you, Mr. Williams." He dropped the envelope atop the suitcase.

"What's this?" muttered the man.

"Have a good day." Domingo turned around. He wasn't obligated to explain himself, only to serve the subpoena in the flesh. "And while you're at it, pay up to your ex-wife." He dashed to his Pontiac.

It always worked. The key was to wait until the target was halfway between the car and a building. The person wouldn't know which direction to run.

The man gave him the finger before dragging his ass, the envelope, and his suitcase to the motel.

Domingo smiled. That was his last subpoena for the day, but he needed to stalk a woman whose court papers would be served in a couple of days. The legwork of checking her routine and finding the best place to serve the subpoena had to be done beforehand. But first, he checked his phone for email messages.

When he raised his gaze, a big family passed by him as though in a procession. Brown skinned, but not Asian. Most likely Hispanic. Everyone carried a plastic bag of groceries and two-liter bottles of soda. Nope, this wasn't a family, but just a large group of people. They trooped into a ground-floor room at the motel.

Multo. These were undocumented immigrants who were as invisible and unwelcome as ghosts. No tourists or businesspeople packed themselves like sardines in a single room in a cheap motel on a gritty stretch of Route 9. These ghosts were probably waiting for the coyote who'd smuggled them across the border. Perhaps this was their holding pen until they scattered in different parts of the country.

Well, he apprehended only criminal undocumented immigrants who had been ordered for deportation. No point in speculating what these people's circumstances were. None of his business. He tapped the GPS app on his phone and typed the address of his next destination for directions.

He nosed out of the parking lot and onto the highway. Fifteen minutes later, traffic slowed down. There were cars stopped in the opposite direction, but this highway consisted of only two lanes on each side, and some drivers had to slow down out of curiosity. The culprit: a fender bender involving a white van and a red car. A bald guy got out of the van and directed the cars to go around the accident. Was the guy wearing a bulletproof vest? Perhaps SWAT? What the hell was going on?

As Domingo drove past the gridlock, he got a clear view of the writing on the back of Baldy's blue vest: ICE.

The image of the group of migrants entering a motel room came back to him. *ICE raid!* Who knew how many undocumented immigrants were staying at the motel?

His instinct to help others took over. Perhaps it was empathy or compassion or just nosiness, but he couldn't explain the impulse that drove him. He veered onto the next exit, got off the highway and onto a back road. He needed to return to the motel to warn the migrants without getting entangled in the traffic jam on the highway. What would he tell those desperate hopefuls? What if ICE wasn't raiding that motel?

No time for dillydallying. He raced back to where he'd come from. Someone at the motel must have tipped off ICE, which was aggressively rounding up undocumented immigrants based on the current White House policy. Often, the raids targeted the victims, people who'd spent their life savings for a chance to cross the border illegally, instead of the criminals who raked in the money by smuggling migrants.

His Pontiac screeched to a stop in the parking lot. He hopped out and strode to the ground-floor room. TV noises could be heard from outside. He rapped on the door. "ICE is coming! Open the door."

The TV went silent, but nobody answered.

He knocked again. *"La policia viene!"*

They might not know what *ICE* meant, but surely they understood *police*. The door opened a tad, and a middle-aged man peeked out, eyes wide with fear.

"There's going to be a raid," warned Domingo. "You and your *compañeros* better get outta here."

A lot of whispering in Spanish behind the door. Domingo switched to Spanish to inform them about the ICE van just a few miles away. The man asked who he was.

"Un buen samaritano." A Good Samaritan, Domingo said. By sheer luck, Domingo was a US citizen, but he knew what it meant to be unwelcome in this country. As a foreign-born American, his legal status would always remain conditional, a sobering thought that kept him grounded and magnanimous toward the less fortunate. "You better get out now. Go to the mall or the movies or the supermarket. Anywhere but here."

The whispers behind the door grew louder. These desperate hopefuls had twenty minutes, tops. The fender bender wouldn't take long to sort out.

At last, the man stepped out. He was clearly the leader—*El Jefe*—by the way he'd shut the door behind him to protect his group.

Not a word of English, but Domingo understood. They came from El Salvador. There were others, Guatemalans, at the opposite end of the parking lot. The coyotes who'd smuggled them would come back tonight to transport the group to another motel under the cover of darkness. They'd been traveling for three days, from one motel to another. They'd crossed the border in Texas, but they didn't know their final destination.

No shit. These people had traveled over two thousand miles. What to do? He glanced around. At least there were no people in the parking lot, just cars. Domingo asked the man where they'd gotten their groceries. The man pointed behind the motel.

Good enough. He told him to get his *compañeros* to return to the supermarket where they had gone shopping and stay there for a while.

The man nodded and knocked on the door.

When it opened, El Jefe went in, and Domingo saw the messy room with empty soda bottles and food wrappers on the floor. He counted six grown men, two teenage boys, and two adult women. How on earth did they fit in the tiny room?

"*Que hay de los Guatemaltecos?*" asked one of the women. Everyone turned to Domingo for an answer.

"The Guatemalans? You're worried about the Guatemalans? You have no time. Go now." He motioned for them to come out.

But, no, they needed their backpacks and plastic bags and whatnot. Everyone talked at the same time. Where would they go? How long would they be gone?

Domingo stayed outside the room to keep an eye on the road for the ICE van. He alternated between glancing at the El Salvadorans inside, then his wristwatch, then the road. One second passed. Two. Three. Four. Five. "*Vamos, vamos,*" he urged them.

When El Jefe came out, everyone followed. Again like a procession.

"Go, go." Domingo gestured toward the back of the motel. He went back to his car, where he would wait until the El Salvadorans were out of sight. But the group stood in the middle of the parking lot, watching him.

What were they waiting for? El Jefe shuffled toward Domingo, all sheepish.

Domingo got out of his car. "Chief, what's up? I told you to go." Would the man ask for money? Did he expect to shake hands and exchange bro hugs? Before he could get an answer, the noise of cars pulling over stopped him and El Jefe both.

The ICE van and an unmarked SUV were parked in front of the main building where guests checked in and out. Only about twenty yards away, but the motel office blocked the sight of the desperate hopefuls.

El Jefe sprinted toward his companions, calling out "*Vamonos!*" Domingo was at their heels. They all ran toward the back of the motel.

An old man emerged from one of the rooms and gave them the stink eye.

How long would it take before the man understood what was going on and informed the ICE agents? The supermarket had ceased to be an option. They wouldn't make it that far.

Domingo gazed up. The motel had an exterior corridor. A janitor's cart stood outside a door on the second floor. The building was only two stories high, so it was the farthest they could get away from ICE within the premises. He yelled at El Jefe to stop and wait by the stairs while he climbed up two steps at a time.

Did they follow his instruction? Nope. Instead, they all climbed the stairs too. Their footfalls sounded like a stampede. *Goddamn it.* He wanted them to wait downstairs. What if his idea didn't work?

No time to waste. The cart propped the door open. He entered the room, where a brown-skinned young woman was changing the bedsheets. "Excuse me, this room isn't ready," she demurred.

"I need your help." He pulled his wallet from his jeans pocket and took out all his cash, two hundred dollars, the amount he'd withdrawn from an ATM last night for his weekly expenses. El Jefe and a few others peeked inside. Domingo raised his palm at them—*wait there.*

"Take this." He extended his hand with the cash. "Please let these El Salvadorans hide in this room until the ICE agents are gone."

The maid stood frozen, mouth agape. He'd just revealed the presence of ICE, perhaps not the wisest thing to do, but there was no time to make a ruse.

Still, she hadn't accepted the cash. Domingo locked eyes with her, willing her to say yes. The El Salvadorans murmured among themselves. The moment of indecision was getting longer. Would she agree, or scream to call the attention of the authorities? *Come on. Play nice.* He didn't want to threaten her with bodily harm as a bluff.

He gave diplomacy and bribery another chance. "Please take this. Consider it a bonus, plus you earn karma points." He took a step closer, money in his hand. "These people need *our* help—yours and mine. This isn't their fault, okay? The scumbags who gave them false promises and took their money are the bad guys."

She neither said yes nor no. Instead, she reached down to the ancient boom box on the floor and turned it on. A country song blasted. Then she snatched the cash from Domingo's hand and motioned for El Jefe and the others to come in.

Yes!

Everyone trooped inside while Domingo and the woman stepped outside. She'd carried the blasting boom box and put it atop the dirty linens in the cart. The music camouflaged the noises of the El Salvadorans. Good thinking.

"How long would I need to hide them?" she asked. "Are you gonna come back to get them?"

She was probably in her early twenties. Perhaps a Latina, but not a trace of accent.

"I'm going to call a lawyer who works for La Esperanza Network."

"What's that?" She narrowed her eyes.

"It's a nonprofit group that helps undocumented immigrants. Just keep them here for as long as you can."

"What if someone checks into this room—"

A commotion in the parking lot interrupted their conversation. They both looked down. The ICE van lurched and blocked the parking lot's entrance. Agents hopped out of the vehicle and strode toward a ground-floor room, but to Domingo's surprise, they passed the room of the El Salvadorans. They were going after the Guatemalans.

Domingo counted four agents wearing bulletproof vests and two others wearing ICE T-shirts but without vests.

"Call the lawyer now," the maid urged Domingo. "I'm gonna lose my job if Randall finds out."

Domingo followed her gaze. Down in the parking lot, a barrel-shaped man stood by the white van, watching the agents who were banging on the door.

"Is that Randall?" asked Domingo "Is he the manager?"

"Assistant manager. He's an asshole."

"He tipped off ICE?"

She nodded. "He's done it before. ICE pays him each time."

Son of a bitch. Hotel operators were not obligated to help ICE and certainly not to act as the agency's spies. In fact, it was illegal for Randall or anyone to discriminate against motel guests based on their race or legal status.

"Call the lawyer now," the woman repeated. "I can't hide these people forever."

"All right. I promise I won't leave until I get them safely out of this motel." Domingo speed-dialed the hotline for La Esperanza Network. He motioned for the maid to stay outside the door.

The woman nodded.

He went downstairs to get a better view of the ICE agents. The Guatemalans were being herded like cattle into the van.

Thank goodness the lawyer picked up his call. He told her about the El Salvadorans. After the lawyer agreed to pick up the group herself, Domingo hung up.

The bald ICE agent was talking to Randall the Rat, who was pointing at the room occupied by the El Salvadorans. There was no doubt what would happen next.

Domingo couldn't stand around without arousing suspicion, so he sat inside his Pontiac, his phone against his ear. Anyone would think he was talking to someone.

He gazed up to the second floor. The maid went into the next room, though the cart with the loud boom box remained where it was.

Randall led the ICE agents to the El Salvadorans' room. Baldy rapped on the door like crazy. After a moment, Randall opened the door with a key. The agents rushed inside.

Holy crap. It was like watching a movie, except this raid could mean detention and devastation of eleven El Salvadoran lives.

His phone rang, startling him. It was still pressed on his ear. Now he didn't have to pretend to talk to someone. "Hello?"

"It's Cheryl. Tessa Woodridge wants you to fly to Folsom tomorrow. No questions asked. You can fly first class or charter a private jet or do whatever you have to do. Just get there by four p.m. I'll text you the address where you need to be."

"What?" The call had been so unexpected that he glanced at his phone to make sure it wasn't a prank. It was legit. Cheryl's phone number showed on the screen. "Why do I need to go to Folsom?"

"Because she's paying you to do so?"

"Cheryl, I'm not kidding."

"Neither am I. All I know is she wants to meet with you in person in California."

"Please tell me this doesn't have anything to do with Julian Alondra."

"Brace yourself—Tessa and Julian are still together despite your warning about Dulce and your information about the DEA. Apparently, Julian broke up with Dulce one month before he started dating Tessa, but Kevin Godfrey wasn't privy to that information. Of course, Girl Boss was only too willing to forgive Julian for not mentioning Dulce to begin with. She spent last weekend with Julian in Mexico."

"What? And nobody kidnapped her?"

Cheryl chuckled. "Tessa and Julian are getting serious. Grammy and her sister, Alice, have already met Julian, but Tessa's introducing him to the rest of her family in two days at Alice's birthday party."

"I'm meeting with Tessa tomorrow, and she's introducing Julian to her family the day after our meeting. Why do I get the feeling that whatever Tessa is going to tell me tomorrow has something to do with Lover Boy."

"That's what I think too. You better show up so you can tell me all about it. It's tomorrow at four o'clock in Folsom. Got that?"

"Cheryl, I'm in New Jersey watching a reality show of ICE agents busting the asses of desperate hopefuls in real time—"

"Oh, good. So you're in your groove. That's a great way to segue into your next case. By the way, I just contacted Joe Medina on behalf of Tessa about your retainer."

"Are you her assistant or BFF?"

"What does it matter? She's paying me good money to do it. Just like she's paying *you* to be at her beck and call. Gotta go now. Enjoy the reality show."

Cheryl had ended the call with her teasing cackle.

Domingo didn't remove the phone from his ear as he watched the authorities climb into the van and the unmarked SUV. They must have assumed the El Salvadorans had escaped. But they'd caught the Guatemalans. Randall the Rat appeared smug as hell.

Domingo exhaled a great sigh when the ICE vehicles drove away. He'd bought the El Salvadorans some time. They would at least be given a fair chance to apply for asylum.

He would wait until the lawyer picked them up. The migrants and the maid ought to remain nameless to him. It was best to leave this encounter anonymous for everyone's safety. No one could rat out anyone they didn't know.

He digested Cheryl's news. No wonder Tessa never got back to him, even though he'd requested she call him after confronting Julian about Dulce. His assumption that Girl Boss had simply moved on was wrong.

Damn. One call from Cheryl had changed his to-do list. He ran a mental note: *Book the next flight to Sacramento. Touch base with Joe Medina about new assignment. Find a substitute process server for pending subpoenas.*

His phone pinged. Cheryl's text appeared. It was the date, time, and address for Domingo's meeting with Tessa Woodridge.

And he'd thought he was through with the heiress. The strange pull of the unknown nudged him. Who knew what surprises awaited him? A pulse of anticipation cycled up his spine like no subpoena he served ever could. He was a sucker for solving real-life jigsaw puzzles. He glanced at his watch, hoping the lawyer would arrive soon.

CHAPTER 13

What to Do If ICE Tries to Bust You

Even though you're undocumented, you deserve respect. The majority of Americans are good people who believe in treating their fellow human beings humanely. Neither the Republican Party nor the White House is above the law. ICE is not the Gestapo. So if ICE agents give you a surprise visit, do the following:

- *Don't open the door. Ask the agents to show an ID through the peephole.*
- *Ask for a search or arrest warrant signed by a judge. If there's no such warrant, keep the door shut. Stop talking to the agents. Call La Esperanza Network for help:1-800-MIGRANT.*
- *If the agents have a warrant, ask them to slide it under the door so you can examine it.*
- *If it's an arrest warrant, the agents can legally enter your home. If you're on probation with a search condition, they can legally enter your home. If it's a Form I-205 for removal or deportation, they CANNOT enter your home without your consent.*
- *If you open the door, it means you're allowing them in. Don't tell any damn lies or show any false documents. Don't sign anything without talking to a lawyer first.*
- *If agents force their way into your home, don't resist. Tell them:*

I'm exercising my right to remain silent. Then shut up. Call 1-800-MIGRANT immediately.

◆ ◆ ◆

Domingo's encounter with the El Salvadorans yesterday had inspired this chapter of his book, but he didn't finish writing it because his plane had just landed in Sacramento.

He proceeded with great efficiency. *Make a pit stop at the men's room, check. Rent a car at Avis, check. Drive to Folsom, check.*

He parked the rental car, a gray Toyota Camry, on the side of the street. Four o'clock on Saturday afternoon, as instructed. He walked up to the front door of the colonial-style house and rang the doorbell. No gates in this posh neighborhood, just wide front lawns and ample driveways.

"Hi, Sunday." Tessa Woodridge herself opened the door. Her flowing white dress with spaghetti straps gave her the aura of a happy bride. Yeah, she'd spent last weekend in Mexico with Lover Boy. "Come in. This is my grammy's house. I live close by, so I spend a lot of time here."

Yep, Cheryl had given him the backstory. After Tessa's parents died, her grandma had bought this house and raised Tessa and Alice here.

A narrow foyer with a console table brimming with white roses greeted him. In the living room, a middle-aged woman sat in an armchair next to the marble fireplace. She was talking on the phone.

Tessa smiled at her. "That's Aunt Laura. She's in town for Alice's birthday. The official Woodridge invasion will happen tomorrow afternoon when my other relatives arrive for the party."

Neither the grandmother nor the sister was in the living room. The crystal chandelier hanging from the high ceiling was the single most extravagant thing he'd ever seen—about eight feet long in three tiers. It shone brilliantly even when it wasn't lit.

Tessa sashayed in her strappy sandals with a kind of casual luxury that rich people exuded. She led him to the backyard.

A couple of guys were setting up chairs and round tables while another man was setting up an industrial-size grill in a makeshift outdoor kitchen.

"Is this all for Alice's party?" asked Domingo.

"Yes. She's turning thirty-seven tomorrow," said Tessa. "Let's find a quiet spot where we can talk."

The patio was set on the high-bank lawn overlooking Lake Natoma. The trees formed a natural canopy. According to Cheryl, the Woodridge matriarch bought this property so Alice and Tessa could look out across the lake and find some solace in their new life as orphans. The lush, airy waterfront view must have cost millions then and twice as much today.

They sat on oversize rattan chairs, side by side so they both enjoyed the view. A pitcher of ice water and glasses lay on the table. There was a small bowl of fresh lemon slices and another with sprigs of mint.

Tessa poured water into two glasses and dropped in pieces of lemon and mint using tongs. She gave him a glass. "Did Cheryl tell you about Dulce?"

He thanked her. So this was how the wealthy drank water. "Yep. Julian broke up with Dulce one month before the two of you reconnected. But, of course, Kevin Godfrey was clueless."

"Julian and Dulce broke up because she got pregnant and the baby's not Julian's." She crossed her legs, very demure. "That part of the story is closed. It's all in the past."

"Okay. Which chapter are we in the saga now?" he teased.

But she didn't even smile. "I asked you to fly here for two reasons. First, I want you to continue looking for Raul and Maria Beltran. You said they might be in the Napa Valley area."

"Yes, in Ravine."

"Ravine is only a couple of hours away. You can start your search today."

"Okay." Domingo took a sip of water. "Is Julian coming here for Alice's party? Does he know I'll be looking for his parents?"

"Yes, he's arriving tomorrow morning. No, he doesn't know that I've hired you to look for his parents." She gripped her glass with both hands. "I haven't come clean about you and Cheryl. He doesn't know that you're a bounty hunter and Cheryl's a PI." She sipped her water. "I didn't tell Julian that you talked to Lou Harold. And that's the second reason why I need you. I've decided to meet with Lou, and I want you to arrange it. I'm willing to see him in Sacramento. I'll text you the address of a restaurant where he can find me at eleven in the morning, two days from now. Tell him he can take it or leave it. I'm having lunch at the restaurant that day whether he comes or not."

"What made you change your mind about Lou?" asked Domingo.

"Mexico City."

Domingo gave her a questioning look.

"You know how I've always wanted to see where Julian lives? Well, last weekend I was finally there in Mexico City. And I could have sworn that a car was following us wherever we went. This time it wasn't Lou Harold following us but two men. And when I told Julian about them, he brushed it aside just like before." She set her glass down and looked away, as though deep in thought.

A mild breeze from the lake tempered the summer heat. The air reeked of dried grass. From their perch, the two bridges in Historic Folsom were visible. One was an old footbridge, where a few people jogged and walked.

When at last she trained those astonishing green eyes on him, she said, "I'm going to ask Lou Harold if those men in Mexico City were his. And if not, does he know who they might be. I want to hear what he has to say about Julian and Tio."

"It's the right call." Domingo drank his water. "What do those two men look like?"

"One is older, maybe fifties, and the other one is younger, maybe twenties. They're brown skinned, possibly Hispanic. They have strong similarities. They could be father and son. They're both wiry and about the same height, five-nine or five-ten. The older man is balding, but the younger one has thick curly hair." She uncrossed her legs and smoothed down the front of her dress. "You know what else?"

"What?"

"That night I told Julian about the two men, we went back to his place around eleven. I was beat, so I was asleep shortly after that. When I woke up at around two in the morning, Julian was not in the house. He was gone for almost two hours. I pretended to be asleep. The entire weekend I waited for him to volunteer the fact that he'd snuck out in the middle of the night, but he didn't. That's when I decided to hire you again." She laced her fingers on her lap. "Tell me what you're thinking."

He pointed to himself. *Me?* "I don't know what to say." He would rather not express his opinion that Girl Boss's relationship bordered on *Fatal Attraction* loony. They both knew her true rival for Julian's attention was the Malverde Cartel, a demanding and downright dangerous "mistress" that apparently followed Julian around and summoned him in the wee hours. This must be the reason why Julian had avoided inviting his girlfriend to Mexico City for as long as he could. It was crazy for Tessa to continue seeing the guy.

"You must think I'm this ditzy, pathetic girl who's desperately clinging to her boyfriend," she said.

"No, not at all." Not ditzy or pathetic. Desperate, maybe. Definitely fixated on a guy who'd appeared out of the blue on the day she lost her parents. Pure coincidence—not a miracle or true love or destiny or any of that jazz. He bit his tongue.

"Hi, baby girl!" A woman's voice interrupted their conversation.

Both Domingo and Tessa glanced over their shoulders. "Hi, Grammy!" Tessa waved. She turned to him. "I told my grandmother and sister that you're a supplier. It's the same cover story as in Las Vegas—"

"Cheryl and I run Prime Meats," Domingo interjected. "We're doing business with Giant Burgers. Got it."

Mrs. Woodridge approached.

Domingo rose to shake hands with her. She reminded him of another rich, old white lady, Mary Reed, who'd hired Domingo to find her stepdaughter, Monica Reed. Mary had succumbed to cancer two years ago, and Monica's case was closed, but the lessons from the case stuck with him like an old scar.

He'd bonded with Mary, but he never imagined she would include him in her will. She'd left him two valuable antiques—a gilt-framed map of the thirteen American colonies circa 1775 and the original blueprint of a Virginia cottage circa 1800. Joe Medina had advised him to get them appraised by an antiques dealer, while Domingo's mother, whom he called Mamang, wanted him to take the items to the *Antiques Roadshow*. He'd done neither, so far.

"It's nice to meet you," he said. "I should go, ma'am."

"You can't leave without eating first." Grammy motioned for him and Tessa to follow. "The caterer sent a tray of sample appetizers. Why don't you have a taste?"

Two white women emerged from the house. The one holding to a walker had to be Alice. She wore a summer dress and eyeglasses.

He ran through Tessa's sister's background in his head. *Alice's main problem was balance and depth perception due to cerebral palsy. Some learning disability, but not intellectual disability. Homeschooled by special tutors throughout her childhood.*

The other woman, clearly a caregiver, was patting Alice's mouth with a tissue.

Tessa, Grammy, and Domingo walked toward the two women who had just sat down at one of the party tables. Everything had been set up; the workers had left. On the table, there was a tray of appetizers, surrounded by a pitcher of iced tea, glasses, small plates, cloth napkins, and forks.

Tessa introduced Domingo to Alice and Susie before entering the house with Grammy. They had to speak with Aunt Laura about "logistics," which he guessed must have something to do with tomorrow's party.

He'd assumed correctly that the other woman, Susie, was a nursing aide who cared for Alice around the clock. Alice tended to drool because of muscle weakness on the left side of her body, including her face. Her mouth was lopsided. Her wobbly neck made her look like a baby learning to hold her head up.

"Help yourself, Sunday," Susie urged him. She sported a pixie haircut that flattered her high cheekbones. She was spooning food onto two plates. One for her and another for Alice.

The tray contained grilled salmon bites, cucumber canapés, and fancy-looking cheesy pastries.

Domingo poured iced tea into three glasses for all of them. He picked a couple of each appetizer. He gobbled the bite-size pastries with some kind of fruit preserve on top. "Wow, this is delicious. What is it?"

"Brie . . . cup," answered Alice.

"It's the family's favorite cheese," added Susie.

"I can see why." Domingo washed it down with iced tea. "Have you guys met Julian?" A bail enforcer worth his salt never wasted any time shooting the breeze without getting any information in return.

Susie nodded. "You know him?"

"I met him in Las Vegas a couple of weeks ago, when he and Tessa were there."

"Julian's been here a few times." Susie nudged a canapé toward Alice. "Tomorrow he'll get to meet the extended family. Everyone's looking forward to seeing him."

"Are Tessa and Julian getting engaged? Is that why everyone's coming? I mean, in addition to Alice's birthday."

Susie shrugged. "Not that I know of."

"From what I saw in Vegas, Julian and Tessa looked very happy together. I wouldn't be surprised if they got engaged soon. They look great together . . ." He was terrible at small talk. Just as he was about to give up on the conversation, Alice swayed her head, which he took as a sign that she was about to speak.

"He . . . he . . . saved . . . Tessa . . . in . . . in the desert." The rectangular eyeglasses suited Alice's round face. The black rim and thick lenses gave her the air of a no-nonsense young woman.

He shoved the salmon bites in his mouth. "I heard. What an incredible story of how they first met."

"He's . . . very handsome." Alice's lips curled into a mischievous smile.

The suddenness and the smoothness of her remark surprised Domingo; the innocence of her admiration touched him. "He looks like a movie star, doesn't he? Like Leo DiCaprio. Hell, Julian's more handsome than Leo." Yes, handsome, but *dangersome*, if ever there was such a word.

Alice wobbled a big yes.

"You know, girls who are crazy about Leo suffer from a serious form of injury—they've been DeCapri-*tated*."

Both women chuckled. No doubt Julian had charmed Alice and Susie.

They continued eating and sipping iced tea. Susie dabbed the corner of Alice's lips every now and then. And when the breeze blew, she brushed the hair out of Alice's eyeglasses with her fingers, the way a mother might have done with a child. Susie was clearly very protective of Alice. He himself couldn't help but feel protective as well.

After they finished eating, Alice asked Susie if they could go to the front yard to watch the birds.

"You guys go ahead. I'll take the dirty dishes to the kitchen," volunteered Domingo.

Susie thanked him and told him where the kitchen was. She helped Alice with her walker as they shuffled around the house toward the front yard.

Domingo hauled the used dishes indoors. Tessa, Grammy, and Aunt Laura were at the kitchen island talking on the phone with the speaker mode on. They were talking simultaneously about who was arriving when and who was staying with whom.

Tessa got up and took the dishes from Domingo and deposited them in the kitchen sink.

"I'm headed to Ravine," he told her. "When I find the Beltrans, what do you want me to do?"

Tessa gestured for them to proceed to the living room. "I would like to speak with them in person. You can tell them I'm dating Julian and I would love to meet them."

"Okay. Are you going to tell Julian, or is this still meant as a surprise?"

She pouted. "I'll talk to his parents first, and then I'll tell him. Otherwise, he might stop me. I'm afraid he's not telling me everything about them."

No kidding. How could a son not know where his parents were? Sure, they're undocumented, but Domingo dealt with parents like the Beltrans all the time. They sent their hard-earned money to their kids and other relatives back home. Or they went broke paying human traffickers to try to bring their children stateside. They didn't just cut off family ties without a reason.

Meanwhile, Julian's uncle sent him to college in Arizona, and the guy reinvented himself as Jules Alexander and conveniently "lost touch" with his undocumented parents. Was he embarrassed by their social status now that he was going places? Whatever it was, Julian wasn't being forthcoming.

Tessa and Domingo crossed the living room, but before they could reach the front door, a young blonde with a roundish face and figure walked in.

"Bella!" Tessa rushed to hug her. She introduced Domingo to the woman, who turned out to be her cousin. Bella had just flown in from Los Angeles.

He said goodbye and left the cousins gabbing in the living room.

In the front yard, the late-afternoon sunlight seeped through tall trees and dappled the vast lawn. A white sedan was parked on the driveway. It hadn't been there before. It must be Bella's car. He himself had parked on the side of the street.

Susie and Alice sat on the bench under an oak tree, the walker beside Alice. Numerous bird feeders and wind chimes hung from trees surrounding them. They were both gazing down at a blue bird foraging at the base of a tall multiplex birdhouse near the bench.

"Hi." Domingo approached them. "What kind of bird is that? What a beautiful shade of blue."

Susie turned to Alice. "I'm afraid I don't know my birds. Alice? She adores birds and knows their names."

"It . . . it's . . . the . . . Cali . . . fornia . . . scrub . . . jay." Alice's neck wobbled in her struggle to speak.

"I've never heard of it before," admitted Domingo. "I thought it was the blue jay."

"It's . . . it's the . . . cousin . . . of . . . the blue . . . jay."

"Ha!" Domingo shifted on his feet. "I sure hope the scrub jay is a decent cousin, unlike my good-for-nothing cousin Nardo in Manila who never paid back the twenty pesos he borrowed from me in 1997."

Alice smiled, lips parted as though about to say something clever. But perhaps she didn't because it would've taken too much effort. A pocket of silence hung in the air.

"Are you Filipino?" Susie broke the ice. "I hope you don't mind me asking."

"No, I don't. I was born and raised in the Philippines. I'm a naturalized US citizen."

A honk interrupted their conversation. They all turned toward the driveway. A midnight blue Audi Sportback pulled over behind the white sedan. A guy in khaki pants and a polo shirt climbed out of the car.

It was Julian.

Domingo's heart pounded. *Fuck.* Julian was a half day early.

Julian's dark hair was not slicked back this time but tousled in a boyish manner. Boat shoes, no socks. Very cool.

"He's . . . he . . . here." Alice beamed her lopsided smile. She rose with the help of Susie.

Domingo couldn't ignore Julian since they'd met before. He also didn't feel like chatting with the guy and pretending to be a meat supplier, not when he was about to search for his undocumented parents without his knowledge. He did neither. He said goodbye to the women with a quick flick of the hand and, ever so casually, to Lover Boy, as well.

Julian's big grin, meant for Alice and Susie, wavered. His expression was unsure, like he couldn't remember Domingo's name or where they'd met.

"Good to see you, man," Domingo called out as he strode away.

CHAPTER 14

Domingo had never felt so relieved to get in a car. He sat back and just savored the sensation of his heartbeat slowing down to normal. Why had Julian come earlier than planned? Maybe he just wanted to surprise Tessa. Thank goodness Domingo was, in fact, on his way out of the house when Julian arrived.

He turned on the GPS app on his cell phone and wondered how heavy the traffic would be at this time on I-80 en route to Ravine, near Napa Valley. He'd passed by it before on the way to San Francisco, but he'd never visited the place.

According to the app, the drive would cover seventy-seven miles, estimated to take one hour and twenty minutes. *Not bad.* He should get to a motel there before dark.

A wail pierced the air. He jerked his head toward the big house, the view of which was blocked partly by cars parked on the driveway. Was it Alice or Susie? He hopped out of the rental car and jogged up to the driveway and onto the front lawn.

Susie and Alice stood facing the house, tall and imposing with its wide windows and gabled roof. Sunlight bounced off its white facade. Susie's arms were wrapped around Alice's shoulders.

Domingo stopped beside Susie. "What happened?"

She pointed at the roof. "The blue bird's trapped. Alice is worried it might die."

Alice was teary.

"The bird's okay." Domingo waved in the direction of the roof. "He's snug in the vent. He knows to keep still. Otherwise, he'll break his wings or his legs."

Alice swallowed. "He's . . . he's very . . . smart."

"That's right." Domingo smiled. "I'll rescue the scrub jay, I promise."

"Will . . . will . . . you?" Alice's eyes grew wide.

"Yes, of course. We don't want his cousin, blue jay, to get mad at us."

Alice glanced at Susie in a conspiratorial manner, then smiled at Domingo. Yep, the three of them shared an inside joke.

Tessa and Julian burst into Domingo's view. They'd come from the backyard.

Shit. No way of avoiding Lover Boy, who exchanged nods with him. So be it.

"What's wrong, Alice?" Tessa stood before her sister, panting.

Susie repeated what she'd told Domingo. The bird shrieked, prompting everyone to look up. Its head poked out, but its body was caught between the slats of the pitched roof's vent.

The roof was too steep and the two-story house too tall. No wonder birds roosted under the eaves. It must be hard to clean those eaves regularly.

Grammy, Bella, and the aunt emerged from the house and joined the others in the front yard.

"Good Lord," Grammy gasped. "Somebody call 911. We need the firefighters to rescue that bird."

Julian retrieved his cell phone from his pocket. "I'm calling right now."

"No need. Let me get up there." Domingo stepped forward. "Mrs. Woodridge, you have a tall ladder?"

"It's in the garage," the old lady said.

Julian clapped Domingo's back. "Sunday, let me do it. I'll climb."

A knight in shining armor. Julian Alondra saved Tessa's life before, so it was only natural that he would do something equally heroic for the sister.

"Honey, your boat shoes are not meant for climbing," warned Tessa. "Sunday's sneakers have more traction."

"She's right," agreed Domingo. "Besides, I already promised Alice."

"Let's go get the ladder, huh? I'll be your assistant," sneered Julian—tall, fit, and poised, like only a man aware of his own charm could be.

The sneer wasn't lost on Domingo, but he let it slide.

They went to the garage through the house, Julian leading Domingo as though to say that *he* knew this house. He opened the door connecting the house to the garage, switched the lights on, and grabbed the folding ladder.

"Let me help with that," offered Domingo.

"No, I got it." Julian carried the ladder. "Tessa told me she just chose Prime Meats as a supplier. Congratulations."

"Thanks." Domingo snatched a pair of work gloves hanging on a rack.

"But where's Cheryl?" asked Julian.

"She couldn't make it. I don't mind traveling, so I volunteered to come."

"You just like volunteering, don't you? A regular Boy Scout." Julian chuckled.

"Like they say . . . those who can, do. That's Cheryl. Those who can't . . . volunteer. That's me." Domingo laughed a little too loudly.

Julian smiled woodenly before pressing a button. The garage door opened.

Domingo's eyes landed on Tessa, who pinned him with a gaze that said *Don't get busted.* He waggled his eyebrows up and down. *I got this.* He and Julian stepped out of the garage at the same time.

"Here it is," announced Julian. He unfolded the ladder and positioned it against the side of the house. "It's about a couple of feet short."

All eyes on the ladder and the roof.

"Isn't it pretty steep?" Grammy shaded her eyes against the sun with her hand. "Is it safe for Sunday to climb?"

"Don't worry, ma'am. I've climbed trees in the Philippines that are taller," Domingo assured Grammy. Nobody needed to know the real reason he'd climbed tall trees in his native country. One time, it was to evade ruffians who'd tried to extort his earnings from bootlegging. The second time, it was to scout the neighborhood for the same ruffians to avoid crossing paths with them. He had honed his climbing skills under the most stressful conditions. Of course he could climb the damn roof.

Alice's face scrunched. Whether she was concerned for Domingo or the bird, he wasn't sure. Maybe both.

"It's okay, sweetie." Tessa rubbed Alice's back. "Sunday will get the bird out of there."

That annoyed Julian, who shot Domingo a reproving glance. "*Ay, cabron.* What are you waiting for?"

Domingo put the gloves on and waved at Alice before taking the first step on the ladder.

"You know, I wanted ask you—"

Julian's voice stopped Domingo.

Lover Boy's dark eyes bored right through him. "Did you really have to come here on a Saturday to close a deal with Tessa?"

Fuck. The man knew Domingo was keeping a secret, but did he suspect it had to do with his own damn secrets? He decided to play it cool. "Don't tell me you're jealous."

"Should I be?" Julian's eyes sharpened. Territorial as a wolf.

Jesus, Lover Boy really was jealous! Domingo couldn't help but chuckle. "Bro, just look at you. When you walk into a room, you bring your own atmosphere. You positively raise the temperature and make the ladies hot. Your shadow has one hundred percent more chance of getting noticed than *all* of me, even if I'm buck naked."

Julian pointed at him with a roguish smile. "I like your self-deprecating humor."

Domingo was applying Joe Medina's rule number two: Stroke a person's ego when asking for a favor—or in this case, avoiding the wrath of the man who was steadying the ladder for his ass. At last, he climbed the rungs.

The summer sun glared down. He wished he'd brought his sunglasses. He climbed up without stopping until he could go no farther. He loomed on the highest rung. Without glancing down, he absorbed the tense silence below.

His extended arms touched the roof, but he couldn't reach the vent. He gripped the edge of the roof and hoisted himself up, one leg at a time, his heart knocking with fear and thrill both. If he fell, he'd be a goner. He wasn't a daredevil, but he felt sorry for Alice. He didn't want a dead bird to ruin her birthday party.

Now he balanced on the roof like an acrobat—or a feral animal on the prowl—while the world below watched with anxiety. He crouched and plucked the bird from the gable vent. He cradled it with both hands.

The women cheered. Julian's expression was tight. Was it because Domingo had stolen his thunder?

Domingo turned his face toward Alice and raised the bird.

It was Tessa who waved in acknowledgment, though her sister looked up at Domingo with slack-jawed wonder.

Domingo descended, right hand clutching the ladder, the other hand carrying the bird. "Easy now, scrub jay. Easy, buddy," he whispered, lest the bird get scared. He held his breath.

When his feet touched the ground, everyone burst into wild applause.

He walked straight to Alice and presented his catch. "Wanna say hi to scrub jay?"

Alice touched the bird's small head and its long tail. The bird cooed.

"Do you think he's ready to fly?" asked Domingo.

Alice nodded.

He lowered the bird to the ground. It hopped as if in a daze. Then it flapped its wings and flew, to everyone's delight. The crowd looked up, enthralled, until the bird disappeared on the horizon.

The women thanked Domingo at the same time. But it was Alice's smile of gratitude he cherished most. "I promised you, didn't I?" He took off the gloves and patted Alice's shoulder.

Lover Boy clasped Tessa's hand with both of his hands, proprietary as always, announcing to the world that, yes, he owned this beautiful heiress's heart.

Domingo handed the gloves to Julian, forcing Julian to let go of Tessa's hand.

"You're the man," Julian mumbled. But his tone meant the opposite.

"Well, I better go now," Domingo said.

"Why don't you stay awhile? Unless you have another deal to close." Julian's voice dripped with sarcasm.

The last remark made Girl Boss blush, guilty as sin for lying to her boyfriend.

"No, I don't, but I'm driving to San Francisco to catch up with an old buddy of mine," said Domingo. "You know, enjoy some downtime this weekend."

"That's cool." Julian curled his lips into a smile, but his gaze revealed something else.

An understanding passed between Domingo and Julian. Julian understood that Domingo wasn't truthful about coming to Folsom as a meat supplier, and yet he didn't know what Domingo's real business with Tessa was. There was one thing, however, that they both knew for sure. If Domingo could climb the roof like a crazy-ass tightrope walker just to save a little bird, he would go to great lengths to do whatever needed doing.

"Have fun in San Francisco," Tessa chimed in.

"That's the plan." Domingo waved without looking back.

CHAPTER 15

Don't Let Your Kids Be Taken Hostage

It was a sad day when America began separating migrant families caught crossing the southern border. The internet was full of images of wailing infants and toddlers being ripped—literally—from their parents' arms. The adults were put in shackles and led away in vans while the children were sent to shelters with no process in place for reuniting them with their families. It's called the "zero tolerance" immigration policy. The public outcry and multiple lawsuits filed by advocacy groups pressured the White House to end it.

If you're reading this and you're planning to cross the border illegally with your family—please DON'T. Here's what you need to understand: ICE continues to separate families if any of these three conditions exist:

- *At least one of the parents has a pending legal infraction in the US, no matter how innocuous. If you've been charged with jaywalking or loitering before (even if it happened ages ago), you will be locked up and your children will be taken away from you.*
- *No legal proof that the children are yours. Same deal.*
- *If ICE suspects you will endanger your children in any way. This could mean anything at all. Maybe you look nasty or unhappy or left your fly open. That's all it would take for ICE to take your kids hostage.*

If you have kids, please don't put them in harm's way. The white man in the White House will take them away from you, call it a "deterrent," and get away with it. Make no doubt about it.

◆ ◆ ◆

Saint Michael's Catholic Church stood on top of a hill in Ravine, with its skinny bell tower visible from miles away. It was Domingo's first stop today. He was following up the lead from the Mexican American manager at the Tucson-area winery who'd remembered that this church had helped Raul and Maria Beltran after they left Arizona for California.

Inday, Joe Medina's niece and researcher at Immigrants Bail Bonds, had cross-checked the lead with immigration advocates in the San Francisco Bay Area, who gave her the name of the priest who helped undocumented immigrants like the Beltrans. It turned out to be the Saint Michael's parish priest.

Domingo couldn't do his job without Inday, whose real name was Alexandra. She was twenty-three years old, and a recent engineering grad. For every new case, Inday did background research for Domingo. The kid knew how to dig up information and piece together seemingly unrelated facts, from newspaper articles to social media to government databases and historical archives.

Background also included crucial information about a subject, such as social security number, IRS filings, DMV records, and credit card information. This kind of research entailed paid sources in government agencies and credit card reporting companies. With a foreigner like Julian, however, Inday only got his credit card information, and only because he happened to have American credit cards. Joe Medina didn't have paid sources in Mexico.

Domingo sat at the parish office waiting for the woman who had ushered him in, a volunteer named Carrie, to return.

He glanced at his writing. One of these days he would publish his work, which was not so much writing as remembering. He would publish it not to make money, but for what? An advice or warning? He had only the vaguest idea of giving it away online to whomever cared to read it or pass it on to would-be immigrants.

"I'm sorry to keep you waiting."

The woman's voice cut his thoughts. She was small, with massive frizzy hair that overwhelmed her narrow face. She'd come back as quiet as the sunbeam streaming from the lone window in the office, which looked like a catchall room. Lots of boxes overflowing with art supplies. A desk cluttered with paperwork. A landline phone ringing.

"Saint Michael's parish. This is Carrie." She spoke on the phone while clearing the desk, shoving pencils in the drawer and then dropping papers in the garbage can at her feet. "Father Jim is in Spain, gone till next month. May I refer you to the monsignor?"

He stuck his little notepad and pen in a pocket of his cargo pants. He raised his gaze. Father Jim was in Spain? *That* was the priest who probably knew the Beltrans. *Shit.* What to do now?

He looked at his wristwatch. Alice's birthday party was yesterday, and today Tessa was having her meeting with DEA Special Agent Lou Harold, probably right about now. Their meeting might change everything. Girl Boss might finally regain her good sense and break up with Julian. She'd be insane to continue dating a drug cartel's civil engineer.

Carrie hung up the phone.

He cleared his throat. "I can't help but overhear what you said on the phone. So Father Jim's not around?"

"That's right. He's on a pilgrimage to El Camino de Santiago in Spain for one month." She grabbed an elastic from a drawer and bunched up her big hair into a ponytail. "What can I help you with . . . Sunday, right?"

He nodded. "I was hoping to talk to Father Jim about a couple, Raul and Maria Beltran."

"Tough luck. Father Jim's in the middle of a five-hundred-mile hike. You heard of El Camino?"

"The Way of Saint James, yeah. I saw the movie with Martin Sheen."

"Come back next month."

No way. He hoped this investigation would end within the next few hours when Tessa woke up from her Snow White slumber, not because of Prince Julian's kiss but because of Lou Harold's tornado warning.

He got up and pulled a business card from one of his pockets. He wrote the names of Julian's adoptive parents on the back. "I'm looking for this couple. They moved from the Tucson area to Ravine several years ago. They're undocumented immigrants. I believe Father Jim helped them."

"You said you're not ICE." She gave him an accusatory look. Her puffy hair reminded him of cotton candy. "The Roman Catholic Church doesn't advocate for illegal immigration."

"I'm not ICE. I'm a bail enforcement agent doing a private investigation for the, uh . . ." How on earth would he explain Tessa Woodridge's convoluted connection to the Beltrans? He scratched his head. "Okay, so here's the deal. The Beltrans have a son, Julian, who's lost touch with them for almost two decades. He's engaged and hoping to find his parents before the wedding."

"For a reunion at the wedding? Oh, I see." Her expression loosened up, a small smile on her lips. "I'll tell Father Jim when he returns. When's the wedding?"

"As soon as I locate Raul and Maria Beltran. Their son doesn't want them to miss it."

"Of course not."

A white lie in exchange for a dead end. Time to check out of the motel. He thanked her and left.

He drove back to the motel and left his rental car there. He strolled to a Filipino grocery store with a little café to grab a bite, hopefully with Filipino pastries for dessert. When he worked in a strange city, he spent half his time making phone calls and waiting for people to return his calls. What better way to kill time than to indulge his sweet tooth?

The café was nothing but a cordoned-off space with a few tables within the grocery store. He sat at a table with a cup of coffee, a steamed pork bun, and a piece of rice cake called *bibingka*.

He planned the rest of his day while he ate. A stop at the local newspaper's office and the public library might yield something useful. In small cities and towns, those places tended to employ longtime residents who knew people and remembered events. Someone might know somebody connected with vineyard workers in the area who could lead him to the Beltrans.

His phone pinged. It was an email from the lawyer at La Esperanza Network. As expected, the El Salvadorans he'd helped three days ago had applied for asylum. Some El Salvadoran families took them in so they could live as normal guests while they waited for the government's decision. What saved them from ICE detention was the fact that there was no outstanding warrant or removal order for them.

The asylum application process could take forever, with no guarantees they'd be allowed to stay in the country. But at least they were free from the clutches of the scumbags who'd smuggled them in. They wouldn't have to pay or surrender future earnings to those criminals.

His cell phone rang. Tessa Woodridge's phone number materialized on the screen. He answered the call.

"Where are you?" she asked.

"Downtown Ravine. I was just at the Catholic church. Unfortunately, the priest who might know the Beltrans is overseas. I'll check out a couple of other places this afternoon." He wolfed down the pork bun. "How was your meeting with Lou Harold?"

"It was brief, and it went well." She spoke in a cautious uptalk that made Domingo wonder what really happened.

"And?"

"Julian's coming to my office. We're going to have a serious conversation about what Lou told me."

"Julian's still in Folsom?" He'd assumed Lover Boy had already gone back home to Mexico City.

"He had to drive to Davis for a meeting with a Terra Firma executive. He's on his way back to Sacramento now so we can talk before he flies back to Mexico later this afternoon."

Domingo could hear a pinging from Tessa's office, perhaps from her computer or phone. He could almost see her wide green eyes, the way they made her look very young but also wise.

"Last night, after Alice's party, Julian told me a little bit more about his adoptive parents," continued Tessa. "I'm not sure that it's useful."

"Every little bit of information helps. What did he say?" Domingo pulled a pen and a small notepad from one of the pockets of his cargo pants.

"He calls them Papi and Mamaita."

"You mean *Mamacita*?"

"No, it's Mamaita. Julian couldn't pronounce *Mamacita* when he was little, and his mother thought it was cute."

"Okay." He began taking notes.

"When Julian was thirteen, Raul and Maria both lost their jobs, and they were broke. Raul crossed to Arizona illegally in the hope of finding a job stateside. The couple worked in a vineyard in Valle de Guadalupe before, so Raul hoped he could find a similar job in the States."

"Valle de Guadalupe?"

"Yes. Julian took me there a few months ago, but he didn't say anything at the time. Last night he said his parents used to work in a vineyard there."

So Julian had taken his girlfriend not to some random resort town but to a place with sentimental value for him. Maybe he had even lived there with his Papi and Mamaita. It showed a tender side of Lover Boy that Domingo could appreciate.

"The first time Papi crossed to Arizona, he didn't get very far because he hurt his foot. After several months, he tried again and succeeded. He worked in a winery in Sonoita, near Tucson. A year later, Julian helped Mamaita cross the desert. She joined Papi in Arizona. Julian was supposed to follow them, but he stayed behind to finish high school. Tio took care of him and sent him to college in Arizona. Julian got a student visa. Since Raul and Maria were undocumented, the family decided it was best for Julian to cut ties with them."

"Just like that?" He shoved the last piece of rice cake in his mouth and gulped down the now lukewarm coffee.

"It wasn't his choice. He's still brokenhearted about the whole thing."

Something was amiss, though he couldn't put a finger on it. "Julian was fourteen when he helped his Mamaita cross illegally?"

"Yes."

"The same year you met him in the desert?"

"I guess."

Also the same year Julian had beaten a gang member in a knife fight, but Domingo refrained from bringing it up. "Are you sure Julian's mother wasn't with him when you met him in the desert?"

"He was definitely alone."

"Or maybe you just didn't see her."

"What are you saying?"

Domingo's jumbled thoughts whirred. He shut his eyes, trying to make sense of the bits and pieces of facts. "Here's what we know for sure—Julian was fourteen when you met him in the desert. How many times would a kid make such a dangerous crossing like that?" He opened his eyes. The grocery store was now hopping with shoppers. The tiny café was full. "Maybe when he saw your parents' wrecked car, he let his mother proceed without him because he knew the accident might cause a delay. And he was right, too, because he had to help you, which led to Deputy Alvarado arresting him and—"

"And that's why Julian failed to follow his parents stateside," Tessa finished for him.

They remained mum for a few seconds.

"I really need to talk to the Beltrans. There are so many things I want to ask them," said Tessa.

He himself had many questions to ask. Why had Tio assumed guardianship over Julian, and what was his role, if any, in Julian's separation from his adoptive parents? "Just ask Julian about the Beltrans. And Tio. Don't forget Tio."

"I tried, but I can't force him, you know."

He heard a woman's voice in the background on the other end of the line. After a moment, Tessa said, "I have to go now. I need to take care of something before Julian gets here."

"Good luck with Julian." He hoped she would convince him to cooperate with Lou. But whatever it was she meant to tell her boyfriend, breaking up wasn't on the agenda or she would have called off Domingo's search for the Beltrans. Domingo's internal antenna picked up a signal before his thoughts could process everything. His gut tingled. He rose and got out of the café while he called Inday in New York.

"Julian's flying from Sacramento to Mexico City this afternoon," he told Inday. "Check his credit cards and see which airline he's going to fly with. Once you have the airline, get me the flight number," he barked on the phone. "I'm going to trail him at the airport."

"Why?" asked Inday.

"Because he just met with Terra Firma, a company that can make any unconventional tunneling project a reality. His interest in the company reinforces the DEA's theory that he and Tio are designing a secret high-tech tunnel." He was acting on a hunch and rushing toward his rental car, though he hadn't yet clarified his intuition. His brain told him he ought to stay in Ravine to look for the Beltrans, but his gut told him otherwise. "I think Julian's up to something. I'm driving back to Sacramento."

He jogged back to the motel's parking lot and slid inside the rental car. Sacramento was a couple of hours away, and he needed to get there before Julian left for Mexico.

What he expected to find out or why, he didn't have a clue just yet, but he'd been chasing criminals for twenty-one long years. He just knew when to get going, when to heed an inexplicable urge. In the business of survival, hesitation could be fatal. He took off fast.

CHAPTER 16

While driving from Ravine to Sacramento, Domingo had been caught in a traffic snarl that lasted an hour. He'd felt like part of a flock of geese swooping down I-80 East, gliding at eighty miles per hour. Halfway to his destination, he'd hit a traffic jam, and then he'd become a waddling goose among a honking gaggle. What would normally take less than two hours to drive became almost three.

Inday, back in New York, had followed Julian's credit card trail faster than Domingo could reach the man. Julian was flying on Delta to Mexico City.

Domingo came whipping into Sacramento International Airport like a competitive runner. When he reached the cordoned-off area managed by TSA, he stood in a corner, hands on his knees as he panted. He already felt out of shape after just three days of skipping his daily workout.

This was the farthest he could go without a boarding pass. From where he stood, the sign for Delta loomed large. By Domingo's calculation, Julian would check in his luggage at the counter and enter the security area from the entrance closest to Delta's service counter for passenger screening.

He glanced at his wristwatch. A quarter past four. An hour and a half before Julian's boarding time. Could he already have gone through screening?

Domingo watched a steady stream of people darting toward various airline counters. Women wearing pajama-type pants and squeaky Crocs. Men in baggy pants that sagged halfway down their butts for an unwelcome display of their underwear.

Fifteen minutes passed. Sixteen, seventeen minutes marched on. If Julian traveled light and had only carry-on luggage, it was possible he'd skipped Delta's counter altogether. He hoped Julian would print his boarding pass at the airline kiosk, which Domingo was watching.

What if Julian was one of those people who flashed their iPhones bearing their electronic boarding passes? In that case, he would skip the airline kiosk. *Shit.* Domingo didn't even know what he expected to find out today. All he knew was that he needed to eyeball Julian. He glanced at his watch again. Fifty minutes before Julian's departure time.

When he raised his gaze, he just about jumped for joy. Lover Boy in the flesh—navy blue suit, slicked-back hair, computer bag hanging from his shoulder.

Wait, who were the two guys with him? One was middle aged, wearing a suit, while the other one, a lot younger, wore a polo shirt and jeans. Brown skinned, maybe Mexicans, and wiry like runners. Could these be the men who tailed Tessa and Julian in Mexico City? Were the guys traveling with Julian without Tessa knowing?

Julian and the men ambled toward the long TSA line snaking into multiple checkpoints. They were whispering as though they knew each other well. The older guy brought his face closer to Julian's. They were eye to eye, locked in a somber conversation.

Domingo took a step closer, just enough to get a better view of the strangers' faces. They both had bulging dark eyes too close together, so they looked like angry roosters. Yeah, the men could be father and son. Junior wore spiffy black-and-white Air Jordans with the famous wings logo on the collar of the sneakers.

Julian took out a piece of paper from his jacket pocket. He stared at it. His boarding pass? All of a sudden, he walked away.

The father called out his name, with the pronunciation "Hoo-lee-yan."

Julian waved him off without breaking his gait. He lined up with a couple of other men at the checkpoint marked TSA PreCheck, the expedited screening process. The service catered to businesspeople and frequent travelers who shelled out the cash for the privilege of not having to take off their shoes and belts or take out their laptops from their bags, provided they'd passed a security background check beforehand.

Sometimes TSA randomly gave some passengers a precheck status. It was like winning a scratch-off lottery game. Maybe that was what happened—Julian had looked at his boarding pass and perhaps noticed the check sign embedded in the barcode. *Congratulations, you just hit the random precheck jackpot.* Or something like that. It happened once to Domingo. How nice it had been to leave behind the other suckers waiting in line.

As expected, Julian breezed through the precheck line. The father and son watched Julian until he cleared the checkpoint. They exited, Domingo on their heels.

The men strode out of the terminal and crossed the street. Domingo was following, hiding behind people dragging their roller suitcases—passengers who'd just arrived and were on their way to the parking lots.

Where were the Mexicans going? Which parking lot? Another couple minutes of tailing and it became clear they were headed for the outdoor daily parking lot, whereas Domingo had parked in the hourly garage.

He ducked behind a parked car and watched the two men hop into a generic-looking blue sedan. He jumped to his feet and scurried in the direction of the garage.

He hightailed it out of the garage, but it was impossible to drive straight to the outdoor parking lot. The airport's one-way loop road forced him to exit the airport premises and turn around to get to the daily parking lot.

It was too late. The father and son were gone. Time to regroup.

He drove to the first Giant Burgers he saw and sat down at a table with a cup of coffee. He called Inday, but she wasn't picking up. He texted her instead. Julian went thru TSA precheck. See if he's enrolled.

If Julian was enrolled in the TSA PreCheck program, that would indicate he'd passed security background screening by the feds. That meant he wasn't a criminal, or at least he didn't have a record.

Next, Domingo called Tessa.

"I'm in a meeting," she whispered.

"I won't keep you long. I just want you to know that I'm in Sacramento."

"I thought you were in Ravine."

"I was . . . but . . . to make a long story short, I followed Julian at the airport."

A tense silence.

"I saw him talking to the two men who tailed you in Mexico," he continued. "You're right, they look like they're father and son."

"I have to go now," she said. "Meet me at Grammy's house in an hour."

He couldn't tell whether Girl Boss was pissed that he'd followed Julian. Had she summoned him to her grandmother's house for a dressing-down? She could have just fired him on the spot, but she hadn't, so maybe she wasn't mad at him.

His phone pinged. Inday had texted back with an okay; she would look into Julian's TSA PreCheck status.

CHAPTER 17

At Grammy's house, Domingo didn't even have to ring the doorbell—he found the old lady and Alice sitting on a quilted blanket in the front yard. There were cookies and glasses of lemonade. A picnic. Instead of bird-watching, they were watching Susie fill up a bird feeder with seeds.

At five thirty, a lazy breeze kicking up from the nearby lake made the summer afternoon pleasant. The wind chimes tinkled.

"Good afternoon, ladies," Domingo called out. "Can I help you with the feeders?"

All three women glanced back.

Grammy waved hello. "Tessa called a half hour ago. She's on her way here. Shouldn't be too long now."

"No problem. I can make myself useful while I'm waiting for her." He joined Susie under an oak tree and helped to hang a feeder from a low limb. Susie had a bag of birdseed and was filling four other feeders lined up on the ground. A stepladder stood beside the tree. Most of the branches were too high for the women's reach. Unfortunately, he wasn't any taller.

He picked up a full feeder, climbed the three steps of the ladder and hung it on a tree limb. His face warmed up. He glanced at Alice and Grammy. "Being short sucks, but I have a good excuse. In the Philippines, I'm normal height," he joked.

Grammy's face opened into a warm smile.

Alice's neck wobbled. "Joo . . . lian . . . is . . . tall."

"Yep. Tall and handsome as sin." He stepped down the ladder. It was safe to assume Julian charmed every woman he met, but he was still surprised that Alice had brought up Julian out of the blue.

"Julian filled all the water feeders before he left, bless his heart," said Grammy. "At least Susie doesn't have to do it."

Domingo continued hanging the feeders. The multiplex birdhouse was well stocked, so no need to do anything about that. A mourning dove alighted on a refilled feeder and pecked away.

"Sunday, you want a sugar cookie and lemonade?" asked Grammy.

"I just want a cookie." He plopped on the grass, while Susie sat with the two women on the quilt.

Susie handed him a cookie. Alice raised her left arm, as though trying to call attention to it.

Domingo widened his eyes. What was Alice trying to say? Her head swayed as she struggled to speak. He noticed the wristwatch—pink, a little girl's Barbie watch. "Is that a new watch?"

Alice swayed her head even more. It seemed like she was saying no.

"Joo . . . Joo . . . lian . . . re . . . returned . . . it."

"Did he borrow it? I didn't know he likes Barbie," he teased.

More swaying of the head from Alice. "Not . . . bor . . . row."

"No?" Domingo turned to Grammy for an explanation.

"It's a long story, but I think you'll appreciate it." Grammy sipped her lemonade. "The watch has been through a beautiful journey. Back in 2000, when Julian saved our Tessa in the desert, Tessa gave him that Barbie watch to thank him. It came from Alice's watch collection. Alice had gifted that watch to Tessa only a few months before the car accident. Tessa, in turn, gifted the watch to Julian because it was the only valuable thing she carried. Believe it or not, Julian kept the watch all these years. And yesterday, Julian gifted the watch *back* to Alice on her birthday! Isn't that the sweetest thing?"

No shit. Lover Boy sure knew how to make the womenfolk swoon. "And the watch still works after nineteen years?"

Alice nodded with a big smile.

"No kidding." He shoved the entire cookie in his mouth. Why had Julian kept a child's watch for almost two decades? It couldn't possibly have been worth more than twenty or thirty bucks back then. Was it because he cared for the giver—a case of innocent love between a fourteen-year-old boy and an eight-year-old girl? Yeah, he'd called Tessa *niñita*, a pet name.

Multiple wind chimes quaked in the slow breeze—the cluster of bamboo pieces clattered and the copper tubes jangled.

"I wish we had a hammock. Right there between those two birch trees." Grammy pointed toward her right side.

They all gazed at the trees. Alice bobbed her head. "Like . . . in . . . the . . . old house."

"That's right. We had one in Tucson." Grammy set her empty glass down. "We used to have a double hammock in our backyard. Alice and Tessa used to nap there when they were little. It was a lovely dark-green color with a white trim. My husband had the hammock installed specially for the girls. I almost forgot about it."

"Why can't you have a hammock here?" He rose and wiped the cookie crumbs off his hands. "I can hang it for you. I'd put it right here." He walked the length between the two birch trees. "The most perfect spot for watching birds. What do you think, Alice?"

Alice's neck wobbled in excitement, her hand on her chest. A big yes.

"Mrs. Woodridge, just say the word. I can do it easily."

Grammy sat up straight. "But you're busy. When would you do it?"

"I can pick up a hammock after my meeting with Tessa, and I'll come back to hang it after I finish my work in Ravine. I'm flying from Sacramento to New York, so I have to come back here anyway."

Grammy glanced at Alice, who nodded, and then at Susie, who smiled. They seemed to have a wordless way of communication, something Domingo had seen among people who knew each other so well they could finish each other's sentences.

Tessa's Lexus ES 350 pulled over into the driveway. The car's metallic color shimmered like a moonbeam. It looked brand new. It probably cost about fifty grand, at least.

Tessa got out of the car and walked toward them. "Are you guys having a picnic? Hi, Sunday." She wore a sky blue business suit, skirt and jacket, and high heels without stockings. A laptop bag hung from her shoulder.

He waved a hello.

"Hi, sweetie." Tessa knelt beside Alice and pecked her cheek.

"I . . . want . . . a . . . hammock," responded Alice.

"Is that right?" Tessa glanced all around. "You've been planning a landscaping project while you're having a picnic?" She leaned over to kiss her grandmother's forehead.

"Hello, baby girl." Grammy brushed her fingers against Tessa's cheek. "I think it's a great idea. Sunday's very kind to offer to hang the hammock."

Tessa narrowed her eyes at Domingo. "Really?"

He shrugged. "It's not a problem. I know how to do it."

"Let's chat in the backyard." Tessa rose and picked up her bag. "Gram, do you want to eat out tonight?"

"No. I made meat loaf and mashed potatoes. I'll make the salad right before we eat so it won't get soggy."

"Okay. Sunday and I need to talk about work." She removed her shoes and carried them with her bag.

"Stay for dinner," Grammy told Domingo.

He nodded, though he'd probably bail out at the last minute if he wanted to go hammock shopping. He followed Tessa to the back of the house. She sauntered barefoot.

When they reached the patio, she put down her shoes on the ground and the bag on the table. She sank into an oversize rattan chair. "I'm beat."

He sat next to her. "What did Lou Harold tell you?"

"Everything you said to me. He wanted me to intercede." She was gazing at Lake Natoma.

"And did you tell Julian about your meeting with Lou?"

"Yes." She looked pale. The little makeup she usually wore had faded. "Julian's *not* designing or building a tunnel for the cartel, although they want him to. However, he has information for Lou. He's going to contact Lou directly." Her exhaustion showed, as though someone had wrung the life out of her. The poor girl.

"What about Tio?" he asked.

"That's another matter. Tio has ties to the cartel, but Julian doesn't." She rose and ambled away. She was still looking out at the lake, her back to Domingo.

He ought to feel relieved that Julian was cooperating. But he couldn't see Tio working with the cartel without involving Julian, whether today or eventually.

Tio had saved Julian from the border patrol, served as his guardian, and paid for his college education in America. Julian could have studied medicine or law or whatever, but no, he went into civil engineering. Tio, owner of a construction firm, had clearly influenced Julian's choice. Maybe the old man hadn't known that he would need Julian to build a secret tunnel one day, but if he'd worked with drug lords before, he might have anticipated doing projects for them. For as long as Julian hitched his wagon to Tio, it was probably inevitable that Julian would work for the cartel eventually.

The California sun lingered stubbornly in the early evening. The smell of just-mowed grass rose with a warm breeze. Mrs. Woodridge probably hired a gardener to take care of the huge lawn and the garden and all the trees.

Tessa removed her suit jacket; she was wearing a white silk blouse underneath it. She folded the jacket over her arm and turned around. "So you saw Julian at the airport?"

Domingo nodded. "He was talking to two men, most likely the same men who tailed you in Mexico City."

"I asked Lou. They're not DEA."

"Did you ask Julian about them?"

She gnawed at her lower lip. "He confirmed they were following us because the Malverde Cartel wanted very much for Julian to help them with their . . . construction *project.*" She couldn't bear to utter the word *tunnel*; her disdain was written on her face. "Julian called them the Patricios—a father and son—because they're both named Patricio. Julian admitted that he snuck out that night in Mexico City to ask them to stop following us and sort things out."

"But they were still following Julian. Right here in Sacramento. Ask him about that."

"How? I can't tell him that my meat supplier was snooping on him." A deep flush crawled into her cheeks. Like Domingo, she must have realized that although Julian had come clean about certain things, there were many more questions left unanswered.

"Just ask him if he's heard from the Patricios lately," suggested Domingo.

She made a beeline for her bag and shoes and snatched them and carried the whole bundle. "I still want to talk to the Beltrans. I want you to go back to Ravine and look for them."

"Let me help you with that," offered Domingo.

"No, thanks." She proceeded to walk toward the house.

He followed her in silence. He felt unsettled, like he'd left something important behind. The thought of Patricio Senior and Junior nagged at him.

They entered the house through the back door.

In the living room, Tessa dropped her things on the sofa. "Why did you tail Julian at the airport?" She stood straight, wore no expression this time.

Was this her CEO game face? He assumed that at twenty-seven, she needed an unwavering facade to be taken seriously in the boardroom.

"When you mentioned that Julian met with someone from Terra Firma in Davis, I just had to eyeball him. It was a hunch. Although I found no information about Terra Firma, I saw Julian with the Patricios. It was worth the effort."

The front door opened. "Sunday, join us for dinner," Grammy called out. She and Susie flanked Alice, who inched forward without a walker.

"Mrs. Woodridge, I'm not hungry yet. I have to drive back to Ravine. I could stop by Home Depot and buy that hammock before I hop onto I-80." He turned to Alice. "What color should I pick?"

Alice's face bloomed, her jaw slackened, but she was unable to spit out a word.

Susie peered at Alice's face. "I think Alice wants something pink. It's her favorite color."

Alice nodded.

"Oh, pink would be lovely," exclaimed Grammy. "Let me give you some cash, Sunday."

"You can refund me when I come back with it. I'll be sure to bring the receipt."

With that, he managed a quick goodbye and a smooth exit. Already, his mind was swimming. It was back to square one with the Beltrans.

His thoughts about the Patricios fell into place—he had to assume the hombres were still in the area. They hadn't flown back to Mexico with Julian after all. He could only hope that they were flying home later tonight or tomorrow.

Worse, they had crossed the border to tail Julian even though Lover Boy had already "sorted things out" with them. Why? His gut cinched. Despite Julian's cooperation with Lou, his acknowledgment that Tio was shady, and his admission that he'd snuck out in the middle of the night in Mexico City, he was still lying to Tessa.

CHAPTER 18

Don't Feed Your Children to the Big Bad Wolf

In a previous chapter, I urged you to NOT cross the border illegally, especially if you have young children. If you're counting on American compassion for your children, you're dead wrong. You should know that US immigration courts are classified as civil courts, which means that if your kids get separated from you and they're sent to court, the government isn't obligated to provide a court-appointed lawyer, unlike in a criminal court.

You know how I found out about this? I literally stumbled upon it. One time, a toddler blocked my way in the hallway of the immigration court in Manhattan and tripped me! There was a long line of kids, aged about five to twelve, waiting for their turn to appear before a judge.

In Spanish, they told me there was one volunteer from the Unión Americana de Libertades Civiles who drove them, but there was no attorney representing them. When it became obvious they were too young to care for the crawling toddler, I picked up the boy, took him inside the courtroom, and looked for the volunteer, who turned out to be a college student. Jesus, a bunch of kids left on their own!

The judge called out a long Hispanic name I can't remember anymore—the toddler. The ACLU volunteer planted the kid in front of the judge. Guess what happened next? The toddler climbed the judge's desk! The judge picked up the baby and said, "How old is the defendant?"

"Twenty-six months old," said the prosecutor, an ICE attorney.

"I'm deeply sorry, not to mention ashamed, that we're prosecuting babies," responded the judge. The volunteer took the kid while the judge and the prosecutor huddled. I left at that point to do my job. I was in the courthouse to make sure that an undocumented immigrant I had caught attended his deportation hearing.

Here's my point: Spare your children from the court and from illegal crossings to begin with. Although individual judges may be decent, the immigration court itself doesn't exist to protect you or your kids. It's not even a real court—but that's another matter for next time. Just think of it as an institution meant to keep you out. It's the Big Bad Wolf. It's hungry and it's going to devour your children if you allow it.

◆ ◆ ◆

Domingo sat at an outdoor café in Ravine, writing and sipping coffee and watching the crowd streaming into the Grand Renaissance Theater across the road. It was probably an evangelical rally. Banners and signs proclaimed, **We Stand with Jesus! Love Triumphs Over Evil! Faith, Not Fear!**

This was his fourth day in town. He was growing fond of Ravine's hilly roads, small restaurants, and quirky art galleries, but especially the century-old theater with its gilded cornices and grand pillars.

He'd read the plaque explaining its architecture. With the sun backlighting the building, it was aglow. The theater built in the French Beaux-Arts design made him wish he was in Paris. A sense of nostalgia rolled over him, though he'd never stepped foot in France. Everything he'd ever dreamed about Paris came from Liam Neeson's *Taken* and Jackie Chan's *Rush Hour 3*, both kick-ass movies. Who knew counterfeit nostalgia was possible? Or maybe this wistfulness was just wanderlust.

He called Inday in New York.

"Get this—Julian's a US citizen," began Inday.

"Whaaat?"

"Julian has a TSA PreCheck approval, which means he has an American passport."

"I'm pretty sure Julian's Mexican. He used to be a migrant, as in he was detained by Border Patrol in Tucson back in 2000."

"Only US citizens, US nationals, and permanent residents are given a TSA PreCheck approval."

"Maybe he just got the random precheck designation that one time. Or maybe some foreign citizens are given the leeway."

"Nope. Non-US citizens are eligible for global entry, not precheck, and he's definitely on the TSA PreCheck list since last year."

"I met the sheriff's deputy who arrested Julian after he crossed the border illegally. Why would he endure hiking across the desert if his US citizenship would let him take a Greyhound bus to Arizona?"

"That was two decades ago. Maybe he got US citizenship after that," countered Inday.

"Okay, let me count the ways Lover Boy could have gotten US citizenship." Domingo was imagining a checklist. "First, by having parents who are US citizens. An X for that checkbox—his parents are undocumented! Second, by having US citizen siblings who could have petitioned him. Another X. Julian was adopted with no siblings in the picture. Third, by virtue of marriage to a US citizen. Yet another X."

"Maybe he's a green card holder, not a citizen."

"Let me count the ways—"

"Okay, okay . . . I'll look more into it. Seriously."

Domingo chuckled. "Do that, kid."

He sipped his coffee. Could Julian Alondra's US citizenship be fake? If he were indeed the Malverde Cartel's civil engineer, then his employers could easily secure a fake passport or green card or anything he needed for whatever reason. He doubted Tessa knew about this or she would have told Domingo. Not even Cheryl knew, or she, too, would have told him.

He called Lou Harold.

"Lou Harold here."

The DEA agent sounded cranky.

"It's Sunday. I have a question for you."

"Shoot."

"Can you confirm that Julian's Mexican?"

"No."

"No, you can't confirm?"

A sound very much like the smacking of lips emanated from the other line. Domingo could almost see the DEA agent sucking on mints.

"Here's what I know—he has a US passport," said Lou. "Now, whether he's a Mexican citizen with a US passport is a different question entirely."

"You mean his passport is fake?"

"Or his identity is fake. Or he has dual nationality."

"He'd crossed illegally as a kid. How did he get a US passport?"

"Maybe his present employer secured an American passport for him. Maybe I'll check into that. Forgery of a passport carries a penalty of fifteen years' imprisonment plus a hefty fine. I can use it against him."

In the background, an announcement for a Delta flight came out clear. "You're in an airport, Lou?"

"I'm on my way to Mexico City to see our boy. I expect to get the intel I need from him within the next twenty-four hours. Thank you for connecting me with Tessa. Listen, if I find out anything about Julian's passport, I'll call you."

He swigged down his now lukewarm coffee. "One more question before you go. Do you know a father and son whom Julian calls the Patricios?"

"Patricio Jimenez Diaz, who goes by Patty. His son is Patricio Angelo Jimenez Obligacion, who likes to go by Patrick, but everyone calls him Little Patty anyway. They're card-carrying members of the Malverde Cartel. Why are you asking?"

Their names followed the Mexican and Spanish naming convention of first name plus father's surname plus mother's surname. In the case of Little Patty, he had *Angelo* as middle name to distinguish him from his father. In the Philippines, this convention was screwed up at one point during more than three hundred years of Spanish colonialism there. The Filipino naming convention was first name plus mother's surname plus father's surname.

"The Patricios were at the Sacramento airport yesterday for a little chat with Julian," said Domingo.

"It means they're babysitting Julian. That's how the Malverdes remind anyone who needs reminding that they're being watched."

Domingo thanked Lou, and they ended their call on that note.

Time to follow up with Carrie at Saint Michael's. She'd left a voicemail for Domingo to say Father Jim was taking a break from his five-hundred-mile hiking pilgrimage in Spain because of a sprained ankle. The priest had called Carrie from Spain. His bad luck happened to be Domingo's good fortune.

He whistled as he drove to the church. Carrie had confirmed that Father Jim indeed knew the Beltrans. The priest was supposed to call Carrie with either a yes or no for Domingo. A yes would mean Carrie would give Domingo the Beltrans' current address. A no would mean back to square one. What then? Perhaps a trip to Mexico where the Beltrans used to live? Someone there was bound to know where the couple lived today.

At Saint Michael's, Carrie's hair seemed frizzier and her office even messier than before, with children's drawings spread on the floor. She was working on a kids' art exhibition. "Give me ten minutes to clear the floor, or you'll step on the kids' art," she warned him before slamming the door shut.

Ten minutes later, she still hadn't opened the door. To kill time, he took a walk around the church parking lot and back. Carrie's door remained shut. He could hear her talking. She must be on the phone. Might as well make a pit stop at the men's room.

When he came back, the door was open at last.

He walked in. "Hi, Carrie. Please tell me Father Jim said yes."

She closed the door and motioned for him to sit down. What was up with the door? The woman seemed suddenly obsessed about her privacy.

She eased around her cluttered desk and sat across from him. "Father Jim wants to make sure that Julian is really who he says he is."

That makes the two of us, he thought. Instead, he said, "I can tell you everything I know about Julian. And *you* can tell me if I have the right guy." He tapped his chin with his finger. "For starters, when Julian was fourteen, he saved a little white girl named Tessa Woodridge out in the desert in Arizona. It happened one day after Thanksgiving Day in 2000. Deputy Sheriff Ramon Alvarado arrested him for crossing illegally to the United States, even though he saved the little girl's life."

Carrie raised an eyebrow. "That's public information. Anyone who wants to pretend to be Julian Alondra can check it out at the sheriff's office."

He leaned forward. "Does Father Jim think I'm here on behalf of an impostor? Who on earth would want to pretend to be Julian Alondra?"

"Someone who wants to catch undocumented immigrants like the Beltrans, that's who." She crossed her arms over her chest. "Have you heard of ICE stings?"

"Of course. This ain't a sting."

She shook her head. "Father Jim wants proof of some kind."

"Proof? Like what?"

"Like, maybe Julian Alondra should talk to Father Jim when he gets back from Spain."

"What? And delay the wedding?"

She frowned.

Damn. He wouldn't be able to produce Julian. The guy didn't even know his girlfriend was trying to locate his adoptive parents.

Domingo pulled his smartphone from his pocket and scrolled through the photo gallery. He found Julian's picture, the one Cheryl sent when she asked him to meet with Tessa in Las Vegas. "This is a photo of Julian." He extended the phone. "It's my proof."

She took the phone and stared at the picture. Her expression softened. Yep, no straight woman could deny Julian's good looks.

She handed the phone back. "You could have taken this off Instagram or Facebook or somewhere else. I'm afraid it's not enough proof."

He grabbed his phone.

"I'm sorry, but Father Jim can't break confidences—"

He raised his forefinger, stopping her in her tracks. "Okay, okay . . . here's something that nobody but only Julian and his family know."

"I'm all ears."

"Julian used to have a dog named Amigo, a cream Labrador who was always so dirty, he might as well have been brown."

She scowled. "That's it? That's your proof?"

He gazed up at the ceiling, trying to remember the conversation with Julian in Las Vegas. When he trained his eyes back on Carrie, she smirked.

"When Julian and his family lived in Sonora, Amigo saved Julian from a pack of wolves. The poor dog was bitten by wolves and died from the bites a few days later." He couldn't actually remember whether it had been a pack or just one wolf. "Julian was devastated. He promised never to get another dog."

"That's a sad story, but—"

A staticky noise rose, interrupting Carrie. Domingo looked around. What the hell was that? A woman's voice in Spanish crackled, followed by a sobbing noise. Two words came out clear—*mi corazon*. My heart.

"Whose heart?" He rose. "Who's that?"

Carrie picked up the mountain of folders and papers from her desk and dropped the pile on the floor. It had covered the black landline phone. A green button blinked while more noises emanated from the phone—the conversation was on speakerphone!

"Mrs. Beltran?" Domingo leaned toward the phone. "Is that you?" There wasn't an iota of evidence the woman on the phone was Maria Beltran, but he hoped against hope.

"My heart was broken when Amigo died."

Yes! That single detail had convinced the mother to speak up. He modulated his voice to hide his excitement. "I'm sorry to hear that. How are you, Mrs. Beltran?"

More static. Where on earth was she? In Mexico? He exchanged a glance with Carrie, who shrugged.

"Mrs. Beltran, my name is Sunday. I would like to meet with you about your son, Julian, and his fiancée, Tessa Woodridge. They want your blessing to marry. Miss Woodridge hired me to find you and your husband." *Shit.* He had to keep up his lies about the nonexistent wedding.

He held his breath as he listened to more noises, like someone moving around. More static. "Mrs. Beltran, I'm sorry about Amigo . . ."

"I want to see my son."

His heart skipped. How on earth would he produce Julian? "Your son's fiancée would like to meet with you first. Her name is Tessa Woodridge. She's the white girl your son saved—"

"I remember."

"That's great."

"I want to see her today."

"Today?"

The phone went dead. She'd hung up.

As though on cue, Carrie hauled her crap from the floor and dropped it back on the desk, hiding the phone from his view again.

"Can you please call Mrs. Beltran? She didn't give me her address."

She got up and handed him a yellow Post-it note. "If I were you, I'd call Tessa Woodridge and ask her to come now. The Beltrans will leave for work soon. In the summer, they work all night long, six days a week. People who say undocumented immigrants are lazy parasites don't know a goddamned thing."

Domingo snatched the piece of paper from her hand and glanced at it. *No shit.* The Beltrans' address was right here in Ravine.

CHAPTER 19

Domingo waited for Tessa in a paid parking garage. It took her an hour and forty minutes to drive from Sacramento to Ravine.

When the silver Lexus pulled up, he opened the driver's door like a valet. She was his client, after all. He also wanted to move faster before the Beltrans left for work or changed their minds about this visit.

They were using his rental car. He opened the door on the front passenger side.

"Where do the Beltrans live?" She ducked inside the car. She took off the black blazer she wore over her flowery dress. She wore flats instead of high heels. "Why can't I just meet you there?"

He slid into the driver's seat and put on the seat belt. "Where the Beltrans live, nobody drives a brand-new Lexus. Ravine has one of the highest car-theft rates in the country. It's number four or five."

She sighed. "Okay. Thanks for driving me. How did you find them?"

"Through the local Catholic church." He pulled out of the parking spot and onto the exit. "The Beltrans have lived in Ravine off and on over the years. Finding them was easy. Convincing them to talk to me was another thing."

"How did you do it?"

He stopped beside the payment machine and fed in both the parking ticket and his credit card. *To tell or not to tell.* He hesitated, but only for a second. "I told Mrs. Beltran that I work for you, and that you and Julian are getting married."

"What?" She perked up. "Why?"

"They wouldn't talk to me otherwise. They're undocumented. They don't talk to strangers." The machine spat back out his credit card and ticket. He rolled out of the garage. "Look, you can tell them the truth if you like. My job was to get you some face time."

She sank into her seat. "You said they work six days a week? What do they do?"

"They both work at a vineyard called Napa Vintage. They work in the field—harvesting, pruning, suckering, everything." He'd drawn more information about Julian's adoptive parents from Carrie. He owed her and Father Jim, though he had no idea how he could repay them. Maybe he'd donate money to the church.

"What's suckering?" she asked.

"You know . . . pulling off tiny sprouts that stand in the way of healthy grapes. In the summer, they work nights because it's cooler. That's why we need to catch them this afternoon."

She looked out the window and said nothing more.

They passed by mom-and-pop stores, bakeries, and pawnshops. Ravine wasn't big. The drive took all of seventeen minutes.

The Beltrans lived in a squat house equipped with a security door. He rang the doorbell. It turned out to be a duplex. Sort of. It had two entrances. A young man, tattooed to the hilt, including his bald head, emerged from the second door. He gave Tessa an amused look.

"Ignore the dude," whispered Domingo. "He's not used to seeing white people is all."

"Excuse me?" She slung her bag over her shoulder.

"I'm not being racist. It's a fact. White people don't come here. Just look around you."

She did. Her cheeks flushed.

He banged on the door.

At last, it opened. A boy of about four or five years old wearing an oversize T-shirt and no pants let them in and shut the door with a thud.

Now Domingo and Tessa faced the pants-less boy. A faint scent of garlic, of a meal cooked hours ago, hung in the air. Sleeping bags littered the floor along with toy trucks and a pair of sneakers. A window air conditioner struggled to cool the room.

"*Donde esta la Señora Beltran?*" Domingo asked the boy.

"*Un momento, por favor,*" yelled a woman from a room.

The kid turned on the TV—cartoons with an elephant and a monkey speaking in Spanish.

A woman in a red housedress came out of the room behind the TV. "Sit, sit! Please sit down." She picked up the stuffed bears on the couch and the toys on the floor and shoved them in a toy chest.

"Are you Maria Beltran?" Domingo extended his right hand.

"Yes." It sounded like "jess." She shook Domingo's hand.

He was acutely aware of Mrs. Beltran's accent because of his own accent that sounded more pronounced when he was meeting new people—*boated* instead of *voted*, *mom* instead of *ma'am*, and *refand* instead of *refund*.

Maria Beltran shook hands with Tessa. "You are Julian's fiancée?"

Girl Boss smiled, though anxiety emanated off her like black smoke. "I'm his girlfriend. We're not yet . . . it's really premature to call me his fiancée." She'd left her blazer in the car, and she was smoothing down the bell-shaped sleeves of her dress.

"Please sit down," Maria repeated as she hauled away the sleeping bags and piled them against the wall.

Tessa perched on the sofa while Domingo sat on a plastic stool near the door.

Maria Beltran was teeny, perhaps not even five feet tall. She spoke to the boy in Spanish. The boy turned off the TV and slinked to the other room.

Maria was younger than Domingo had imagined; she could be the mother of the pants-less boy. "Is the kid your son?" asked Domingo.

"Oh, no. Lucas, his grandma, his grandpa—they rent a room here."

He glanced around. The apartment had only *one* other room. The kitchen was in the same space as the living room. How could five people fit in here?

A mustachioed man emerged from what must be the bedroom. Maria grabbed the sneakers from the floor and went inside the room.

"Hello, hello! How are you?" The man was buttoning his shirt as though he'd just woken up. His hair was rumpled, his eyes red. Probably in his fifties, youthful like his wife. "I am Raul."

Domingo and Tessa introduced themselves and took turns shaking Raul's hand.

"Ah, the future Mrs. Julian Lark." Raul clasped Tessa's hand with both of his.

Domingo snapped to attention. *"Joo-lee-yan Lark"? What?*

Girl Boss turned to him with a hard look.

Domingo cleared his throat. "So you don't call him 'Hoo-lee-yan'? And his last name is Lark? That's the surname of his biological parents? Sometimes he introduces himself as Julian Alondra or Jules Alexander."

Raul motioned for them to sit down while he sat on an armchair that didn't match the sofa. "*Lark* means a bird, no? In Spanish, it's called *alondra*. That's why Julian changed his last name to Alondra." He shook his head. "I say to him, 'Nothing wrong with your name.' He say to me, 'It does not sound Mexican.' But he is *not* Mexican. Nothing wrong with American. Many people wish to be Americans!'"

Tessa stared at Raul with grimness. Julian was *not* Mexican. At last, the truth.

Domingo feared she might cry. "Was Julian born here in the States?"

"In Los Angeles."

"Los Ang-hail-es," as Raul had pronounced it. Now Julian's US passport and TSA PreCheck approval all made sense. But it didn't explain his illegal crossing and self-deportation as a teenager, or how he'd ended up in Mexico to begin with. Although *Lark* sounded Anglo, maybe Julian's parents were part Mexican. That must be it.

"I say to Julian, 'You are lucky to be American,'" continued Raul. "Me . . . I almost die crossing the desert just to work in America."

Domingo's mind buzzed with questions. He tossed a glance at Tessa, who sat cradling her purse, shell shocked. "How do you know that Julian was born in Los Angeles?" he asked. "Do you know his parents?"

"Tonio and Rosa know Julian's mommy and daddy," Maria shouted from the room. The walls hid no secret conversations in this home.

"Yes, Tonio and Rosa work with Julian's parents in a motel in Encinitas." Raul flattened his mustache. "They are very young. They cannot take care of Julian. Tonio and Rosa have very many children—six—but we have none. So they take Julian to our house in Sonora, and we take care of him."

Domingo sat amazed at how the Beltrans revealed so much without hesitation, how a face-to-face meeting engendered trust even among strangers.

"Forgive me for intruding." At last, Tessa spoke. "I wanted to meet you and your wife because Julian doesn't like talking about his past. Do you happen to know the names of his biological parents?"

Raul scratched his head, then his arm, as though trying to recall. "The father is Jeremy Lark. The mother, Emily Chambers. They are not married."

The memory of Domingo's first encounter with Julian in Las Vegas played in his mind. The sleek, handsome devil who'd turned heads—tall, light skin, no accent. "Is Julian white? Are his parents white or are they part Mexican?"

"They are white."

The son of a bitch. Domingo turned to Tessa, who flinched. She'd romanticized the image of a Mexican migrant with a heart of gold, except Julian was neither Mexican nor a migrant. She was dating an impostor of the highest caliber.

"Raul, are you or Maria related to a man Julian calls Tio?" continued Domingo.

Raul shook his head. "Tio is a friend. Ah, he do everything for Julian. When the police catch Julian in Arizona, Tio go to Los Angeles to get Julian's birth certificate. Tio tell the police, 'This boy is American! Why do you put him in jail?' After that, Tio take care of him and send him to study in Arizona."

No shit. Domingo cast his gaze at the dirt-streaked window, the early-afternoon sun peeking through. Lover Boy's story got weirder by the second. He couldn't begin to guess what Tessa was thinking.

She set her bag on the floor. Her entire being welled with sadness. "I'm the reason he was caught in the desert."

"Julian say a coyote almost bite you," said Raul.

She nodded. "He saved me. Why did he cross the desert?"

Raul rubbed his mustache again. "He should not have done it—he is American. But he did it because he work for Oldie. You know Oldie?"

"No," Domingo and Tessa said at the same time.

"I tell you about Oldie," Maria cut in. She sidled up to the sofa and sat beside Tessa. "Some boys who work for Oldie call me barren—useless—because I have no baby. Julian is very angry, and he stab one boy, and so Oldie come for Julian."

"Wait . . . wait . . . Is that how Julian got his knife wound on his forearm?" Tessa's eyes grew big. "Who's Oldie?"

Maria responded with a string of Spanish words, then Raul added his own barrage of Spanish. The two of them talked nonstop, their voices overlapping, perhaps not realizing or simply forgetting that Girl Boss understood none of what they were saying.

Domingo let them talk without interruption as Julian's past, like a thousand pieces of jigsaw puzzle, rearranged itself in Domingo's mind. He'd never met anyone with as complicated a history as Lover Boy. It would seem only logical that his *present* life would be just as tangled, if not more so.

Tessa turned to him with a questioning look. "Can you translate everything they just said, please?"

"Sure." Domingo took a deep breath. He began from the beginning, in Nogales, in the state of Sonora, where Julian and the Beltrans, Oldie, and Tio had lived.

Oldie, whose real name was Rafael, was a small-time hoodlum who smuggled drugs and migrants into the United States. He wasn't old, but at the age of thirty back in 2000, he was a senior citizen compared to his "colleagues" in the narco business, who tended to die young. He'd been so impressed with Julian for winning the knife fight against one of his mules that he'd offered Julian a job as a scout in the desert.

Julian had refused, so Oldie had upped his offer. "How about I decapitate your mother's head instead?" he'd threatened. At the time, Raul Beltran had already been living illegally in the United States for a year. Julian had assumed the role of Maria's defender, the man of the house.

Julian had had no choice but to work as a scout for Oldie, but he'd negotiated something else. "You'll have to let Mamaita cross the desert safely so she can join Papi in Arizona," he'd demanded. Only fourteen years old at the time and already making a deal with a criminal! He'd gotten what he wanted too. Maria Beltran had crossed and joined her husband in America, where they'd been working in various vineyards for the past two decades. Julian had meant to follow his adoptive parents, but Oldie had stopped him. After all, their deal covered only Maria's safe passage to the United States. Mainly, he'd needed Julian as a scout.

Tessa's jaw slackened a tad, her green eyes blazing.

"Oh, and by the way, Tio is Oldie's uncle for real and the father of Dulce. So Oldie and Dulce are cousins." If Julian had married Dulce, then he would have been a legitimate member of Tio's family, Domingo wanted to add but didn't.

He paused, trying to read Tessa's shifting expression from surprise to even greater surprise. Latin music blasted from outside, with lots of percussion. He waited until the music receded. It had come from a passing vehicle.

"Oldie used to send Julian to help Tio's construction crew, and that's how Tio became close to Julian," Domingo continued. "The man had saved Julian not once but twice. First, he'd brought Julian back home from immigration detention. Second, he'd negotiated Julian's freedom from Oldie and sent the boy to college in Arizona. After that, Tio had convinced everyone that it was safer for Julian and the Beltrans to cut off their ties."

As far as Domingo was concerned, the last part proved that Tio wasn't any better than Oldie. An unease pooled in his gut. "Did Tio say why he thought it wasn't safe for you to see or talk to Julian? What's the harm of talking to your son even just once in a while? Are you even on speaking terms with Tio?" he asked the couple.

Raul and Maria glanced at each other before shaking their heads.

"We are not legal." Raul rubbed the back of his neck sheepishly. "We do not have the right to ask anything from Tio. He say we are in America, we should be contented. We must forget about our son."

Domingo and Tessa traded glances. *Can you believe Tio's bullshit?*

Their reactions were not lost on Maria, whose mouth tensed. "Tio is just like Oldie. He need our son, so he keep him away from us."

There. Tio wasn't the benevolent guardian of Julian, but an investor who expected a return on his investment. Julian hadn't "lost touch" with his parents. Tio had forbidden him to contact them.

But why had Julian agreed? Could it be because Lover Boy was more involved in Tio's illicit business than he cared to admit? It made sense that he would protect the Beltrans by cutting off ties with them. If he didn't know where they were and pretended to not care, then Tio and the cartel would leave them be. Domingo nodded—a sunburst of clarity after a cloudy stretch—but caught himself and focused back on the conversation.

Tessa peered into Raul's face. "When Julian helped me in the desert, was he working as a scout then?"

"Yes," said Raul.

Tessa cast her gaze down, looking defeated.

Raul yawned. "Excuse me. I work very late last night."

"I'm sorry we woke you up," said Tessa.

Raul's kind face broke into a shy smile. "You want café?"

Both Domingo and Tessa declined with a shake of the head.

Maria pulled something from her pocket. "I want to show you the photographs."

"Oh, I'd love to see them." Tessa accepted the first picture. "Is this little boy Julian?"

Maria scooted closer to Tessa. "Yes. And that is Tonio and Rosa and their children."

Tessa's eyes moistened.

"Can I see it?" Domingo wanted to distract Girl Boss, take the picture away to stop her from crying.

Tessa passed it to him. He stared at the blond boy, maybe five or six, surrounded by dark-haired and dark-eyed people. So Julian had been blond. Was he still blond? Did he color his hair to look like a Latino?

Maria shared two more pictures, which they passed around. The second photo showed the Beltrans with Julian, perhaps ten years old and no longer blond. In the last photo, the trio posed outside a house, but this time, Julian towered over the couple—dark, longish hair, big smile, perhaps thirteen or fourteen. *This* must have been how he looked like when Tessa had first laid eyes on him.

He snuck a peek at Girl Boss. A sad smile crossed her face as she stared at the pictures.

"Tessa, you have a picture of Julian you can show them?" asked Domingo.

"Yes, I do." She retrieved her phone from her bag. She found what she was looking for and showed Maria the screen.

"Que guapo." Maria waved the phone at her husband. "Look how handsome your son is."

Raul leaned forward to accept the phone. He beamed as he stared at the image. "Thank you." He passed the phone back to Tessa. "When is the wedding? Julian want us to come? Will Tio allow it?"

Tessa stared daggers at Domingo. She replaced the phone in her bag. "He doesn't know I'm here today. It's kind of complicated."

"No?" Raul pursed his lips. "So why do you . . . ? Does he need money for the wedding?"

"No, no. It's not that at all . . . I just haven't told him that I'm visiting you today, but I will," stammered Tessa.

"Julian's a civil engineer, and he makes good money," Domingo interjected. He realized that even though the Beltrans remembered the name Tessa Woodridge as that of the white girl Julian had saved, they had no clue she was a bona fide one percenter. Otherwise, Raul wouldn't have mentioned money.

Now Raul spoke in Spanish to Maria, who had turned her face away from Tessa. The mother was crying.

"Ay, Mamaita . . . Why do you cry?" Raul's face was lined with concern. "You hear what Sunday say? Julian is an engineer. *Gracias a Dios.*"

"In my heart, Julian is *my* son." Maria struck her chest for emphasis. Her face, the color of honey, glowed. She had a smooth complexion and taut cheekbones. Her dark wavy hair hung loose on her shoulders. She couldn't have been older than fifty-two or fifty-three.

"I cannot have a baby, but God gave me Julian. His mommy and daddy . . . they left him. I do not understand why Americans throw away the best things . . . why they do not see how lucky they are. In restaurants, Americans buy so much, but they do not eat everything. They waste so much."

"Why do you compare a baby and a restaurant?" Raul clucked his tongue. "It is not the same."

"Yes, it is." Maria snorted. "Some people leave food on the table. Others leave their baby."

"The Americans, they have so much of everything." Raul trained his eyes on Tessa, then on Domingo. "They cannot help but take it for granted."

His tone was kind, not a criticism but a sign of understanding.

Maria sniffled. "I pray to God every night." She wiped her nose with the sleeve of her dress. "I pray Julian make a lot of money, get married, and have many children. Now God answer my prayer. My son is making lots of money, and he will marry you." She locked eyes with Tessa. "I want to see him. Even if he don't invite us to the wedding, he can visit us, no? You come back here with him. After the wedding maybe. I think Tio will allow it, if it is one time only."

Tessa glanced at Domingo. *Help!*

He sat up straight. "Mrs. Beltran? I made a mistake. I thought they're getting married, but they're not. They're both very busy with their jobs. I'm sorry. My bad."

Maria held Tessa's hand, seemingly ignoring Domingo's admission of an epic mistake. "Where does Julian live? He live with you?"

"No, we don't live together. He lives in Mexico City, but he visits me stateside as much as he can."

"Why does he live in Distrito Federal?" Raul made a tsk-tsk noise with his tongue. "It's not good. You should make him live here in California."

"You can do that, no?" Maria gave Tessa an expectant gaze. "Yes, of course. You are getting married. He will do it, if you ask him."

Domingo rubbed his temple. The mother wouldn't let go of the nonexistent wedding. It was his damn fault.

Tessa's lips curled into a small smile. "I, um, I'll try to convince him."

The door opened, and an older woman bearing tote bags full of groceries entered. Raul got up to help her. The little boy, Lucas, shot out of the room like a bullet and rooted in one of the bags, which smelled of fried food. The air had grown stifling, the room bursting at the seams.

Conversations in Spanish ensued. Tessa glanced at her wristwatch, which prompted Domingo to check his own watch. It was almost three o'clock.

Maria introduced Tessa to the other woman, Lupita, who turned out to be the boy's grandma. "This is my son's fiancée. Very pretty, no? Such green eyes."

Fiancée. "Sorry," Domingo mouthed to Tessa, who made a face that underscored her unhappiness.

More rapid-fire exchange in Spanish followed. They were talking about the wedding that wasn't happening.

"Excuse me." Domingo stepped forward. "I'm sorry to interrupt, but Tessa needs to drive back to her office."

Tessa picked up her bag and rose. "Thanks so much for talking to us."

Maria embraced her tightly. "You and Julian, you take care of one another, okay?" When she released Tessa, her expression grew plaintive. "Julian has very good, very loyal heart. If he love somebody, he will do *anything.*" She grew teary again, covering her eyes. "I am to blame. Julian defend my honor. Because of me, Oldie make my son work for him and forbid him to see us. And then Tio do the same."

Raul wrapped his arm around his wife's shoulders. "Ay, Mamaita. No more crying."

The wife pulled something from her pocket. "You can keep this one." One of Julian's pictures.

Tessa accepted it. "Are you sure you want me to have this?"

"Yes, yes." Maria placed her hand on Tessa's arm. She paused for a second before withdrawing her touch. "Take care of my son."

Tessa hugged Maria. "I'll do my best."

CHAPTER 20

Domingo drove in silence while Tessa stared out the window. They could both use the quiet after Hurricane Julian upended everything they *thought* they'd known about the guy. He hoped the visit with the Beltrans had brought the heiress to her senses.

About halfway to the parking garage where they'd left Tessa's Lexus, traffic halted. An old Volkswagen stalled. Cars honked, but Domingo kept his cool.

"You got any marching orders for me?" He stole a glance at her, feeling like an intruder in the private space of her introspection. "Should I stop snooping on Julian? I could catch the next flight back to New York."

"I don't know what to do." She turned to him with a washed-out expression. "How do you think Alice is going to react if I tell her that Julian's a white man pretending to be Mexican?"

"Don't tell her. At least not yet."

She nodded and switched her gaze back out the front window. A couple of guys were pushing the Volkswagen to the side of the road, but now the SUV behind it was trying to turn around, blocking the other lane. Frustrated drivers blew their horns.

On the sidewalk, a group of women pushed their baby strollers in single file like a nursery caravan.

Tessa glanced at her wristwatch, which reminded Domingo that her time was precious. CEOs were not like working stiffs. He read somewhere that the top dog at Starbucks earned ten grand an hour, while the CEO of Weight Watchers made sixteen grand an hour. Who knew there was so much money to be reaped from peddling coffee and weight loss? Girl Boss probably made as much money in one week as someone like him earned in an entire year.

"There's no cop directing the traffic. Let me try something or we're gonna be stuck here forever," he told her. The mothers with the strollers had crossed the street, and the sidewalk was clear, so he jumped the curb and drove on the sidewalk to get around the gridlock.

Everyone honked at him. *Only those who risk win. And only those willing to risk a violation ticket get out of the traffic jam.* He crept on the sidewalk until he reached an intersection, where he swung right. "Sorry about that." He glanced at her.

She smirked. "Where did you learn to drive?"

"In Manila. The *only* driving rule there is, there are *no* driving rules."

At least she smiled.

Driving in Manila took tremendous guts. He used to drive Tito Mando's stick-shift Datsun, which required hand-eye-foot coordination and a kind of dexterity unnecessary in driving an automatic car. Once he'd learned stick shift, driving just about any vehicle in any kind of situation became easier. It gave him the self-confidence to drive any car anywhere.

How else would he have survived driving and at the same time ducking from gunfire? Yep, a bad hombre had once sprayed him with bullets during a chase on a highway outside Washington, DC. Domingo had been struck by three bullets, but he'd still managed to apprehend the fugitive. He would forever be grateful to the surgeon who had removed the bullets and stapled closed the holes in his intestines.

Now he weaved in and out of congested roads for another ten minutes before finally arriving at the parking garage. He pulled over beside her Lexus. "If you don't need me anymore, I'm going back home ASAP." He ran through his to-do list in his mind. *Book a flight home.*

Call work for next assignment. Return rental car and fly home. Get a hot-stone massage. Jump-start daily workout routine.

She unzipped her shoulder bag and rooted inside. "I'm going to tell Julian about my meeting with his parents in person. I want to visit him in Mexico City, so I'll see him in his natural environment. It's going to be a surprise." She pulled out a ChapStick and swiped it on her lips.

His thoughts snapped back into place. He'd fully expected a breakup, but now she wanted to see him? He shifted in his seat as he digested what she'd said. "So you're going to visit Julian as a surprise, plus you'll surprise him with the news that you found out he's been passing as Mexican all this time."

She dropped the ChapStick inside her bag and zipped it. "Call it a double delight."

It was too much, if anyone asked him, not that she would. Her double whammy of surprises would not only disrupt Julian's groove but Tio's, who would probably not appreciate it. It was like sticking one's arm inside a glass tank of sleeping snakes—surprise! Meanwhile, Lou Harold was probably meeting with Julian right now, and who knew what would come out of it. He shook his head.

"What is it?" said Tessa.

"Two things. One, Mexico City is probably the worst place for a surprise trip. There were more than seven hundred kidnappings there last year alone. God knows how many more are unreported since Mexicans don't trust the police. I hate to say this, but you're a prime candidate for kidnapping." He tapped the steering wheel for emphasis. "Two, do you really want to rattle Tio's cage by showing up in his turf uninvited? Did Julian introduce you to Tio the first time you visited Mexico City?"

"No."

He drummed his fingers on the steering wheel. "There's probably a good reason for that. You've heard the Beltrans—Tio is not the loving, generous benefactor we thought he was. Tio is the real reason Julian's in deep shit today."

She placed her hand on her forehead and closed her eyes for a beat.

If the gesture meant she wanted him to shut up, too bad. "I think Julian's more involved with Tio's business than he's letting on. I think Julian himself has disconnected from his parents to spare them any trouble because he knows whatever it is he's doing with Tio is dangerous."

Tessa opened her eyes and shot him a sidelong glance. "Don't you think I know that? If his way of sparing the people he loves is by discarding them, then it's only a matter of time before he leaves me."

"Not if *you* leave him first." He kept his gaze forward, but he felt the intensity of her stare.

"You know I can't do that." She turned her torso toward him, so he was forced to meet her eyes. The air of defeat about her was gone. She was all business now. "I'm going to Mexico City, and I want you to come with me."

Her ability to go from a vulnerable orphan one minute to a decisive Girl Boss the next never ceased to amaze him.

"You want me to be your bodyguard?"

"My shadow." She tucked her hair behind her ear, revealing a diamond stud earring. "I don't want anybody to know that you'll be in Mexico, not even Julian."

"You want me to follow you around secretly?"

"Exactly. That's what you do, isn't it?"

He smiled. And he thought she was naive. Perhaps he'd underestimated her before because of her youth and her privileged background. The girl was cunning. If she flaunted her wealth by bringing a bodyguard, she'd be twice as much a target for random criminals. Not only that, but Domingo's presence would encourage Julian to hide his true colors even more.

He glanced around as he mulled over the situation. A man got out of a van and blipped it shut. Someone's car tires squealed in the distance. "Tessa, have you considered breaking up with Julian? It would make your life so much easier, not to mention safer."

She locked eyes with him. "Even if I break up with Julian, he'll always be in my heart."

"Okay, I get that. So you can stay friends. Trade emails or phone calls, but stop seeing him. The DEA shit's gonna hit the fan soon."

"Julian saved me. Now it's my turn to save him."

The way she'd straightened her spine told him she was determined to keep Julian. But he just had to ask, "You're gonna save him from the cartel?"

"I'm going to save him from himself. He and Tio can deal with the drug cartel." She opened the car door and stepped out.

Domingo did the same. "I guess your mind is made up."

Her green eyes, always striking, turned steely. "I told you before: Julian is nonnegotiable to me."

He raised a palm. "I get it. So when are you going to Mexico City?"

"In two days."

"Two days?" His mental to-do list just went down the drain.

"I'd go today if I could. This trip is important to me, and I want you to treat it with urgency." She walked the few steps to the driver's side of her Lexus.

"Understood." Domingo followed her. "That means I have to leave tomorrow. I'm your advance party. I need to get to your destination at least one day before you do. Text me your flight number, as well as the time and place of arrival in Mexico. I need to equip you with a tracking device."

"What kind?" She unlocked her car using the key fob.

Domingo opened the door for her, and she slid inside. "Don't worry. It's not obtrusive. It's the size of a lighter. It has an SOS button, so I'll know when you need me."

"Let's hope I don't need to push the button at all." She shut the door and started the car. Then she lowered the window. "Are you going to be armed in Mexico City?"

He bent his head so they were eye to eye. "I can't enter Mexico with a gun, but I can borrow one from a local contact. Yeah, I'll be armed."

"Have you worked as a bodyguard before?"

"You could say that. I've escorted criminals and fugitives to ICE or to prison. I've even delivered some of them to the Policía Federal in Ciudad Juárez."

"Good. I don't doubt your qualifications. I'm just curious." The corners of her mouth were turned up in a small smile. "I need to go back to the office to finish up a project."

"And I'm driving to Folsom to install Alice's hammock," he said.

She widened her eyes, as though she'd forgotten all about it. "Are you sure you can do it today? I can ask someone else."

"I promised Alice, so I'm going to do it."

She thanked him with a smile. "I'll text you my flight itinerary." She closed the window and drove away.

He stood there as the Lexus receded from his view. He'd never known anyone like Tessa Woodridge, never met any girl before who was secretly writing a diary addressed to a guy for nineteen long years. She wasn't even in denial. She understood Julian's dangerous cartel ties. Still, her love was nonnegotiable.

No one, certainly not him, could convince her to forget Julian. All he could do was keep the girl safe so she might one day rouse her own damn self from her batshit-crazy love.

CHAPTER 21

It was almost six in the evening when Domingo arrived in Folsom, but the summer sun still hung in the sky, blanketing rooftops, treetops, and lawns in a warm hue of amber.

Grammy, Alice, and Susie were in the kitchen making dinner. Alice and Susie were seated at the table as they prepared a five-bean salad. Open cans of beans lined the table. Some kind of pasta was baking in the oven, the rich, cheesy smell blooming. Grammy was carving roasted chicken on the kitchen island.

"You want a cup of coffee or tea?" asked the old lady.

Domingo declined. "But I'll take a tape measure, scissors, and a drill while you're at it. I bought a hammock yesterday. I'll install it now. It won't take long."

"Let me get the toolbox." Susie rose. "You want me to bring it to the front yard?"

"That would be great. I might as well get started."

He proceeded outside. The leaves on trees fluttered, and the wind chimes knocked around in the breeze. Only a few cars passed by. Nobody on the streets, although he could hear a dog barking in the distance. It was the kind of languid evening that would dissolve into a tranquil night.

He took out a big box from the trunk of the rental car and laid it on the ground. He appraised the two birch trees Grammy had chosen to hold the hammock, running his fingers on one of the tree trunks. Both trees appeared healthy with no signs of disease or stress.

Susie arrived with the toolbox. "Alice is very excited about the hammock."

"I picked a striped fiber in pink and white. She's going to love it." He rooted inside the toolbox for a tape measure. "How was Alice's birthday party? Julian was here, right? How did the relatives react?" He tried to sound nonchalant.

"It was Alice's party, but Julian was the man of the hour." Susie smiled in a knowing way. "All the relatives loved him. You should have seen how everybody couldn't get enough of him. He won the Woodridge family over by a landslide. Remember you asked us on Saturday whether we think Tessa and Julian are getting engaged?"

"Well, are they?"

"I don't know, but everyone at the party wished they would, especially Alice." Susie ran her fingers through her pixie hair. "You need anything else?"

"No, I'm good. You go ahead and make that salad."

After she left, he measured the distance between the two trees while mulling over Alice's growing fondness for Julian. With Alice's and the rest of the family's blessings, Lover Boy would be foolish to pass up the opportunity to marry a beautiful heiress who was madly in love with him.

He wrote down the measurement on the surface of the hammock package. Next, he measured the trunk of each tree and jotted down the numbers as well. He hadn't called Lou Harold, but it was on his to-do list. He hoped Julian had given the DEA agent the information he needed to save his own hide and spare Tessa the risk of being an accomplice.

He took out a pair of scissors from the toolbox and ripped open the packaging containing the hammock. The three women emerged through the front door just as he was laying out the parts.

Grammy spread the same quilt blanket from yesterday under a tree while Susie accompanied Alice to the bench. No walker for Alice this time.

"Sunday, give us something to do. Let us help you," offered Grammy.

"Sure. I'm going to need the extension chains. If you can take them out for me, that would be great. Same thing with the hammock. Please unwrap it to make sure the fabric isn't damaged in any way." He handed Grammy the plastic bag with the chains and another one with the fabric.

When Susie joined them, he asked her to measure the chains according to the length he'd written down.

Alice waved at him. Perhaps the poor woman felt left out.

"You wanna help?" he called out.

She nodded a wobbly yes.

He couldn't think of a task for her, but her Barbie watch caught his attention—a bright pink. It didn't look like it was nineteen years old. That gave him an idea.

He walked toward her. "Do you want to time me? See how fast I can put the hammock together?" He knelt before her. "We can put your awesome Barbie watch to use. Can I take a look at it?"

Alice extended her wrist, and Domingo removed the watch. On closer inspection, it wasn't a child's watch, but for ladies, with a leather band, not plastic. It made sense because in 2000, Alice was eighteen years old, and this had been part of her collection.

A kid's watch typically had a digital counter, but this one had hands for hours, minutes, and seconds. Barbie's mug was on the watch's face. Although the front looked in mint condition, the markings on the back were barely legible. The trademark sign was clear enough: *Barbie*™. The copyright symbol and the year it was manufactured were clear—©*2001*.

The realization came to him with a zap of surprise. This watch was manufactured *one year* after Julian met Tessa in the desert. Julian had lied.

"It's very nice, but I don't think this is your watch." He replaced it around her wrist. "It's a lookalike. Your real watch was manufactured in 2000 or earlier, but this one was made in 2001."

Alice's head swayed. "Joo . . . lian said . . . this is . . . the . . . one."

"You believe him?"

She nodded with a smile. Saliva pooled in the corners of her lips.

He glanced back at the two other women. To his surprise, they were assembling the hammock. Grammy was reading the instructions out loud while Susie inserted a stick through one end of the hammock's width. The kit came with two sticks called spreaders, which would keep the hammock open and prevent it from folding.

He turned back to Alice. She wiped her lips with the sleeve of her T-shirt. How could he explain that Julian Alondra might not be the Prince Charming she wanted for her sister? That he was an impostor who most likely worked for a drug cartel?

"Alice, do you trust me?" he asked.

She nodded. "You . . . save . . . saved . . . the . . . scrub . . . jay."

It was his turn to smile. "Will you promise me that if you feel unsafe, you're going to call me?"

She gave him a blank expression.

"For example, if you feel like someone you know might hurt you, call me."

She opened her mouth, struggling to speak. "Who?"

"Julian."

Her eyes widened. Her eyeglasses had slipped lower on the bridge of her nose. Would she rat him out to Tessa?

"What I mean is, you don't really know him. He lied to you about your Barbie watch. He could be lying about other, more serious things. You understand what I'm saying?" As soon as he'd said the words, he realized his argument could backfire. He himself was practically a stranger. He was lying, too, pretending to be a meat supplier. Why should Alice trust him over Julian? He was at a loss.

Alice's face grew pink from her struggle to speak. "You . . . would . . . save me . . . like . . . the scrub . . . jay."

"Yes, absolutely."

Alice blinked slowly. "I don't . . . have . . . your . . . your number."

He couldn't give her his business card showing he was a bail enforcement agent, so he pulled a pen from one of the pockets of his cargo pants and wrote his cell number on the back of a gas receipt. He handed it to her. "Do you have a cell phone?"

Alice wobbled a yes.

"Add my number to your contact list, okay? Just in case you need to call me."

Alice studied the paper, as though committing the number to memory.

Thank goodness she understood. Who knew saving a bird would serve as proof of his integrity?

"Sunday! We're done," Grammy called out. "Should we hang it now?"

He glanced over his shoulder. "I'll be there in a sec!" He turned to Alice. "Let me go see what Grammy and Susie are up to. Don't forget your promise, okay?"

Alice swayed her head. "Call . . . you."

Her vulnerability stabbed at his heart. In case of danger, would she be able to cry for help? Even if she were to call Domingo, she'd struggle to speak. They needed a code word.

"Alice, if you call me because you feel threatened by Julian, just say *blue bird*."

Her face clouded with confusion.

"It's our secret code. Call me or text me. I'll know what I have to do."

She smiled. "Blue . . . bird."

He patted her hand. "That's right." He loped back to the two women and asked Susie to help Alice time him once he started tying the hammock to the trees.

"Alice likes to help. That's a wonderful idea," cooed Grammy.

Susie walked over to the bench.

He picked up the hammock and inserted an extension chain to the rope on one end. To Susie and Alice, he yelled, "Are you guys ready to time me?"

Both women nodded.

"Let's do this." He tied the rope on one end of the hammock to one tree and bolted the screws with a drill to secure it. Then he tackled the other end. He couldn't wait to finish the job.

His next destination: Mexico City. Far from his own turf, but closer and closer to the truth that Julian Alondra was hiding. Domingo had peeled off a few layers already about Julian's racial identity, his previous work as a desert scout for Oldie, and the nature of Tio's "mentorship." The biggest question remained: Was Julian Alondra, a.k.a. *El Genio*, designing a secret tunnel for the bad guys?

Tessa wouldn't even dare to think of it. But Domingo saw the possibility. Two words crossed his mind: Terra Firma. Julian's interest in the company's nascent technology for developing a cutting-edge tunnel boring machine that could go deepest, fastest, and safest underground like no other was the clearest indication that he might be designing a tunnel for the ages.

CHAPTER 22

Why the "Big, Beautiful Wall" Won't Work

The border between the United States and Mexico spans two thousand miles, out of which about seven hundred miles are protected by fencing and other forms of barrier. Drug and human smuggling and illegal crossings continue despite the barrier. You know why? Because there are so many ways to go around, over, below, and beyond the damn wall.

I surveyed people I know—desperate hopefuls, ex-cons who have served time for smuggling drugs and migrants, law enforcement personnel, and fellow bail enforcement agents—about the wall's effectiveness. I asked all of them the same question: ***Do you think the president's "big, beautiful wall" will work?*** *The unanimous answer was no. They gave examples of different ways determined criminals could beat the wall:*

- *use ladder or rope*
- *enter illegally by sea*
- *blow up sections of the wall*
- *fly over wall in light aircraft*
- *bribe Border Patrol agents to look the other way*
- *bribe flight attendants or truckers to smuggle drugs*
- *enter through airport legally and never leave*
- *use drones to smuggle drugs*
- *use tunnels to smuggle drugs and migrants*

- *hide drugs (or migrants) with legitimate goods transported via tractor trailers*
- *use catapult or cannon (drugs only, not people!)*
- *customize a submarine to deliver drugs via sea*
- *plant explosives to blow up the fucking wall*

I admit my survey is unscientific and my list is short. You can bet that a list by smart criminals who profit from smuggling drugs and migrants would be exponentially longer and mind-blowingly inventive.

◆ ◆ ◆

Domingo had arrived in Mexico City yesterday. The flight from Sacramento had taken seven hours with one stop and given him ample time to write a few pages of his book. Today, he had a scheduled rendezvous with Lou Harold in an area known as Centro.

This wasn't Domingo's first time in Mexico, which he liked for the obvious reason that it shared many things with his native Philippines. Both countries were colonized by Spain. They shared a Roman Catholic heritage, the prevalence of Spanish names and surnames, their love for big families, and predilection for superstition. And, as the Filipino American comedian Jo Koy once noted, Filipino and Mexican moms even shared a preference for Vicks VapoRub as a remedy for every ailment. Crazy but true.

The cab dropped him off at the plaza in Zócalo, teeming with vendors' booths and tables. There was an artsy-fartsy festival of some kind going on. Under the late-afternoon sun, the plaza exploded with colors—bright scarves, big sombreros, watercolor paintings, and backyard sculptures amid the hubbub of vendors and shoppers.

Domingo scurried through the crowds toward the looming double tower of the Metropolitan Cathedral. He was running late.

When he'd called Lou yesterday, he'd expected the agent to be back in San Diego already. As it turned out, Lou was still here in Mexico City. Their paths continued to crisscross each other with Julian Alondra at the heart of it. On the phone, Lou's voice had given away nothing, but he guessed the DEA agent needed something from him or he wouldn't bother with a face-to-face meeting.

Even from afar, he spotted Lou without any trouble—shaggy hair, plain gray T-shirt, and baggy jeans. A pair of sunglasses sat atop his head like a headband. Domingo tipped his baseball hat at Lou.

Lou strode toward him. "Keep walking. Let's tour this plaza."

Bad news was written all over the agent's face. Two days ago, Lou had met with Julian, who was supposed to have revealed important information about the drug cartel's plan for a high-tech tunnel. Tessa confirmed the meeting had taken place, though she wasn't privy to the outcome.

Domingo kept in lockstep with Lou. "What's wrong?"

"Julian lied to me. The info he gave me? It's bullshit."

His stomach dropped. "What did he tell you?" He didn't need this crap right now. Girl Boss was arriving in a few hours. There wasn't enough time to conduct reconnaissance, though he was familiar with Mexico City. He could protect Tessa on a level playing field without too many unexpected variables.

"Julian admitted the Malverdes wanted to build a high-tech tunnel, but it was more wishful thinking than an actual plan because they didn't have the right technology to do it. He gave me a location in the desert where he claimed the Malverdes are building a tunnel, which was far from cutting-edge today, but they hoped to turn into an advanced tunnel eventually. My team went in there and found a tunnel already in use. We caught some lowly coyotes. Nobody important and nothing substantial. You know what else? The tunnel caved in!"

"Maybe that's why the cartel needs a better tunnel."

"Nope. That's not it." Lou slowed down at the tables displaying leather belts and bags, pretending to browse. "Julian gave me a shoddy little tunnel, something expendable, to divert us. A talented engineer like him and a savvy businessman like Tio couldn't have built it. The Malverde Cartel wouldn't have hired them if that's all they could do.

The tunnel doesn't even belong to the Malverdes. It belongs to *former* Malverde members. Julian's playing me."

They moved on to a booth selling trinkets.

"What's going to happen now?" asked Domingo.

Lou picked up a sugar-skull key chain and studied it. "I have a proposition for Tessa Woodridge."

"What? Can't you just leave her out of this? You should go after Tio instead."

"Believe me, I am. Why do you think I asked to meet with you here?"

"Why?"

"Tio and his wife, Sofia, are attending Mass in the church. I'm tailing him."

"You're doing it yourself? He's that important to you?"

"Yes, he is. Listen, Sunday." Lou motioned for him to keep walking. They sidled away from the tables and resumed strolling. "The drug cartels operate like transnational corporations," continued Lou. "They own a variety of businesses across the world. From narcotics to gas and oil to iron and copper, even cheese. They have franchises and subsidiaries and contractors. The annual revenue for the narco transnational industry is estimated at a whopping three hundred billion dollars." He let out a low whistle. "That's about as big as Singapore's annual GDP. It's nothing to sneeze at. And that's a conservative estimate. Nobody really knows the exact figure. It's not like they disclose their earnings. So . . . Is Tio *that* important to me? Hell yeah."

They'd reached the edge of the plaza. The sun slunk lower on the horizon, painting the sky a light orange. They paused behind the pickup trucks parked on the side of the street.

Lou crossed his arms over his chest. "Here's the beauty of the cartels behaving like corporations. The Malverdes are building the tunnel, but they'll let the other cartels pass through it for a fee, kinda like a toll system. That means the different factions will forge an agreement of some sort. There's a whole new game being played out there. And I need Tessa Woodridge to convince her boyfriend to reveal the tunnel's location and give up the blueprint, or face the consequences."

Domingo's skin had grown clammy from the walk. He wiped the sweat on the crown of his nose with the back of his hand. "What kind of consequences?"

"I have a feeling you know what they are."

Indeed, he did. He removed his hat and fanned himself with it. If Julian were convicted of aiding and abetting to distribute illegal substances by building a goddamn high-tech tunnel, he'd be doing twenty years in prison. And if Tessa were found to be conspiring with her boyfriend, she'd be looking at the exact same penalty.

He put his hat back on. "What's your proposition?"

"I want Tessa to look for the blueprint in Julian's laptop." Lou slid on his sunglasses.

"You want her to spy on her boyfriend?"

Lou jerked his head toward the cathedral, and they resumed walking. He didn't answer Domingo's question, didn't even slow down. "I'm positive that Julian has the plan for a state-of-the-art underground system with ventilation, lighting, and security features. I have no idea how far along the project is. We can't afford to have that tunnel operational. We might as well open our border and dedicate an express lane for illegal drugs and migrants if that happens."

The hair on Domingo's nape rose. How would he break this kind of news to Tessa? She was still grappling with the fact that Julian was neither a Mexican nor a migrant, but an impostor. "Did you know that Julian's a white man pretending to be a Mexican?" he blurted out.

That got the agent's attention. "What?" He stopped dead in his tracks. They were blocking a stream of people trying to get by.

Domingo moved aside and Lou followed.

"Okay, tell me what you know." The agent put his hands on his hips. "Is that why Tessa is flying here today?"

"To talk to him in his 'natural environment.' Her words, not mine. And that's because we found out from Julian's adoptive parents that his real name is Julian Lark. His parents are white. They were young and unmarried and broke in Encinitas, California, where they left Julian with a Mexican couple who ended up giving the kid to the Beltrans."

"Damn." Lou removed his sunglasses and looked Sunday in the eye. "And I thought maybe the cartel got a forged US passport for Julian. Excellent job, Sunday. A hell of a job sleuthing," he conceded. He glanced around.

Domingo could tell Lou's mind was speeding on the highway of possibilities. How could he use this new information to bargain with Tessa or to nab Julian?

"Let me get this straight—Tessa wants to continue dating Julian despite the lies?" Lou asked.

"That's right. She's coming here to sort things out with him."

"And you're here as the bodyguard because . . . why? I don't get it. If she doesn't trust Julian, she should just dump him."

"Yes, I'm here to keep her safe. It's true, she doesn't trust Julian. But no, she'll never dump him."

"That's crazy. But it's good news for me because I need her." The church bells tolled, jolting Lou. "Fuck! It sounds like a million bells."

"Just twenty-five, actually," Domingo corrected him. He'd been inside the cathedral before. He liked to visit touristy places when he had a chance to mix business with pleasure.

Lou glanced at his watch. "Let's go back to the church. Tio will be out soon."

They strode toward the massive building.

"Sunday, tell Tessa Woodridge if she wants to save her beloved boyfriend from prison, then she needs to get me the information about the *real* tunnel. If she can't convince Julian to give up the location and the blueprint, she needs to steal it."

"That's a tall order for anyone, but especially for Tessa. She's not a criminal."

"She should stop dating a criminal then."

"What if she won't do it, or if she *can't* find it?"

"Well, this is my last offer to her."

The bells clanged again. The front doors of the cathedral burst open. Lou sped up, then began to jog in earnest. Domingo stopped and watched him go.

Lou glanced back. "You have forty-eight hours!"

No shit. Two short days to convince Girl Boss to betray the man she was obsessed with, search for the secret blueprint, and steal it for good measure. The air grew as thick as clay. It was as though he was breathing through a mask.

He glanced at his wristwatch: 5:05. In a couple of hours, Girl Boss would arrive. How on earth would he relay Lou Harold's offer? They were supposed to avoid communicating with each other if possible. Only *she* was supposed to initiate contact and only if necessary. The SOS button in the tracking device with her was meant to be a last resort.

He loped back toward the busy street. Time to rent a motorcycle.

CHAPTER 23

Domingo found himself inside the international airport for the second time today. Not his favorite place, for sure. The crowds in this renovation-bound terminal left him claustrophobic. The odor assaulted his senses. Old cigarette smoke mixed with something dank despite the air-conditioning.

Tessa arrived on time. Seven-fifteen in the evening. Girl Boss looked mighty fine in a short red dress underneath a cropped black blazer and medium heels.

Julian was waiting for her at the customs and immigration section, where long lines snaked. He wore dark jeans, a black shirt, a black sports jacket, and his hair was slicked back. He looked every bit of the Latin Lover Boy—except he wasn't Latin.

Tessa had told her boyfriend about this visit only this morning. He'd protested initially, according to her, but she'd put her foot down. "I want to see you on *my* schedule for a change," she'd told him.

Now Domingo followed the couple as they navigated their way out of the long lines.

Julian led Tessa by the hand to a counter nearby, where two men stared at a computer screen. No line there. Julian barged in, shook hands with both men. Tessa handed something, perhaps her passport, to one of the guys, who inspected it. She'd brought just one duffel bag on wheels.

Five minutes later, the couple was out of customs and immigration. Yep, Julian had pulled some strings, or he wouldn't even be allowed inside an area exclusive to passengers and employees. Domingo himself had finagled his way into the passenger area by pretending that he'd lost a bag from his flight earlier. He'd been sent from one department to another, and he'd conveniently veered toward Tessa's arrival gate, following her from there.

Outside the airport, dusk had descended, the air giving off the stench of sweaty humanity. Tessa and Julian hopped in a black SUV waiting at the curb. They sat in the back, which meant whoever was driving was hired help, not a friend.

Domingo watched the car flow through the traffic. No need to rush to the motorcycle he'd rented. He would find them, thanks to the tracking device he'd given Tessa, which worked anywhere in the world as long as there was mobile phone reception.

He straddled the black motorbike, a BMW G650GS, small but powerful. He checked the tracking app on his smartphone. Julian's SUV hadn't gone very far. Yep, traffic in Mexico City was gnarly, which was why he hadn't rented a car. Oddly, he felt at home here because it reminded him of Manila, from the brown-skinned people to the dense, elbow-to-elbow population and smog. He stuck his phone in one of the pockets of his cargo pants, put on the helmet that had come with the bike, and took off.

He followed Tessa and Julian, first to his house in a hip neighborhood in Roma, presumably to drop off her luggage and freshen up, because they stopped for only twenty-three minutes.

Next destination: a restaurant called the Mustang in La Condesa, a short drive of less than three kilometers from Julian's house, or less than two miles in Domingo's Americanized way of thinking. The restaurant must cater to expatriates, judging by its name and the English signs outside. He parked across from the restaurant. He stayed perched on the motorbike and left his helmet on, ready to bounce if a cop hassled him.

Julian and Tessa sat at a booth by a glass window with the view of the busy street.

He used a burner phone to text her. Need to talk ASAP. Wait for my next text.

Could he go in, order food, and somehow pull Tessa for a quick chat? Nope, it wouldn't work. The restaurant was well lit. He wouldn't be able to slink in and out without Julian noticing.

He turned on the ignition and drove away from the fancy restaurants and shops. He stopped at the first hole-in-the-wall taqueria he spotted. After chowing down, he drove back to the Mustang, just in time to see Julian's chauffeured SUV drive away.

He throttled up. He was getting the hang of the BMW motorbike. He'd learned to ride back in the Philippines—on a badass Kawasaki, no less—with a maximum speed of 186 miles per hour. By contrast, this BMW could push only up to 105 miles per hour. His old Kawasaki motorbike in Manila had been perfect for fleeing extortioners who'd targeted him for bootlegging.

Tonight, he didn't need speed but flexibility to weave in and out of tight spaces as he followed Tessa and Julian. The black SUV pulled over outside El Diablo, a trendy club in Roma. Julian and Tessa hopped out of the SUV. She'd removed the blazer; her short, sleeveless crimson dress showcased her slim figure and shapely legs.

They bypassed the long line of well-dressed millennials and Gen Z patrons at the entrance. Instead, they entered through a side door. Lover Boy apparently knew the right people wherever he went.

A dark and crowded dance club offered more opportunities for Domingo to catch Tessa and relay Lou Harold's proposition than a quiet restaurant. His immediate challenge: how to get in without having to line up with the gazillion people at the entrance. He might wait all night long and still be turned away.

He circled the area until he found a paid parking lot for the motorcycle. Then he strode straight to the club's side door. He banged on it like he had the right to do so. His heart thumped just as loud as he thought out his plan.

A man's voice boomed from the other side of the door. *"Quien eres tu?"*

Domingo straightened his back. "Who am I? I'm with Jules Alexander! Open up."

The door opened a tad; a guy peeked out. Lover Boy's name served as a password around here. Domingo spoke in Spanish, introducing himself as the bodyguard of Jules Alexander's American girlfriend, the green-eyed woman in a red dress who'd passed through this door holding hands with Jules fifteen minutes ago.

The guy opened the door wider, revealing his massive build. He appraised Domingo like a German shepherd sniffing out a cadaver.

Domingo pulled up his T-shirt to reveal the Glock tucked in his waistband holster. No bodyguard worth his salt worked without a concealed weapon. The gun was courtesy of an undocumented military veteran he'd deported to Mexico. ICE periodically outsourced the legwork. When that happened, Domingo's boss provided a package deal, from catching the fugitive to ensuring the perp's court appearance all the way to deportation. In this case, the vet became Domingo's buddy and a useful contact in Mexico. No way in hell would Mexico grant tourists like Domingo a weapon's permit. It was ironic that the deluge of illegal firearms in this country came from the US. Maybe Mexico needed to build a wall to separate itself from America, not the other way around.

The big guy waved Domingo in.

Fuck yeah. He entered like a prince.

Inside, the dance music blasted. No doubt this was Mexico City's party central. He paused to let his eyes get accustomed to the dim lighting. The sharp odor of weed hung in the air. Pulsating lights bounced off the ceiling. Thick fog rose from the packed dance floor, playing around the legs of the couples grinding their bodies together.

He inched up as he scanned the vast interior. There was an L-shaped bar and tables overflowing with gregarious hipsters. There were sofas in every corner. In one nook, Julian was doing an elaborate handshake with a guy—hands clapping, knuckles locking, their shoulders meeting in a cordial bump. *Very gangsta.* Lover Boy would never do this type of greeting stateside. Tessa was right to visit him in his true environment.

When Julian sat on the sofa, he pulled Tessa onto his lap. *No shit.* She didn't seem the kind of woman who would sit on anybody's lap in public. Another girl also sat on another guy's lap. The two couples were surrounded by three dateless guys. Everybody was talking and sipping beer.

Domingo ordered a Corona at the bar. He texted Tessa. Meet me outside the ladies' room. Urgent.

"*Bailen todoooos,*" the DJ screamed. An angry Spanish hip-hop song blared.

The other girl with Tessa bolted up, tugging at her date's hand toward the dance floor. Julian and his friends were teasing the guy.

Julian's arms were entwined around Tessa's waist, but his attention was on the other couple. Tessa was staring at her phone.

At last, the other couple went to the dance floor amid the group's hooting.

Domingo proceeded to the back of the club. He waited for Tessa outside the restroom. As soon as the red dress came into view, he met her halfway and led her by the elbow toward a standing table. With his glass of beer, they could pretend to be having a normal conversation instead of a crisis meeting.

He told her everything: Julian's decoy tunnel that caved in, the Malverde Cartel's plan to impose a toll fee on other cartels once its high-tech tunnel became operational, and Lou Harold's offer to exculpate both Tessa and Julian if he shared the tunnel's location and blueprint.

Tessa's lips pinched together in a tight knot. Every word out of Domingo's mouth seemed to wind her tighter and tighter.

"You have to convince Julian to give up the real location of the tunnel," he went on.

She wrapped her arms around herself like she was freezing, though the air in the club was stuffy. "What if I fail?"

He drummed his fingers on the table. In another minute, Julian might start looking for her. "If you can't make Julian give up the blueprint, then Lou wants you to copy the document from Julian's laptop."

"Copy?"

"Okay, steal." Domingo gulped his beer. "Lou wants you to steal it."

"I can't believe this is happening to me." She gave him a bitter little smile. "I haven't even told Julian that I met his adoptive parents."

"Tell him you know he's white and you know he lied to the DEA." He finished his beer. "That's two strikes against him, so he's going to beg for your forgiveness. And if you really want to save him from himself, tell him you're going to forgive him *only* if he cooperates with Lou Harold. You'll be saving him from twenty years in prison."

She dropped her head almost to her chest. Of course, Lou's message had shredded her.

"Tessa, if Julian loves you as much as you love him, he'll do what's necessary."

She raised her gaze to his. Her forehead closed into a line of wrinkles, her expression suffused with hurt. "I need to go back now."

"Lou's offer expires in forty-eight hours. Contact me before then." He was counting on her to put on her CEO game face and tackle this crisis head on.

She lifted her chin and nodded, the return of her self-confidence falling on him like a ray of sun in this dark cave of a club. Then she pivoted back to Julian and his friends.

CHAPTER 24

Domingo sat on the BMW motorcycle as he watched Julian's two-story house from the intersection. He wore the helmet to hide his face. A messenger bag hung across his chest.

Early this morning, Tessa had texted him on his burner phone. Need to talk. Going shopping in Roma this AM.

Out of an abundance of caution, he'd brought two burner phones for a short trip to Mexico City. Burner phones were untraceable. He'd also equipped Tessa's phone with a special app that would let her send a text to his burner phone anonymously.

Tessa cared too much about Julian to get busted with secret texts, while Domingo's professionalism compelled him to protect his client's privacy. None of this stalking on foreign soil would ever connect Tessa to him.

With neither a time nor a specific store mentioned in her text, his only choice was to tail her. Since Julian lived in Roma, he anticipated the couple would walk to the nearby boutiques.

Julian's front yard consisted of a small patch of grass flanked by tall trees. The black SUV sat in the driveway, visible through the wrought iron gate. The house reminded him of the brownstones on the Upper West Side in Manhattan, except this one came with a little porch.

He glanced around. Big old houses and apartment buildings. Mercedes-Benzes and Audis on leafy driveways. Julian's neighborhood was quirky like the Village in Manhattan and hip like SoMa in San Francisco.

At ten minutes past eleven o'clock, the front door opened. Tessa came out in skinny jeans, a white sleeveless blouse, and flat shoes. Julian trailed her, placing a wide-brimmed hat on her head. He pecked her on the lips. Very sweet. There was no hint of any tension or friction between them. Did it mean Girl Boss had persuaded him to come clean to the DEA? He hoped she would have good news.

While Julian was locking the front door, Domingo texted Tessa. Go inside Augusta.

Tessa pulled her phone from her shoulder bag, glanced at it, and shoved it back. Julian opened the iron gate for her and shut it behind them with a clang. Like Domingo had expected, the couple strolled along the tree-lined streets, headed toward the shops, restaurants, and art galleries.

Domingo started the motorcycle and zoomed ahead. He had about twenty minutes before Tessa and Julian arrived at La Casa de Augusta, a lingerie store and the only place he deemed possible to talk to her this morning without her boyfriend.

He'd paid in advance an hour ago for a parking spot at a bakery across from the store and befriended the girl who worked behind the counter. He stayed inside the bakery as he kept an eye on La Casa de Augusta.

A vintage clothing store and a fruit stand exploding with the sunny colors of fresh mangoes, papayas, and bananas flanked the lingerie shop. Japanese tourists bearing a group-tour flag marked **VIAJE REAL** lined up at the fruit stand for drinks.

At last, Tessa and Julian arrived at Augusta, where they lingered outside, chatting. Domingo slapped on a baseball cap, slinked out of the bakery, and blended with the Japanese tourists as he studied the juice menu.

Girl Boss ought to enter the shop already, but they seemed to be discussing something. Did Julian want to accompany Tessa inside? Was she trying to convince him otherwise?

If Julian went in with her, Domingo's plan would fail. He was counting on Julian's machismo to prevent him from following his girl around in a lingerie shop.

He was right too. Tessa entered Augusta while Julian crossed the street and entered the very bakery where Domingo had been.

He exhaled and followed Tessa in the store, a little bell hanging from the door clinking.

The cashier was chatting with a customer, while another clerk helped two women.

Domingo slid up beside Tessa and whispered, "It's me."

She covered her mouth. "You startled me."

He grabbed a bunch of stuff from a rack and gave it to her. "Tell the ladies you're going to try these on. Leave the door open, and I'll follow you there."

Tessa approached the clerk, who opened a fitting room for her.

Domingo eased behind the racks of underwear and around the shelves of lotions and soaps to get to the fitting room. The shop employees and the customers continued yakking.

He entered the room with the door left ajar. Tessa shut it behind him.

"Did Julian agree to give the blueprint to Lou?" he asked.

Tessa took off her hat and leaned against the floor-length mirror, her bag hanging from her shoulder. "No. He denied having the blueprint. He even denied lying about being a Mexican."

"What?"

"When Julian's parents abandoned him, this country accepted him unconditionally. The only love he's ever experienced came from Mexicans. In his mind, he *became* Mexican. He's given up being an American. He identifies as a Mexican from the bottom of his heart."

He took off his cap. "*That* is the biggest pile of bullshit ever."

"Julian has transracial identity." She chewed her lower lip.

"What does that mean?"

She let out a sigh. "It's like being a transgender . . . like a transgender woman is a female trapped in a man's body—"

He raised his forefinger to stop her. "I understand transsexuality and transgender identity. But this transracial . . . thing . . . Are you kidding me? Race isn't fluid."

"In Julian's mind, he *is* Mexican."

"You believe his shit?"

She nodded. "It explains his willingness to be detained and deported as a migrant."

"Okay, so he believes he's Mexican, but he's lying about the tunnel."

"He came clean about the tunnel. He admitted he was under such duress that he gave away the first tunnel he could think of."

"The *first* tunnel? So there are many tunnels?"

"Lou himself told me the different cartels have built more than two hundred tunnels originating from Mexico over the years. Julian said Tio has been working for the Malverdes to save Oldie's life. Remember Oldie?"

"How can I forget?"

"Oldie was in prison for a long time. Thanks to the Malverdes, he's out now, and he'll stay alive as long as Tio cooperates. Julian said there's no blueprint, at least not yet, because the whole project is impossible. It requires advanced technology, which the Malverdes don't have."

"That's bullshit." He plopped his cap back on his head. "The cartel doesn't have the technology, but you know who does?"

"Terra Firma." Her shoulders stiffened. "But Julian said the company isn't anywhere near ready to develop the right kind of machine that's small enough to be undetected and powerful enough to dig to the right depth in days, not months. They're at least a decade away. His meeting in Davis was a letdown."

Domingo shook his head. "Nope, that's bullshit. Julian knew the technology isn't ready, and that's why he approached Terra Firma. According to David McCoy, Julian wants to connect Terra Firma with some Mexican investors. Can't you see that the Malverdes are the investors? The cartel will finance Terra Firma's R&D. With the right financing, the right tunnel boring machine will be ready sooner than later."

She puckered her eyebrows; her eyes welled. "I don't know what to believe anymore, but I can't give up on Julian. He's really trying to cooperate with Lou. And he's doing his best to make Tio understand that the project is impossible because the technology they need isn't there."

They stopped talking when they heard footsteps. The salesclerk was letting a customer into the next fitting room.

Tessa appeared to be holding her breath, pressing her hat and shoulder bag against her chest.

Domingo glanced at his wristwatch. They'd been talking for only a minute, but the giant clock ticking inside his head made it seem longer. "What am I gonna tell Lou?" he mouthed.

"Tell him the blueprint doesn't exist—yet," she whispered.

"Plan B then. You need to check Julian's laptop for the blueprint."

She gaped at him. "There's no blueprint."

"What if he's lying? Check his laptop."

The woman in the next room coughed.

Domingo mouthed, "Check his laptop." He gestured for her to go out first. He grabbed a couple of negligees and handed them to her. "You gotta buy these. You've been here too long."

She snatched them from him, opened the door, and got out.

The customer next door was moving around. He needed to get out before she did. He peeked from the door. The coast was clear. He sidled out of the room.

Tessa had just finished paying for her purchases. New customers arrived, keeping the salesclerk busy. But the cashier's eyes grew wide upon seeing Domingo, apparently unaware of his presence before then.

He wanted to flee, but he could see through the glass door that Tessa and Julian were just outside the store.

The cashier eyed him suspiciously.

He smiled. In Spanish, he asked her about the soaps and lotions. Did they have something made of lavender or aloe vera? She showed him a gift set of lavender bar soap and lotion. He knew cash was king in Mexico. Thank goodness he had a wad of Mexican pesos. He paid for it in cash, plus gave the cashier a tip. For her trouble, he'd told her.

It was the only time she'd smiled at him.

At last, Tessa and Julian were gone. He left the store with the soap and lotion. Well, he was sure Mamang would appreciate them.

CHAPTER 25

How Anti-Immigration Supporters Unwittingly Help Smugglers

"Build a wall" supporters think that the louder they scream, the more likely they'll scare desperate hopefuls from crossing illegally into this country. WRONG. They only help make the business of migrant smuggling more lucrative.

A decade ago, migrants paid one hundred dollars just to be taken to the staging area along the border. From there, they paid the coyotes—the guides and the fixers—one to three thousand dollars for the privilege of hiking all the way to America. A lot of people never make it in the unforgiving desert temperatures that could rise to one hundred twenty degrees during the day and plummet to as low as minus thirty-five degrees during the night. Their blood could boil in extreme heat, or their organs shut down in freezing cold. The coyotes made money whether their clients lived or died. How's that for a business model?

With the anti-immigration sentiment in this country surging, prices have gone through the roof. Getting to the staging area now costs from five to ten grand, plus another ten to fifteen grand to cross stateside. There are extra fees if you bring children or if you're pregnant or if you have a medical condition, all of which require additional attention.

Smugglers claim it's much harder to cross the border in the light of the ICE crackdown. They say their risks are greater because of increased law enforcement. That's bullshit. The desert remains the same, so the deadly crossing is no different now than before. The risks are also the same, though the bribes to corrupt Border Patrol agents have skyrocketed. The conditions haven't changed, but smugglers are capitalizing on the current anti-immigration fervor to drive their profits. I learned all this firsthand from coyotes I've apprehended and their poor victims.

The bigots in this country have made migrant trafficking more lucrative than ever and illegal immigration worse than before. So thanks but no thanks, assholes!

◆ ◆ ◆

It was almost two o'clock in the afternoon. Domingo had been sitting for an hour on a bench in a park in Coyoacán, a neighborhood named after the damn coyote—the animal, not the criminal. The statues of two coyotes in a fountain inspired the page he'd just written. He shoved the writing pad and pen inside his messenger bag.

Today he needed to get close enough to Tessa to hand her a burner phone. She had texted Domingo earlier. Need burner with camera. Only one of the two burner phones he'd brought had a camera.

He slipped on his sunglasses and baseball cap and walked the short distance to the restaurant where Tessa and Julian were having lunch with Tio and his wife, Sofia. This was important for Tessa. Julian had finally introduced her to his surrogate parents. It might also explain why Domingo hadn't seen any sign that the cartel was "babysitting" Julian. Neither the Patricios nor anyone else had tailed Lover Boy. Most likely, Tio had told the goons to back off.

Why did Tessa need a burner camera? Whatever it was, it must have been something she didn't want on her personal phone. Therefore, it had to be the blueprint. How on earth was Domingo supposed to hand her the burner? All he could do was stalk her and keep an eye out for an opportunity.

Lou Harold's forty-eight-hour deadline would end tonight. And yet he refrained from nagging Tessa about it. They'd agreed to keep texts or any form of communication to a minimum lest Julian found out.

Fifteen minutes later, Julian and Tessa emerged from the restaurant, their hands clasped together. A bespectacled man and an elegant woman trailed them. *Santiago Sepulveda de Santiago a.k.a. Santiago Santiago a.k.a. Tio.* He and his wife appeared to be in their sixties.

The two couples chatted. Perhaps they were waiting for their ride. Tio wore a brown suit. With his eyeglasses, neat mustache, and receding hairline, he looked like a retired high school teacher or someone's uncle. No wonder they called him Tio. Mexicans were like Filipinos in the sense that everyone called everybody *uncle* or *aunt*. Domingo called all his mother's girlfriends *Tita*, and even the lady who owned the Filipino store he frequented in Flatbush. None of them was a real aunt.

Tio was a far cry from stereotypical characters associated with drug cartels and mobsters. He'd imagined a Marlon Brando type, like in *The Godfather*, or Joe Pesci in *Goodfellas*.

It hit Domingo that these were Dulce's parents. Was Dulce as delicate looking as her mother? Did she have Sofia's curly hair, dark eyes, and thin lips? Domingo wondered if Tessa was thinking similar thoughts. Julian had almost married Dulce, after all.

A silver Mercedes-Benz arrived. The chauffeur hurried to open the passenger door. Just as Deputy Sheriff Alvarado had recalled, Tio walked with a prominent limp. His left leg was shorter than his right.

To Domingo's surprise, Julian and Tessa didn't ride in the Mercedes. They both waved goodbye as the car drove away. The couple crossed the cobblestone street and strolled toward the park where Domingo had just come from. Where were they headed?

He maintained a good distance from them.

In the park, Julian and Tessa traipsed past the fountain with the bronze coyotes. They proceeded to a nearby monument in honor of the revolutionary Miguel Hidalgo.

Tessa and Julian laughing together in a park evoked a dreamy sense of ease and fun—the good life. It was like staring at a tourism advertisement in a travel magazine. She wore flats and a flowery wrap dress that hugged her slim figure. A leather bag hung from her shoulder. Julian exuded effortless charm in a pair of khaki chinos, white cotton shirt, and boat shoes.

They held hands all the time. Lover Boy might as well be playing upon an exquisite violin with Girl Boss answering to his trill of the bow. The glow of happiness about her, plus her body language, showed that she was under his spell. Domingo doubted the lovebirds even noticed the white veil of haze that made him clammy—smog.

From the Hidalgo monument, Julian and Tessa strolled toward the adjacent church. Tourists milled about the plaza in front of the church. And where tourists gathered, vendors followed to hawk T-shirts and hats, postcards and trinkets, and other merchandise. Domingo positioned himself near the benches, about thirty feet away from the couple.

Tessa broke away from Julian and stopped before the steps leading to the church's front doors. She gazed up at the bell tower that stood four-story high, a hand shielding her eyes from the sun. The building's austere design resembled more of a fortress than a house of worship.

Julian called out Tessa's name, and when she glanced back, he snapped a photo with his cell phone.

The church doors opened. Hordes of people in black clothes streamed out, adding to the congestion of tourists and vendors. Domingo took off his sunglasses and stood atop a bench to get a better view. The surging crowd had separated Tessa and Julian, both of them waiting out the flow of humanity.

To Domingo's surprise, some women were crying. They had just attended a funeral Mass, judging by the black outfits of everyone streaming out of the church.

Tessa craned her neck, apparently searching for her boyfriend. As she stepped back, she hit the elbow of a man wearing a loud Hawaiian shirt—a middle-aged, skinny, and unshaven guy. He gestured in an urgent manner while Tessa leaned closer. Were they having a conversation? Was the guy begging for coins or hassling her?

The thought of a possible mugging prickled Domingo's sweaty skin and made him anxious. Tessa was shaking her head, backing away, when Mr. Hawaiian Shirt yanked the bag off her shoulder and scampered off with it. *Motherfucker!*

"My purse," Tessa screamed. "Julian—heeelp!"

A group of men carrying a coffin came out of the church, followed by a procession of mourners. It was impossible to spot Julian in the throng.

Domingo jumped off the bench and sprinted after Hawaiian Shirt, cutting through the funeral procession. *"Ladrón! Ladrón!"* Thief, he yelled, hoping someone would stop the son of a bitch.

Because Hawaiian Shirt kept glancing back at Domingo, he stumbled into a line of fruit vendors. The bastard fell face first, knocking down the vendors' makeshift tables. Bananas, pineapples, oranges, and papayas rolled on the ground. Curses in Spanish exploded.

Shoppers swarmed to help the vendors pick up the rolling fruits. Domingo dove for Tessa's bag, snatched it from the thief's grasp, and crouched behind the toppled tables partly blocked by the vendors scooping up produce. Hawaiian Shirt appeared dazed as he got up and looked around. He seemed to realize just then that he'd lost the bag in the commotion.

Domingo stayed low, hiding from Hawaiian Shirt, but also planning his next move. He needed to find Tessa to hand her the burner camera plus her bag.

Hawaiian Shirt bent his head, apparently still looking for the bag among the scattered fruits, baskets, and crates. Out of nowhere, someone lunged at him. It was Julian! The shoppers shrieked.

Julian seized Hawaiian Shirt by the neck and slammed the crown of his head against the guy's face—a whopping headbutt. The scoundrel fell backward. The crowd drew back.

Domingo scrambled away and ran back to the plaza, where he bumped into Tessa. "I have your bag."

"Thank you so much." She was panting. "Have you seen Julian?"

"He's kicking the mugger's ass." He pulled the burner phone from his pocket and stuck it in Tessa's bag. He thrust it to her. "Why do you need a camera?"

"The blueprint is on paper, *not* in his computer. I'm going to take a picture of it." She snatched her bag from Domingo, brushed past him as though she didn't know him, and bolted forward. "Juliaaan! I got my bag back!"

Domingo glanced over his shoulder.

She ran into Lover Boy's open arms. *Julian the Savior.* Tessa's hero forever. He enveloped her with a tight hug and kissed the top of her head. He swept the surroundings with a quick gaze.

Domingo turned around and barged past a cluster of onlookers. He hoped Julian hadn't spotted him.

CHAPTER 26

Five hours after the attempted mugging of Tessa, Domingo was eating barbacoa—the real deal with goat meat—at a table outside a little cantina in Centro.

He handed his buddy, Alfonso, a Kellogg's box containing the borrowed Glock instead of cornflakes. "I can't thank you enough for this."

"You used it?" Alfonso set the box on the empty chair beside him. His friend hadn't changed in five years. Still sported a mustache like Jack Black in *Nacho Libre*, still spoke with his mouth full.

"Nah. It's just insurance."

"How do you like Smog City?" asked Alfonso. He meant Mexico City, his home since Domingo had deported him.

"It doesn't bother me one bit. Remember, I came from Smog City, Philippines."

"True, true." Alfonso chuckled.

The guy had grown up in New York, undocumented like his parents. He could have lived under the radar forever, but he wanted to serve his country—he was American at heart if not by birth. He'd joined the army and served not once or twice but *four* times in Iraq in hopes of gaining American citizenship. He'd almost made it, too, but after a drunken brawl, he'd landed in jail, posted bail, and tried to "disappear" before his immigration hearing. Well, Domingo had caught him, escorted him to his hearing, and delivered him to Mexican authorities in Ciudad Juárez after ICE outsourced the deportation legwork to Domingo. Lo and behold, Alfonso and Domingo had struck an unlikely camaraderie during the long drive from Manhattan to Juárez.

Domingo swigged his soda. "Do you miss New York?"

"Of course. I still think of myself as American. See this?" Alfonso lifted his T-shirt to show the Lady Liberty tattoo on his chest. "I got this last year—four years after America dumped me. Other dudes etch the name of their wife or girlfriend on their chest. Me? I chose the country I love. Too bad it doesn't love me back."

"Sorry, bro." Domingo was apologizing for the inherent injustice in a country where O. J. Simpson got away with murder while a war veteran like his pal got deported for a brawl.

They ate without speaking for a while. All the other customers were crammed indoors, but Domingo didn't mind dining outdoors, despite the hubbub of cars and motorcycles on the street. The air was thinner tonight, the sky clear enough for the stars to shine.

"How's your job?" asked Domingo between bites of the tender goat meat.

Alfonso shrugged. "It's okay. I work ten days straight; then I come home for five days. You're lucky you caught me on my time off." He was snarfing down a mushy pile of rice and beans. "At least you didn't have to drive two hundred miles just to borrow a box of Kellogg's."

They both chuckled.

"I owe you big time." Domingo raised his soda can, which Alfonso clinked with his own. He admired the guy's magnanimity. Alfonso never showed any bitterness toward Uncle Sam, hadn't succumbed to job offers from drug lords. Instead, he'd taken a job with the *policía comunitaria*, a local militia, in Guerrero. If he couldn't serve as a soldier in America, he'd rather be a vigilante in Mexico.

Domingo's cell phone pinged. A text from Tessa. Will drop paper bag outside the house, Concepcion Street. Search bushes after 11 PM.

Julian's house stood at the intersection of Avenida Obregon and Calle Concepción. Tessa meant the chest-high bushes on the side of the house. The paper bag would likely contain the burner phone with the camera. A picture of the secret tunnel's blueprint would please Lou Harold. Hell, it would probably push him up a couple of pay grades. He could almost taste the sweetness of triumph but stopped short of calling the DEA agent. Only George W. Bush and damn fools would declare *mission accomplished* without proof positive.

He wiped his plate clean and drank his soda. "Since it's your night off, you want a tequila instead of dessert?"

"Sure. I know a joint nearby." Alfonso burped without care. *"Vamonos."*

They walked one block to a bar where laughter and loud conversations drowned out the live guitar music. Domingo sipped a Coke while listening to Alfonso describe his commute to and from Guerrero, where the poppy farmers who funded the militia had been hit hard by the declining prices of opium. Domingo refrained from drinking alcohol, because this workday was far from over.

For the next hour, he just observed. The forlorn guitarist exited the makeshift stage after playing to a tittering, uncaring audience. Middle-aged hombres were openly snorting white lines on their table, and young couples smooched without shame. He gasped for breath amid the ripe smell of sweat, stale perfume, smoke, and booze.

When his cell phone rang, he was glad for the excuse to get out of the room. He burst outside with a great breath of relief and answered the call. It was Lou Harold, who was back in San Diego.

"Don't you stop working?" Domingo was standing several feet away from the bar, on the curb.

"Sunday, I can't relax until you tell me you have the blueprint or new information or something. I'll take *anything*."

"I wanna make sure what I've got first. How about I call you first thing tomorrow?"

"Can you give me a little hint?"

"I don't wanna raise any false hopes."

"Okay. Tomorrow morning, then."

"I'm curious about your forty-eight-hour deadline. If I don't deliver, would you subpoena Julian and Tio?"

"They're both clean. Not even a traffic violation."

"So what would you do?"

"We would have to get creative."

Like hack into Julian's computer or ransack Tio's house in the guise of burglary. He couldn't voice his thoughts. Instead, he teased the agent. "When I hear *creative*, I'm reminded of some crazy-ass abstract painting that looks like a splash of vomit, or an art installation of a banana duct-taped on a freaking wall."

Lou chuckled. "Have you heard of the saying 'creativity is intelligence having fun'? Whoever said it is absolutely right, hence the vomit and banana."

"Albert Einstein said it, according to a poster."

"Really?"

"I saw it on Amazon for nineteen bucks."

"You're a bottomless well of pleasant surprises."

"I always aim to please, Lou."

They ended the call on that note, and he went back inside the bar. He would hang out for another thirty minutes with Alfonso before he headed for Julian's house.

◆ ◆ ◆

At eleven o'clock, Julian's neighborhood in Roma was already asleep, engulfed by shadows. The night air smelled of trees ripened by summer. A dog barked not too far away.

Domingo strolled along Calle Concepción and stopped outside Julian's house. He searched the row of evergreen bushes that served as a hedge between the wrought iron fence and the sidewalk. Nothing there.

He crossed the street and perched on the motorcycle. At this hour, he could double-park beside a Nissan without consequences. If a cop showed up, he would just leave. This side of Julian's house had no windows, and therefore there was no danger of Julian seeing him from inside. He could afford not to wear his helmet for cover.

The dog's bark grew louder—a guy out for a walk was struggling to control a beagle. Although Domingo heard the noise all along, he hadn't spotted them on the dim street until they were about twelve feet away. The man yanked the leash to no avail, the beagle still yapping at Domingo.

Damn it. The last thing he needed was for someone to remember him staking out Julian's house. He put on his helmet and zoomed away. He was familiar with the area by now. He cruised by the bakery where he'd bribed the employee for the privilege of parking and then passed by the hole-in-the-wall taqueria he liked. A densely populated place like Mexico City had a dearth of parking space. No wonder Julian never drove himself. A driver picked up him and Tessa and dropped them off, or they walked to their destinations. After the disrupted mugging, Julian and Tessa had gone to the Frida Kahlo Museum on foot. Domingo had followed them until it was time to meet Alfonso. He'd been monitoring the couple's movement through the tracking app since then.

He eased off the throttle and turned around, back to Julian's house. This time, he kept the helmet on as he rummaged through the dense bushes. No paper bag. He glanced at his wristwatch: 11:41. He sat on his double-parked motorbike and waited. In the best-case scenario, Tessa would emerge from the back door and lob the burner phone over the fence. Domingo would pick it up from the bushes, and everyone would live happily ever after.

A white car passed by, then a scooter. In the middling-case scenario, Tessa would text to say she would keep the camera. She and Domingo were catching a flight back to Sacramento in a few hours, after all. Couldn't she manage to keep it safe from her boyfriend until then?

At midnight, Domingo removed his helmet and carried it with him as he circled Julian's house on foot. He wondered if there were surveillance cameras. Nope. Tessa wouldn't have chosen the bushes as the drop-off point if there were cameras. She would have seen a monitor inside the house, or maybe she'd asked Julian about it. He trusted that she'd done some due diligence.

The lights burned indoors. He kept up hope. Maybe Tessa was just waiting for the right time to sneak out. Maybe she and Lover Boy got busy under the covers like a normal lovestruck couple. In the worst-case scenario . . . well, he refused to think of it. He slipped his helmet back on, hopped on the motorcycle, and took off.

He rode through a commercial area still abuzz with traffic. No art galleries here, but strip clubs and beer joints spilling over with tipsy men. Hordes of people streamed out of a movie theater. Some of them raced to a bus stop where passengers lined up to board the metro bus.

At half past midnight, he retraced his way back to Calle Concepción and searched the bushes again. *Nada.* Frustration sometimes triggered his worst fears, the kind that leaped over logic and straight to the starkest possibilities. Was Tessa all right? He checked the tracking app. She was inside Julian's house. She hadn't pushed the SOS button on the tracking device. Of course she was fine.

He straddled his double-parked motorcycle and waited. Surveillance required a tremendous amount of patience, something he'd developed over the years. He embraced the blank spaces of time as a respite, as a natural form of meditation. In times like this, he focused on situational awareness. He took in the stock-still night without the benefit of moonlight or breeze, the wailing siren in the distance, and the rhythm of his breath underneath the helmet.

Sometimes sad memories ambushed him. He could see Monica Reed just as she'd stood at the Greyhound bus station the first time he'd caught her. Young, brunette, dark eyes blazing at him. Taller than him too. She was fair, thanks to her mixed Filipino American race. Hers was the kind of beauty that melted his heart. She'd been in love with a married white man who looked like he'd stepped off a *GQ* cover. Domingo had been contented to love her only in his mind, but even that was impossible today.

He glanced at his watch. At a quarter past one in the morning, the lights in Julian's house continued to glow. Would Lover Boy leave them on all night? Some people did that as a deterrent to burglars.

His phone pinged. A text from Tessa. Sorry no blueprint. Julian proposed.

He read it again. Here it was, the bad news he'd been dreading—a complete reversal in the situation. In a span of just eleven hours, Tessa had changed from a willing informant against a drug cartel back to her old infatuated self, a vulnerable young woman too blinded by her obsession to refuse a marriage proposal by her impostor boyfriend.

CHAPTER 27

Five Things You Need to Know About Immigration Courts

Thousands of migrants flock to the southern border and seek out Border Patrol agents to request safe haven. They think if they can only face an immigration judge, all will be well. WRONG. US immigration courts are NOT real courts. I mentioned this in a previous chapter, so let's dive in.

Just to be clear, I'm not saying these courts are fake. What I mean is that they're not part of the judicial branch. So if you're undocumented, please don't ever think that an immigration judge will take your side. Nothing could be further from the truth.

Here are five things you need to keep in mind before you cross illegally and demand to see an immigration judge:

1. *In America, judicial independence means regular judges decide cases by interpreting the law, not based on political influence or popular public opinion. Immigration judges DON'T possess such impartiality.*
2. *Immigration courts are under the jurisdiction of the Department of Justice. That means the US attorney general can overturn an immigration case without rhyme or reason. Just like other federal employees, immigration judges are beholden to the administration currently in power.*
3. *Today there are only about six hundred immigration judges,*

sixty-eight immigration courts, and three adjudication centers in this country. Over two million cases are pending in these courts. So when you get to one of these courts, expect an overworked and stressed-out federal employee who must decide thousands of cases.

4. *Unlike criminal courts, an immigration court has zero obligation to provide a court-appointed lawyer for you. You're lucky if you get a translator. Volunteers in nonprofit organizations that advocate for immigrants are your best bet for help.*
5. *For God's sake, don't cross illegally!*

◆ ◆ ◆

The airplane took off eleven minutes late. Domingo stopped writing and shoved his notepad and pen in his messenger bag, which he stowed underneath the seat in front of him. He occupied an aisle seat in coach while Tessa was in first class. If he were a freeloader, he would be in the same section at her expense. But he hadn't been brought up that way. This flight wasn't even risky. They'd left the muggings and other dangers behind. They were almost home free.

At the airport, they'd waited separately and avoided contact. His job was to shadow her. Socializing was uncalled for. Besides, one day after Julian proposed, the couple had been inseparable until it was time for Tessa to enter the secured area. Domingo had worn sunglasses and a baseball cap pulled low to hide his face, while he observed them. Girl Boss had carried a small gift bag and her purse. The gift had probably come from Lover Boy, something precious she hadn't wanted to check in with her luggage.

He was glad the two guys who sat in his row were not blabbermouths. The guy in the middle seat wore earbuds that announced *Don't bother me*, while the one slumped in the window seat got busy with his laptop.

As soon as the seat belt sign went off, a woman three rows ahead leaped to her feet and proceeded to the front cabin. One of those people who couldn't sit still. He called them ACHDs, for "attention-challenged hyperannoying douchebags." Did *douchebag* apply only to men? What was the female version of a douchebag? A *douchebaguette*?

The other passengers stirred, conversing in Spanish. This was an Aeroméxico flight originating from Mexico City, after all.

He would deplane with Tessa in Sacramento and get his instructions. Julian had thrown a curveball with his marriage proposal. Perhaps she would terminate Domingo's services today and he could catch the next plane to New York. Further investigation into Julian's affairs was unnecessary. She would marry him for better or for worse, federal charges against him be damned.

Douchebaguette returned to her seat, a sourpuss look on her face. She wore slacks and a blue button-down shirt, the epitome of business casual. A flight attendant had stopped her from wandering into the first-class cabin.

He'd put his phone on airplane mode. No new texts would show up. Fine by him. He didn't want another text from Lou Harold reminding him of his missed deadline. He would call the DEA agent after he got the whole story from Tessa. It had been wise to withhold the information about the paper blueprint. Lou didn't know that it existed at all, so Domingo would just say Tessa hadn't found anything relevant on Julian's computer. The DEA would have to steal the information it needed by other means.

When the plane stopped in Las Vegas for a layover, everyone went through the US customs and immigration checkpoint. Afterward, Tessa walked inside the VIP lounge for first-class passengers and Priority Pass members, where she stayed until it was time to board their next flight. Domingo kept close but didn't seek her inside. There wasn't any need.

Guess who'd tried to crash at the first-class lounge? Yep, Douchebaguette. What was her problem? Did she want a free cocktail so bad she'd risk humiliation? At least Douchebaguette hadn't resisted the airport employee who'd turned her away. No arguing or cussing or drama.

By the last leg of the trip, Domingo couldn't keep his eyes open. He had been up the night before till the wee hours waiting for the blueprint that had never come. The next thing he knew, the plane crew were reminding passengers to buckle up and remain seated for the landing.

Seconds after the plane landed, he turned off his phone's airplane mode and texted Tessa. Will shadow u. Where can we talk?

Sacramento was her home turf. It was best to keep his distance, in case anyone she knew happened to be in the airport. Since nobody knew about his role as her bodyguard, it would be hard to explain his presence.

His phone pinged. A text from Tessa. Will take Uber Black. See you at pickup spot.

◆ ◆ ◆

Domingo hadn't used the restroom on the plane, so his first stop was the men's room. His tracking app showed Tessa's location: the women's room next door. He hurried up so he would be outside when she emerged from the restroom.

He carried his duffel bag as he tailed her. The messenger bag was hanging across his chest. He always traveled light. Tessa, on the other hand, had checked in her bag. Now she had to retrieve it.

Girl Boss looked like an ordinary girl, not a rich boss, in her plaid blouse, skinny jeans, and flat shoes. A simple gold necklace with a pearl pendant adorned her neck. Nothing about her flaunted her wealth, which made his job easier.

When she got on the escalator, he waited until she was halfway down before hopping on. A bird's-eye view of the entire baggage-claim area unfolded before him. *Well, well, what do you know? Douchebaguette.* A short muscular guy accompanied her. They were craning their necks and sweeping the area with their gazes as if waiting for someone.

Tessa. The hunter in him sprang to attention. His racing thoughts tumbled into place—Douchebaguette had followed Tessa from Mexico

City to Las Vegas to Sacramento. The constant checking in first class and in the VIP lounge suddenly made sense. But the woman's job was only to follow Tessa. Like a relay race, she was passing the baton to the douchebag with her. The man was the real perpetrator, the one who would harm the heiress. *Son of a bitch.*

Tessa got off the escalator. Douchebag and Douchebaguette slinked behind her.

Adrenaline rushed through Domingo, making his every muscle tight. The escalator was packed so he couldn't go down the steps. What to do? The ground was about four feet below. He slung his duffel bag's strap over his right shoulder, planted both palms on the railing, and jumped off the side of the escalator. He landed on his feet. *Easy peasy.*

In five huge strides, he got to about five feet from Douche Couple while they maintained a distance of about seven feet from Tessa. They carried no luggage. The woman's purse was hanging over her shoulder.

He couldn't initiate any move without ascertaining whether they meant to harm Tessa. He could do nothing but wait for Douche Couple to try to grab or stab or shoot the heiress. The man was the same height as Domingo, though thicker, and his sidekick was no Zoya the Destroya wrestling type of woman. Domingo was unarmed, but he could whip these jokers' asses with his bare hands.

The pair accelerated their pace, so Domingo did the same. Douchebag pulled something from his trouser pocket and clasped his hands behind his back. Wait a minute . . . Was he hiding something in his hands? A knife? No, too small. An ice pick?

Domingo strode faster to get a closer view of what Douchebag was trying to hide. A syringe? Yes, definitely. *What the fuck?* It could be a knockout drug or anesthetic to incapacitate Tessa. Worst-case scenario, something poisonous to kill her.

The airport was crowded, but unlike in New York, Sacramento wasn't teeming with cops. Still, he couldn't afford a fistfight in front of hundreds of witnesses, not to mention surveillance cameras. On this floor, he guessed the cameras would be monitoring the conveyor belts for any luggage theft. He was halfway to them.

He took the baseball cap from his messenger bag, slapped it on, and pulled it low to hide his face. *Focus,* he reminded himself. All he needed to do was get rid of the syringe and warn Tessa. He didn't have to eliminate Douche Couple.

Douchebag didn't suspect anyone observing him, certainly not from behind. Even as he tried to conceal the syringe, he did so with the laxness of someone unaware. The surprise factor and proximity boosted Domingo's self-confidence. What was his chance of stopping the scoundrel? About 90 percent. *Now or never.*

He took a deep breath. When he exhaled, he glided right behind Douchebag and slapped the hand clutching the syringe, which hit the floor and skidded away. "Run, Tessa," he yelled. She took off, the plaid shirt suddenly out of his view.

Douchebag jerked his head back to see who had knocked the syringe from his hand, but the sight of Tessa scampering away distracted him. A split second was enough—Domingo chopped each side of the bastard's neck with a simultaneous knife-hand strike, aiming for the vagus nerve. Douchebaguette squealed and ran in the opposite direction, back to the escalator. An amateur, for sure.

Douchebag's knees buckled from the assault, but Domingo caught him in a rear bear hug. Domingo wrapped his arms tightly around the man's chest, squeezing the air out of the bastard's lungs without murdering him. He just about crumbled down.

The people around them parted. "Oh my God!" gasped a woman wearing a straw hat.

"He's all right," said Domingo. "His knees gave way. He has a balance problem." With his arms still locked around Douchebag's chest, he dragged the man farther away from the baggage carousels and the surveillance cameras.

Douchebag was sprawled on his back, dazed. A vagus strike slowed down the heartbeat and breathing, sometimes to the point of fainting. Domingo needed to run before an airport employee noticed them.

"He dropped his medicine!" The woman with the hat picked up the syringe and handed it to Domingo.

"Just put it on the floor beside him," he instructed her. He didn't want his fingerprints on the syringe. "I'm going to find a doctor or nurse upstairs. I'll be back." He broke into a run. *Adios, Douchebag!*

CHAPTER 28

After the near-miss encounter with Douche Couple, Domingo was finally talking to Tessa outside the airport in a parking lot reserved for Uber and Lyft pickup and drop-off. She hadn't summoned a ride yet. They needed to regroup. This was the safest place for now. They were surrounded by cars and passengers who came and went within minutes. No scoundrel could hide in the constant motion, and certainly not Douche Couple.

"Where do you think those two people went? Do you think they'll come back?" asked Tessa. Her duffel bag on wheels was at her feet, but she gripped the small gift bag with both hands. Her purse was hanging across her chest, messenger style. *Good.* She'd learned her lesson from the mugging attempt in Mexico City.

"They're not coming back," Domingo assured her. "Whoever hired them can't be so stupid as to send them back now that we know what they look like."

After he abandoned a spread-eagled Douchebag, he caught up with Tessa, who had been frantically looking for the sheriff's department's office at the airport. Thanks to the tracking device, he'd found her before she'd reached the bureau. He'd stopped her just in time. He couldn't imagine the complications that could result from reporting the incident to the authorities. He'd convinced her there was nothing to report—Douchebag hadn't actually hurt her. If anything, it was Domingo who'd assaulted the guy.

She'd calmed down after that, and they'd waited a half hour at the Starbucks kiosk before claiming her luggage. Tessa had picked up her bag while Domingo shadowed her from twenty feet away. There had been no sign of Douche Couple, no paramedics, no indication of anything out of the ordinary. It was as though Domingo's epic karate chop on both sides of the bastard's neck hadn't occurred at all. The man must have picked up after himself, syringe and all, and called it a day. He'd failed to accomplish his mission. His sidekick had fled. His first instinct must have been to save his sorry ass and disappear.

"You haven't told me what happened last night. Where's the blueprint?" asked Domingo.

She shook her head. "Julian caught me while I was studying the blueprint. I felt so stupid to be caught in the act! My only consolation is that he didn't see the camera. I asked him outright if it was the blueprint Lou wanted. He said yes, but that it's far from finished. I was so furious that he lied to me. I yelled at him and threw a book at him. I was hysterical by then. He apologized . . . and there was so much drama." She looked away and stared off into space.

"Is that when Julian proposed?"

She turned back to him, those green eyes bulging out. "How did you know?"

"I'm just guessing." He suspected that after their fight, they'd had make-up sex, and then Julian had proposed, but he couldn't voice such thoughts. "So when's the wedding?"

"What?" She blushed, apparently shocked by his prying.

When her face contorted, like someone in pain, Domingo realized his mistake. She wasn't shocked but mortified. "Wait . . . You rejected Julian? You're not marrying him?"

"Of course not."

"No shit."

"I broke up with him."

"But you were holding hands at the airport."

"So what? We broke up, but we're still friends, and we can hold hands."

He scratched his head, embarrassed by his wrong assumption. He should have known that Girl Boss and Lover Boy's relationship defied logic.

"Last night, I asked Julian to give up the blueprint and cut his ties with Tio and the . . . you know . . . his associates. But he refused," she continued. "And so I said we're through." She cast her eyes down at the gift bag; her shoulders dropped.

Tessa and Julian's breakup happened less than twenty-four hours ago, so Tio and the cartel might not have known about this development yet. They'd sent the Douche Couple to hurt Tessa with the ultimate goal of ending her romance with Julian, because they hadn't known the relationship they'd deemed too risky was already over.

So much sadness welled up from Tessa, and so much discomfort nudged at Domingo as he watched her struggle in putting up a neutral facade. He pointed his chin at the gift bag. "Is that a gift from Julian?"

"Yes. He bought this for me before we broke up when we visited the Frida Kahlo Museum." She took out a framed picture and showed him. "It's a reprint of one of Frida's many self-portraits."

He put his duffel bag down and held the picture with both hands. It was a standard frame, about nine inches wide and eleven inches long. Of course he'd heard of Frida Kahlo, or rather he'd heard of Salma Hayek playing Frida in a movie.

His eyes were drawn to the woman in pink at the center of the painting despite the riotous images competing for his attention—the sun, the moon, the American flag, chimney stacks spewing smoke, flowers, and skyscrapers. It was labeled **Frida Kahlo, Self-Portrait Along the Borderline Between Mexico and the United States, 1932.**

Art couldn't have been more remote and incomprehensible than this painting. He was no art connoisseur. "Wow. This is quite . . . something. I don't even know where to look." He handed it back to her.

She replaced the picture in the bag. "Do you think Julian hired those two people to kill me?" Her eyes brimmed with tears.

"I don't think so. Maybe his, uh . . . associates—like you said—hired those two idiots. Maybe they meant to scare you." He modulated his tone with diplomacy and stopped himself from thinking out loud.

If Tessa had remained in Mexico, someone might have simply shot her to death, as the drug cartel was inclined to do in its own turf. Maybe Tio or his bosses were unhappy that their golden boy was dating an American woman who could jeopardize their tunnel. But because Tessa was already crossing back into the States, the cartel might have been forced to adopt a hasty, dumbass murder-by-syringe plan. Perhaps the bad hombres couldn't find better mercenaries than the bumbling Douche Couple on such short notice.

In hindsight, he should have snatched the syringe for testing. He would forever be wondering about its contents. Had it been a fatal mixture of cocaine and fentanyl—two of the cartel's bestselling products? If Douchebag had succeeded in injecting Tessa, she could have looked like a drug abuser shooting up in an airport. A rich white girl like her would have fit the profile of a naive recreational user, fresh from a vacay in Mexico, who had accidentally overdosed.

Jet planes roared in the background. The coming and going of Uber and Lyft cars and traditional yellow cabs surged. It was the peak of the rush hour.

He rocked on his heels. "You did the right thing breaking up with Julian."

She blinked her tears away. "Do you think he loves me?"

The unexpected question, so personal, froze him for a moment. His face grew warm, though he had no reason to feel embarrassed. "Are you asking me if his marriage proposal was sincere? Or if he loves you?"

"Both, I guess."

"I think Julian loves you, but his sudden marriage proposal might have had an ulterior motive."

She gave him a questioning look.

"Okay, so . . . there's something called spousal immunity," he explained. "Under federal rules, prosecutors can't force a wife to testify against her husband. Of course, she may waive that right. But any woman who truly loves her man would never do that. Julian must have felt vulnerable after he'd told you so much. He probably thought that marrying you would guarantee you wouldn't betray him." He exhaled in relief. *There.* Sad but true. It reminded him of a Filipino saying. *Ang taong gipit, sa patalim kumakapit.* A desperate person would cling to a knife. Julian had risked rejection by proposing because he probably felt it was his only option.

Tessa nodded with a wounded expression.

The marriage proposal might have been suspect, but it was true Domingo believed Julian loved Tessa. The man's PDA was such that he all but bowed at her feet. With Julian's good looks, he could have easily found another woman, perhaps someone local, who would condone his cartel ties and whom the cartel would approve of. Tessa simply wasn't cartel-wife material. She was too rich, too smart, too law abiding, and an American citizen to boot. Their long-distance relationship, which had risked angering the cartel, had had an equally long shot of succeeding. At least now they didn't have to face that risk anymore.

"You did the right thing leaving Julian," he repeated. "I'll call Lou and tell him about it. The feds won't bother you again."

Her eyes teared up anew. "Julian kept saying the right technology for the project didn't exist . . . and yet, there it was. I saw it. The blueprint is in Spanish. Why did he draw it if it's impossible to build?"

"Maybe it's for Terra Firma's R&D engineers, like a set of specifications for when they start developing their advanced tunnel boring machine. Maybe the Malverdes will pump enough cash to incentivize Terra Firma to speed up its R&D." He rolled back his shoulders. "I suggest you don't tell anyone about the blueprint. It could be dangerous." The less he knew about the freaking blueprint, the better. He wouldn't have to lie so much to Lou Harold. But no, Girl Boss needed to vent.

"It's a delicate sketch of lines and blocks marked in Spanish. There are several schematic diagrams with lots of numbers. The specs are very fine. They're handwritten. The only thing I understood was *Naco* and *1.60 kilometers*. I've heard of Naco, back when we lived in Arizona."

"It's a town, a port of entry on the Arizona-Sonora border. It's also the name of a town in Sonora."

"The two towns have exactly the same name?" Tessa asked.

"Yeah. Why?"

"On the blueprint, it's actually *Naco*^{2}."

"Naco *squared*? It must refer to the two Nacos." No shit. He really didn't want to hear more about the blueprint. He picked up his duffel bag. "So I take it I'm done snooping on Julian? I could catch the next flight back to New York."

"Can't you stay as my shadow?" Her voice wavered. She wiped the corner of her eyes with her fingers.

Indeed, he couldn't imagine what would have happened if he hadn't traveled with her to Mexico. In his job, luck was a skill, but even his skills might not be enough in the long run in the face of a vicious drug cartel.

Although Domingo never liked Julian—the guy had wrapped Tessa around his little finger—he didn't doubt Lover Boy's feelings for Girl Boss. Julian wouldn't physically harm Tessa, but Tio and the cartel were another matter.

"You need a security specialist as your bodyguard, someone who's local," he advised. "Cheryl's ex-husband, Dan, owns a security firm that protects rock stars and politicians. Dan can help you. I'll call Cheryl or Dan directly if you like."

"It's okay. I'll call Cheryl when I get home." She bit her lower lip.

Her vulnerability couldn't have been more transparent. And what about Alice and Grammy? Jesus, if something bad happened to these women, he wouldn't be able to live with himself. "How about I stay in town until Dan's guy arrives?"

"Will you? Please."

"Sure, no problem. Dan provides VIP security in Silicon Valley. I'm sure he can send someone from the Bay Area within twenty-four hours."

"Thank you." She rubbed the pearl pendant hanging from her necklace. "I really would like to see Grammy and Alice now."

"I'll ride with you to your grandma's house to make sure everything's fine. Then I'll rent a car and stay at the closest motel."

"Can I keep the tracking device?"

"Yep." He smiled. "I'm just one pressed button away, I promise."

She pulled her phone from her purse and started tapping on icons. An Uber Black ought to arrive within a few minutes. He got busy planning his next moves.

Number one: Ask Lou Harold to dig up the identity of Douchebaguette. She had to be on the airplane manifest. No such luck with her partner in crime, though.

Number two: Ask Lou to leave Tessa and the Woodridge family alone. Enough with his "propositions." Mental note: Don't mention the blueprint, or the feds would continue to hound Tessa, the only person on this side of the border who'd eyeballed the document.

Number three: Relay all critical information and notes to Dan and the bodyguard he would deploy to Sacramento.

Girl Boss was on the phone talking to Grammy when their ride glided in, a shiny black Escalade. He carried his own bag with one hand and picked up her luggage with his other. He was eager to wrap things up. The crisis was over. The heiress was safe. The impostor was out of her life.

But somehow, the aftermath felt eerie. What was he missing? The quiet he sensed was reminiscent of when small birds suddenly flee a tree because they know a hawk is about to swoop down and snatch one of them.

CHAPTER 29

One Month Later

What's Love Got to Do with US Citizenship?

Are we, Americans, the hottest, most irresistible lovers in the world? Or are we considered a good catch because marrying us is the shortest path to gaining US citizenship? I'm a naturalized US citizen and a magnet for green-card-seeking women, if I may say so. They don't even care that I'm a bail enforcement agent who catches criminal undocumented immigrants for a living, which means there's no way in hell they're gonna be able to con me. But still, a few have tried before.

Sham marriage used to be the go-to immigration strategy for desperate hopefuls who could spare upward of fifty grand to pay for a professional husband or wife. I once caught an undocumented woman who married an enterprising polygamist who'd been married eight times. The man hadn't even bothered to divorce some of his ex-wives. In another case, an undocumented male immigrant I escorted to court claimed to be happily married to a green card holder, but he couldn't even talk to his alleged wife! The guy, a native of the Ivory Coast, spoke only French, while the woman, a refugee from Laos, spoke Hmong. In broken English, the couple claimed to be married in front of an immigration judge, who promptly issued a deportation order for the lying groom. I told the guy that he and his partner in crime were les imbéciles.

ICE has gotten wiser and tougher ever since a study showed that up to 30 percent of marriages between Americans and foreigners might be fake. Here are the ways fraudsters circumvent the law to marry a US citizen for the sole purpose of obtaining citizenship. You can bet love's got nothing to do with it.

- *A foreigner whose culture allows arranged marriage uses it as a ruse to pay for a sham marriage with a US citizen.*
- *A foreigner marries a for-hire partner who's a US citizen just long enough to get citizenship. These professional spouses marry and divorce for a living.*
- *Women from around the world willingly become mail-order brides of US citizens. They may or may not stay married after they become citizens.*
- *In a divorce-marry-remarry scheme, a foreigner divorces a spouse to marry an American citizen. Upon obtaining citizenship, the foreigner divorces the American to remarry the original (foreigner) spouse.*
- *Criminal US citizens marry vulnerable foreigners for sex trafficking or other exploitative purpose.*
- *Foreign heartbreakers go through the motion of courtship and marriage and dupe lovestruck US citizens only to dump them as soon as they get citizenship.*

◆ ◆ ◆

Lulu, a Filipino nursing assistant, entered the party room, bearing Mamang's cake. Everyone burst into an exuberant rendition of "Happy Birthday." Domingo stopped writing and stuck his little notepad and pen in the side pocket of his cargo pants.

Lulu set the cake on a rectangular table brimming with food. **HAPPY BIRTHDAY MAMANG!** The words were written in white icing on top of the purple sheet cake. The cake was made of *ube*, purple yam from the Philippines or Hawaii, which Mamang had ordered from a Filipino bakery.

A rich aroma rose from a platter of rice noodles called *pancit bihon*, meant to bring good luck and good health to the birthday celebrant. The long noodle strands symbolized a long, healthy life. There were also platters of roast pork, spring rolls, and paella. It was Saturday, two o'clock in the afternoon. This was neither a lunch nor dinner party. Was there such a thing as *linner* or *dunch*?

After the singing, Domingo's mother blew out the numeral candles revealing her age: seventy-two. He could tell she'd prepared for this special day. Her gray hair had been trimmed into a bob; plus, she'd worn makeup. Even her pink outfit, a matching set of slacks and blouse, was new.

Moving Mamang to Vista Nursing and Rehabilitation Center was one of the best decisions he'd ever made, though his guilt crept up on him time and again. Filipinos took care of their elders, but he and his mother lived in America without the benefit of a network of extended relatives. Mamang, however, attributed his inability to care for her to his failure to find a loving wife with whom he could raise a happy brood. She deemed a contented family life that brimmed with caregiver relatives the ultimate measuring stick for a man's success.

Domingo braced himself for another motherly reminder of his failure to marry, especially because there were two women in the room whom Mamang considered ideal wife material.

"Did you make a wish?" Lulu asked Mamang. "Tell us your wish."

Domingo counted twenty-two people surrounding his mother at the table, including a dozen Filipinos.

"I have only one wish," replied Mamang.

He knew what would come next. He stepped back from the crowd so he could take pictures with his smartphone.

"I have the same wish every year." Mamang trained her dark eyes on him—her voodoo eyes trying to cast a spell on him. "My only wish is to see my son settle down with a nice Filipina and give me a couple of healthy grandchildren before I die."

Yep, whatever. He took one picture and another, aware that the attention was on him. Thank goodness for an old lady who chirped, "May your wish come true!" It shifted the focus back to Mamang as everyone swarmed her with hugs, kisses, and presents.

From the moment his mother moved to Vista's rehabilitation center, she'd attracted friends and well-wishers. Her social life at the center almost made up for the hip-replacement surgery that had brought her here to begin with. At least she'd moved out of the rehab wing and into this building for more independent residents who needed only minimal care. She'd ditched the wheelchair and walked on her own now, although sometimes she still needed a walker.

Lulu sashayed to Domingo's side. "Your mother's happiness is in the palm of your hands. All you have to do is make a move," she whispered with a coquettish smile.

Mamang rooted for Lulu, her favorite caregiver, as the top contender for the empty spot in Domingo's life. The fortysomething divorcée was a green card holder, so she wasn't interested in his US citizenship, which made her more dangerous. She wanted a new husband for real, forever. She was Public Enemy Number One as far as his bachelorhood and freedom were concerned.

He managed a papery smile. "Thanks for organizing this party. I owe you a big one." *Damn it.* He shouldn't have said that.

"When?" She batted her fake eyelashes.

"When is what?"

Her eyelashes always reminded him of rubber spiders and Halloween. Even her scrubs, with their dizzying pattern of teddy bears, flowers, and hearts, looked like a bad costume.

She shifted her weight to her right hip. "When are you taking me out to dinner?"

"When did I say that?"

"Two seconds ago." She pouted. "You owe me a big one, remember?"

"I was thinking more of a restaurant gift card. I'm just too busy to go out. You like Olive Garden or Chili's? Your choice."

"*Mahirap gisingin ang nagtutulog-tulogan*," she harrumphed. It's hard to wake up someone who pretends to be asleep. It was an old Filipino saying.

On the contrary, he was wide awake and aware of what she was trying to do. He bit his tongue.

"Hi, Domingo," Elena cut in. "Can I ask you something?"

Lulu glared at the woman before stomping away.

One gone, one more to go. "What's on your mind?" he asked.

At least Elena wore no artificial eyelashes, no crazy-ass-patterned outfit. She was dressed in a sensible knee-length denim skirt, plain blouse, and flat sandals. It was autumn now, but unseasonably warm.

"I'm wondering if you'd speak to my students about your work as a bail enforcement agent. We have a career day later this year."

"Me? I'm a terrible speaker." He stuck his phone in his pocket.

Elena, a thirtysomething Filipina, was more subtle than Lulu. She knew how to stroke his ego with a speaking invitation. She even knew to use the term *bail enforcement agent*, which he preferred over *bounty hunter*.

"You'll speak for just fifteen minutes," Elena continued. "After that, you'll be answering questions from the kids. It's just a conversation with them. I'm sure you'll do great."

"Let's get something to drink while we chat." Domingo pointed at the coolers in the corner. They walked a few feet, and he picked up a Diet Coke while she grabbed bottled water.

Elena was among those highly educated professionals recruited from overseas by public schools suffering from an acute shortage of math and science teachers. From Alaska to West Virginia, there were school districts desperate for specialty teachers willing to work long hours for next to nothing. Lucky for one high school in the Bronx, Elena had said yes. Her J-1 visa would expire next year. He suspected she'd rather find an American husband to obtain citizenship and increase her career options instead of returning to Manila without a job or renewing her contract to continue working for peanuts. Either that or he somehow had managed to charm her for real without trying. His cheeks turned warm.

They stood behind the coolers. He opened the Coke can and slurped the hissing soda. "I'm sure you can find a better speaker with a better job."

"You have the most interesting and unusual career," she persisted. "Will you at least think about it? Don't say no yet. I don't need your answer today."

It sure sounded like he'd been propositioned, but he couldn't deny her effective negotiation skills. "Okay. I'll get back to you on that."

"Great! I'll stop bugging you now." She made a phone-like gesture, the thumb pointing to her ear and the little finger to her mouth. "Call me."

"I don't have your—" He stopped, realizing he was about to ask for her phone number, which wasn't his intention.

She flashed an amused smile. "Your mom has my number. Just ask her." She turned away for good measure, playing it cool.

Mamang waved him over. Of course she'd been watching the scene, first with Lulu and then Elena. He shuffled to her side.

"Slice the cake into squares like this, *hijo*. Then put each slice on a paper plate." She put a slice on the first plate on the table and handed him the knife.

"I got this. Why don't you mingle with your friends?" He put his soda can aside and sliced the cake into small blocks.

She scooted closer and whispered, "Do you like Elena better than Lulu? Of course, she's younger. Did you ask her on a date?"

Good Lord. "Mamang, let's not talk about this. It's your birthday, and you should enjoy your party."

"It's my birthday, and I'm asking you for my present."

He tossed her a sideways glance. "You're wearing the watch I gave you. That's your birthday present."

"What I really want is for you to go on a date. Go ahead, ask Elena or Lulu."

He gazed upward.

"Don't roll your eyes."

"I'm not rolling my eyes."

"You were about to! And you're holding that knife like a murderer."

"Have you actually seen a murderer wield a knife?"

"Don't change the subject."

Jesus. He resumed slicing the cake.

"When are you going to get married? You better find someone now or you'll be alone when I die. What if I drop dead tomorrow? I couldn't have guessed in a million years your father and brother would die young."

Here we go again. The story of his life. His father had died of tuberculosis when Domingo was ten. You'd think one tragedy was enough, but no, his twelve-year-old brother had caught the disease and had died soon thereafter.

He transferred the slices of cake to paper plates.

"Your stepfather left the house in your name, so you'll have something to show for when you get married. Well, how long is that house going to remain empty?"

"It's not empty. I live there."

"Don't be a smart-ass. Consider yourself very lucky. You're a US citizen with a house, a car, a job, and two ladies just waiting for you to notice them."

A couple of nursing aides wanted cake and interrupted his mother.

It was true. He was fortunate that Mamang had married Roger Ronan, who had given them their American citizenship. She'd met him through an agency that matched lonely Americans with Filipino women. While most American men picked young wives, Roger had chosen a mature, trustworthy woman. He'd been a Sears repairman who'd remained single until the ripe age of seventy-two when he married Mamang. She'd become Mrs. Aurora Ronan when she was forty-seven.

After the nursing aides left with their plates of cake, she resumed her lecture about his love life.

Domingo's phone rang, but he ignored it. "Mamang, here's the deal. I would love to get married soon, but first, I have to find the right woman. Just give me a little more time." How could he explain that he simply hadn't found someone yet who would replace Monica Reed in the tender spot at the bottom of his heart?

She clucked her tongue. "At the rate you're going, I'll be dead before you get to it."

His phone rang nonstop. He raised both hands in a gesture of surrender. "Okay, you're right. I'm a hopeless loser, so sue me." He pulled his phone from his pocket and headed for the door. He needed some privacy. "Hello?"

Static emitted from the other end of the line.

"Hello? Who's this?" He'd stopped just outside the doorway.

"Blue . . . blue . . . bird."

Definitely a woman's voice.

"What? Who's this?" He glanced at the phone. *Incoming call. Unknown.*

The phone went dead.

A memory, bright as a flare, came back to him. He'd promised Alice that if she ever felt threatened by Julian, he would come if she called him and uttered their code: *blue bird.* The thought hitched his breath. His arms prickled.

He whirled around and faced the room. Someone had mentioned his name. It was his mother, regaling her friends with something funny, their laughter reverberating. All at once, they turned to him.

"Hey, everybody," he yelled. "Something came up, so I have to run. Also, please continue talking about me because the only thing worse than being talked about is *not* being talked about."

His mother frowned, but her friends chuckled.

He fled the room and called Tessa. No answer. He scurried toward the elevators. Every passing second seemed like a gaping hole threatening to suck him in. The mysterious caller hadn't blocked the caller ID feature, otherwise he would have seen *No Caller ID* or *Private* on his phone screen. Even a burner phone would display a number, except it would trace back only to the phone provider, not the user.

He reached the elevator bank. He hung up and pressed the elevator's down button.

His phone rang. He picked it up, expecting Tessa. "Hello?"

A man on the other end of the line said, "Who's this?"

"You called me—who are you?"

"Is this Sunday?"

Domingo glanced at his phone screen. It displayed *Private Number*, but he recognized the voice. "Yes. Julian, where's Alice?" His chest banged.

"She's right here. I saw her making a call, but she already hung up before I could speak with whomever she was talking to," said Julian in a low, calm voice. "I asked her if she dialed 911. She said no. To prove that she was telling the truth, I asked her to call the same person using my phone this time, so I could confirm it. And here we are. So it was you."

Domingo could hear cars passing by in the background and people talking. Julian and Alice were in a public place. So Julian wasn't even hiding Alice. He was obviously not a professional kidnapper. Or at least he was unlikely to hurt Alice in front of other people. So why had he taken Alice an entire month after his breakup with Tessa? His action seemed too extreme even for a guy who was heartbroken. Could the cartel be behind this? But why? What could the cartel want from Tessa after she'd already left their golden boy?

"Let me talk to Alice, please. Let me hear her voice," pleaded Domingo.

"No. I'm the one talking right now." Julian's voice had grown peevish. "I've always suspected that you're not a meat supplier. Who are you, really? *What* are you?"

"I'm a bail enforcement agent. I catch fugitive undocumented immigrants. Now, can I please talk to Alice? I just want to make sure she's okay."

"Take my word for it, she's okay." A pause, as though he was trying to collect his thoughts. "Fine. Alice, say hello to Sunday."

The elevator door opened with a ding, but Domingo was waiting for Alice to speak. He didn't get in the elevator.

"Hi . . . Sun . . . day."

"Thank you, Alice. Sunday, here's what I want you to do," continued Julian. "Call Tessa and ask her to call me this instant. I'm tired of begging her to see me or to answer my texts and calls. She hired a fucking bodyguard to keep me away, like I'm some kind of a pervert. It hurts, the way she's treating me. So I took her sister and left a note saying I just want to talk, and she still won't pick up the fucking phone." Julian snorted. "What's a guy got to do, huh? Tell Tessa, if she wants to see her sister again, she must do two things. First, don't call the cops. Second, call me right now." The line went dead.

Domingo ran to the stairs and made his way down as he speed-dialed Tessa. At last, she picked up the phone. "This is Sunday. You have to call Julian."

"What? No! I just called the police. He kidnapped my sister. One moment she was in the hammock; the next moment she was gone. How did you know . . . ?"

The hammock he'd installed—damn it. "Alice called me and then Julian called me."

"Why would they call you?"

Should he mention the saga behind the *blue bird* code, or would that complicate things? He glanced at his watch—3:02 in the afternoon in New York, and barely noon in California. He'd reached the lobby of the nursing home. He paused to catch his breath. No time to waste. "Tessa, here's what Julian said: If you want to see Alice again, don't call the cops, and call him right now."

"But I already called the police."

"He has Alice—you have to follow his instructions. Call the cops again and tell them that Alice is fine. She's with a friend, and it was a miscommunication."

Silence, followed by a hiccuping noise.

"Hello? Tessa?"

She was sobbing. "Julian came to my house last week, but I refused to see him. My therapist says I have to cut and cut cleanly. I shouldn't see Julian again. Not even answer his texts or calls. He's my addiction and enabler both. I'm going cold turkey."

"Believe me, I understand," he assured her. "This is the last time you'll have to deal with him. I'll do everything in my power, I promise. But right now, we can't afford to piss him off. You gotta do what he says."

She was sniffling. "Okay. I'll call off the police. Will you come here and help us?"

"Yes, I'm on my way there."

"Please hurry. Charter a private plane. You're going to need more than just your credit card to rent one. I'll text you an account number."

"Copy that. I'll be there soon. And you know what? I'll call Lou Harold. He has people in Sacramento. We don't need the cops to spook Julian, but we'll make sure the DEA has our backs."

CHAPTER 30

Two hours after Domingo spoke to Tessa, he was aboard a Cessna Citation midsize jet at Teterboro Airport in New Jersey, waiting for takeoff. Who knew that a bail enforcer like him would fly like a rock star one day? He had an entire plane that could seat eight passengers to himself, with two pilots at his beck and call.

Inday chartered this one-way flight to Sacramento for a cool thirty grand, courtesy of Girl Boss. In Teterboro, there were thirty private jets of all types to choose from. No long lines of grouchy people, no security screening hassle, no shedding of shoes and belt. The aircraft company allowed him to pack heat, although his New York permit to carry a weapon wouldn't be recognized in California. But he'd brought it for insurance.

He reclined his seat and spread his legs wide apart—yep, manspreading. He'd just finished a call with his phone-tracing service. He wanted Alice's and Julian's calls traced to locate them, but no luck. The phone used by Alice was simply unknown, while Julian's phone had blocked his number. Both were dead ends.

Next, he called Lou Harold. His duffel bag sat beside him. A cold bottle of Perrier on his tray table remained unopened. Later, he would chow down on catered food. He'd ordered grilled chicken and pasta. This must be heaven, but the thought of Alice kidnapped punctured the pleasure.

At last, Lou answered. He gave the DEA agent the lowdown on Alice's kidnapping. "Tessa's sister called me from a phone with an unknown number. I subscribe to a phone-tracing service, but even those guys couldn't unmask the number. Julian blocked his number. Nothing they can do about it. Alice's call wasn't blocked. It simply wasn't showing. Can you trace it for me?"

"Maybe," replied Lou.

The agent sounded lukewarm, so Domingo grabbed him by his Achilles' heel. "Did you manage to get the blueprint?"

"We tried."

Domingo suspected as much.

Lou made a smacking noise. Perhaps he was chewing mints. "It's not in Julian's laptop or desktop computer and not in Tio's house or office."

Nope, it was in a drawer somewhere in Julian's house. But because Lover Boy was a millennial, the feds assumed he would be working on a digital blueprint. Tio was old, so they thought he would keep a paper copy. Wrong on both counts.

"Lou, I need to locate Alice without spooking Julian. That means we can't involve the cops," he continued. "Meanwhile, Tessa is going to call Julian. That should buy us time. Best-case scenario is that Tessa sees Julian and they sort things out amicably, and Alice goes home with Tessa. Worst-case scenario . . . Who knows what Julian's capable of doing?"

Domingo never trusted Julian, with his too-white skin and no-accent English, from the day he first saw him in Las Vegas. He knew the guy was too good to be true, and yet even he was fooled into believing that Julian was Mexican. Julian's life was based on a false racial identity, and his successful career depended on a deceptive veneer of respectability, both of which were tied to Tio and the cartel. Without his Mexican benefactors, Julian was nothing. In Domingo's mind, that made Julian dangerous, despite his love for Tessa and his fondness for Alice.

A loud sputtering noise filled the air. Domingo looked through the glass window. A helicopter was landing, the sound and sight of its whirling rotors pressuring him to chop-chop already. "Can you trace Alice's phone call and ask someone in your Sacramento office to be on standby in case I need help? Will you lend me a hand, please?"

"Two hands, plus both of my feet—if you can get me the blueprint."

One of the pilots popped in and mouthed, "Wheels up."

Domingo gave the man a thumbs-up and snapped his seat belt on.

"I'll make sure a local DEA agent will contact you for backup," said Lou. "About Alice's phone call . . . we're not NSA, and we don't snoop illegally. Inform your phone-service provider that you've given the DEA permission to trace your calls."

"Will do."

"Excellent. We're in business."

They hung up. The jet taxied out to the runway.

It seemed like Domingo had been working for Girl Boss for months, though in reality, he first met her over a month ago on a sizzling summer evening. Now it was the beginning of autumn, and still no end in sight for this saga. What was supposed to be an easy gig looking for the Beltrans had turned out to be a prolonged journey without a clear destination. If his life were a movie, it would be called *Planes, More Planes, and Automobiles*, and it wouldn't be nearly as funny as the Steve Martin and John Candy flick.

The Cessna accelerated before lifting off the ground. Even with a private plane, Sacramento remained far, twenty-eight hundred miles away. Six hours of flying time stretched ahead of him.

He went over the facts in his head, the timeline, the places where Julian could have taken Alice. First, Alice required some help. Unless Julian brought a caregiver with him, he wouldn't take her very far. Second, Julian and Alice were in a public place where Alice had made a phone call. Julian had sounded like any desperate boyfriend who'd been dumped, except most men wouldn't go as far as to kidnap anyone. What exactly did he want from Tessa that was so urgent he'd risk getting arrested for kidnapping? The more Domingo thought of it, the more convinced he was that Julian's action was either influenced or dictated by the cartel. But what did the cartel want from Tessa?

Focus, he told himself. He didn't need to know what Julian wanted because it would soon be revealed once Tessa talked to him. His job was to find Alice if Julian continued to keep her hostage.

Maybe Tessa was already talking to Julian right now. If Domingo got lucky, maybe Alice and Tessa would be home by the time he landed. He might just dismantle the damn hammock while he was there.

He uncapped the Perrier and sipped the sparkling water. Did Julian enjoy hiding? If not, then he'd already lost this game, because Domingo thoroughly loved his job.

Blue bird. Domingo wasn't religious, but at the moment, he thanked God for the foresight. Chasing and catching someone, whether legal or undocumented, called for the same set of skills. In Shakespeare's words, hunting by any name would smell as sweet as a rose for the right hunter. Or something like that. Whatever. *Bring it on, Lover Boy.*

◆ ◆ ◆

When he arrived at Sacramento Executive Airport, a soft dusk was just descending. He'd gained three hours and avoided the circus at the regular airport. He rented a car and drove straight to ground zero: Grammy's house in Folsom. While driving, he called his phone-service provider to authorize the DEA to trace his calls. Then he contacted Dan Mott, Cheryl's ex-husband, who had provided a bodyguard for Tessa.

Dan briefed Domingo. In the month since Domingo and Tessa returned from Mexico, a security specialist named Scott Redwood, or Red for short, had been working as her bodyguard as suggested by Domingo. Another guy alternated with Red on his days off.

All the security measures focused on Girl Boss, and rightly so. She led a multimillion-dollar business, and she'd been privy to Julian and Tio's tunnel project. Nobody thought of guarding Alice or

Grammy around the clock, though their home security system had been upgraded. And yet, none of the outdoor cameras captured the hammock. A camera monitored the driveway and the front door, while another camera covered the backyard.

Tessa and Julian's breakup should have been the end of their misbegotten love story. Alice's kidnapping was as unexpected as the Douche Couple's attempt to hurt Girl Boss. And Domingo didn't even know if the kidnapping was Julian's or the cartel's idea. What could the cartel possibly want from Tessa? So it had to be Julian.

Domingo had asked Lou to check the identity of Douchebaguette on the airplane's passenger manifest, but he'd forgotten to follow up on it. He made a mental note to ask the agent. He also needed to arrange for another bail enforcer to babysit the undocumented Pakistani facing an immigration judge on Monday if his search for Alice lasted longer than the weekend. So much work to do, so little time.

A call from DEA Special Agent Jim Havant came in while Domingo pulled over at Grammy's house. Lou Harold's guy rattled off his bona fides. He lived in the suburb of Elk Grove, twenty-six miles away from where Domingo was. He apprised Havant of the situation and asked him to be on standby. Domingo would text him Julian and Alice's location as soon as he found it out.

When Domingo entered Grammy's house, all the women gave him a bear hug—Tessa, her grandmother, and Susie. It was Saturday, and everyone wore lounge clothes. Sweatpants and T-shirts for Grammy and Susie, and sweater and leggings for Tessa. The only other guy present, Red, a towering millennial, was wearing a tracksuit. He greeted Domingo with a flick of a hand.

Domingo had arrived just as the group was about to eat in the dining room, where a spread of Chinese takeout was still untouched.

"You guys go ahead and eat. I already ate on the plane, so I'm good," said Domingo.

"We haven't had lunch, and we're all starving," said Grammy.

Everyone moved quietly, passing paper plates and plastic forks. A greasy smell escaped from the take-out cartons containing orange chicken, beef broccoli, egg rolls, and fried rice.

Tessa sat down at the head of the dining table. "I called Julian. He wants to see me tonight."

"When? Where?" Domingo sat at the other end of the table.

"I don't know yet." Tessa spooned chicken and broccoli onto her plate. "Julian's going to call me again right before we're supposed to meet. I think he wants to be sure there won't be any cops waiting for him wherever we're going to meet. He let me say hello to Alice. I was grateful for that."

"Sunday, is it true Alice called you?" asked Grammy in between bites of chicken. "Why did she call you instead of us? I was so worried!"

Domingo pulled his phone from his jeans pocket and set it to vibrate. "Let me start by saying that I'm not a meat supplier. I'm a bail enforcement agent."

Grammy and Susie glanced at each other. "A what?" said the old lady.

"Sunday is a bounty hunter," explained Tessa. "I hired him to look for Julian's adoptive parents. I didn't want Julian or anyone else to know, so I asked Sunday to pretend to be a meat supplier."

Grammy raised her eyebrow. "Julian's adopted?"

Domingo nodded. *And that is the least of Julian's problems,* he wanted to add. He redirected the conversation, mindful that he ought to be looking for Alice. "Let's talk about Alice—she called me today instead of you because she and I agreed about it in advance," he continued.

He recalled the day he'd installed the hammock, how he'd discovered that Julian had lied about Alice's Barbie watch, and how Domingo had come up with the code words, *blue bird*, in honor of the scrub jay he'd saved on the roof.

"I asked Alice to promise me that if Julian ever made her feel"—he paused, searching for a word less scary than *threatened*—"uncomfortable . . . you know, if she didn't feel like being around Julian, then she should call me and say *blue bird.* This morning, that's exactly what she did."

Everyone mulled this over. A tense silence hung in the air.

"So Julian lied about the watch?" Grammy glanced at Tessa. "Is that why you broke up with him?"

"No, there are other things." Tessa's voice wobbled. She shot Domingo a worried glance.

Yeah, if only they knew about the freaking drug cartel and the goddamned secret tunnel and the DEA wanting to bust Julian and all the shit he and Tessa were trying to keep under wraps. If only he could tell them they were deep inside Crazy Town without causing a panic.

"What *other* things?" Grammy picked at the broccoli on her plate.

Tessa propped her elbow on the table and pressed her hand on her forehead. "I can't talk about this."

The old lady exhaled sharply. "Whatever it is, you and Julian have to deal with your own problems. Why would he involve Alice?"

"He's mad at me, Grammy. Because I refused to see him last week and didn't answer his calls and texts." Tessa looked up from her half-eaten dinner. "This is all my fault. I'm sorry."

Domingo's phone vibrated.

"Actually, I feel like it's my fault," Susie interrupted. "I'm sorry I left Alice in the hammock. I should have insisted on getting her back inside when she asked for lunch, knowing it would take me a while to make a sandwich and soup."

Domingo pulled out his phone. A text from Lou Harold. Alice called from Folsom. Old landline without caller ID. Look for antique but functioning phone.

He raised his gaze, his heart bouncing with hope. Alice was close. He texted Lou back. Tnx. U have ID of female perp from Aeromexico?

Grammy reached out to Tessa with her left hand and Susie with her right hand. "It's nobody's fault, okay?" She turned to Tessa. "Ask Julian to come over, and the two of you can talk. Leave Alice out of this."

"I already called him," protested Tessa. "I'm waiting for him to call me again with the time and place for us to meet."

"Call him again," insisted Grammy. "He wanted you to call off the cops—well, you did that already. Tell him to drop off Alice now, and the two of you can talk here. What's he waiting for?"

And *that* was the big question. There was something else going on with Julian. He seemed to be waiting for something, perhaps instructions from Tio or the cartel. What could it possibly be? A ransom demand for Alice?

"Listen up, everybody," said Domingo. "I need you guys to help me with something." They all turned to him with expectant expressions. "I'm looking for old landline phones in Folsom."

"Why?" asked Susie.

"Because I was able to trace Alice's call to an old telephone right here in Folsom. I need to know where that phone is, and maybe I can go and get her now instead of waiting for Julian to call Tessa."

"Does anybody still use a landline?" Red was snarfing down an egg roll.

Tessa sipped her water. "Businesses use landline phones and older people prefer them."

Domingo glanced at Lou's text again. "Not just any landline, but an old one."

Susie held her fork, a piece of beef dangling, halfway to her mouth. "How old exactly?" She resumed eating.

Domingo shrugged. "Old . . . like antique, maybe, but still working." He wondered if there were dozens of those still around, but surely, not all would be in active use. "When I was talking to Julian and Alice, I could hear cars and people in the background. They were in a public place. Now we know that they were here in Folsom."

"Wait a minute." Grammy's face brightened.

All eyes turned to the old lady.

She bolted to her feet, raising her forefinger. "I know where to find the phone!"

CHAPTER 31

The pub and shopping crawls brought the crowds to Historic Folsom. At half past seven in the evening, laughter and music from the bars charged the autumn air with excitement. Beverly's Antique Nook and all the shops and restaurants were open late.

The sight of the black rotary phone greeted Domingo as soon as he entered the antique store. It was there for the taking—or a free phone call—right by the entrance. It sat atop a side table with a vase of fresh flowers, a bowl of candy, and a stack of business cards. It was an elegant curiosity, about six inches high.

An immaculately coiffed old lady broke from a couple of customers browsing the quilt rack and said hello to him. Grammy had called Mrs. Beverly Palmer, the store owner, in advance to say that Sunday, a family friend, wanted to visit.

Domingo introduced himself and shook her hand. When he asked after Alice, Beverly said she had seen Alice this afternoon with Tessa's boyfriend. She'd met Julian before. He, Tessa, and Alice once visited the shop. Another time, Julian had stopped by with Tessa and her grandmother.

"Does this phone work?" He played dumb. He'd instructed Grammy to withhold the information about Alice's phone call. No need to involve other people in Julian and Alice's "outing."

"Yes, it works just fine. Isn't it a beauty?" She lifted it up to show the logo at the bottom. "See that? It's made in Germany in 1960. Many people want to buy it, but I'm not quite ready to give it up."

Beverly might be the same age as Tessa's grandmother and in the same tax bracket. Her glittering earrings reminded him that diamonds were a woman's best friend. Botox might be another bestie, judging by Beverly's unnaturally taut cheeks.

"So Julian and Alice stopped by to browse?" he asked.

"Yes. I believe they were in the deli, or at least, that's where I thought Alice came from. She was browsing. I was presiding over the events committee meeting right here in the shop when I caught a glimpse of her. And then Julian also came. Such a fine young man."

Just as Domingo had suspected, Julian hadn't even tried hiding Alice. He'd taken the poor woman out for a forced excursion, a leisurely abduction, to pressure Tessa into returning his call.

Beverly picked a business card from the table and gave it to Domingo. Her name was on the card, and it also noted she was Historic Folsom Council president and proprietor of the store.

"Is everything okay with Alice?" she asked.

"Oh, yeah. She and Julian are watching a play at the Sutter Street Theatre. I'm here to pick her up in a little while because Julian needs to wine and dine a prospective client. Alice just wants to go home after the show. Julian's an engineer and a consultant, you know."

"Is that right? A fine young man," she repeated.

"Thanks for showing me the phone. It's as beautiful as Mrs. Woodridge described it."

He said goodbye and left.

Beverly's store was sandwiched between the yogurt shop on the left and a deli on the right. Perhaps Julian and Alice had eaten lunch at the deli, like Beverly had thought.

He walked along Sutter Street and saw the theater. Could Julian and Alice really be watching a play? He checked the showtimes. The play would end in an hour. He wondered if he could get in to check inside, though the play had already started. He would think about that.

Domingo's worries whirled inside him. Alice had been fine earlier, as Beverly had attested, but Alice might be scared by now. She'd been away from home for more than eight hours. Had she ever spent this much time away from Grammy or Susie?

He covered the entire length of the street, checking stores and restaurants. He stopped at the corner of Sutter and Riley Streets, surveying the flow of people streaming in and out of a pizzeria and a Mexican restaurant. A group of young guys trooped inside a pub.

Where could Julian have taken Alice?

The tracking app beeped. He whipped out his phone and saw that Tessa had pushed the panic button on the tracking device he'd given her. His heartbeat sped up.

He tapped the app on his phone. A map appeared with the green button showing Tessa's location. He swiped the screen with his thumb and forefinger to enlarge the view. *Fair Oaks Bluff.* A park near a river.

His phone rang, forcing him to switch modes. It was Red the bodyguard. "Hello?"

"Julian called Tessa, and she just drove off. She didn't want me to go with her."

"Slow down." He exhaled. He didn't want to absorb Red's nervous energy.

"Should I tail Tessa? I can track her through her phone's GPS."

"Nope. She was right—you just stay put. The last thing we want is for some asshole to kidnap Grammy and Susie."

"You mean the idiot couple from the airport?"

"Or someone new. There's no shortage of assholes for hire."

"I'll scout the perimeter as soon as we hang up."

"Good." Yeah, Red needed to expend his surplus of energy. "I'll follow Tessa."

They ended the call.

Domingo entered the park's name on the GPS app on his phone, and the fastest route materialized. Light traffic. Estimated driving time: twelve minutes. Tessa was only 5.6 miles away. *Gotta love technology.*

He sidestepped a group of women trying to cross the street and ran to the parking garage. He started the car and roared out of the building.

◆ ◆ ◆

He slowed down as he entered a sleepy section of Fair Oaks. He passed by two-story houses, real estate and chiropractic offices, and restaurants.

He parked a few feet from the sign that declared, **Road Ends 500 ft**. His car's headlights illuminated an old footbridge up ahead.

He checked the tracking app again. Tessa was definitely here. He switched his phone setting from ring to vibrate so no phone noise could give him away.

His phone immediately vibrated. A text message from Lou Harold. ID'd female perp. She's nonverbal.

Douchebaguette had been identified. He texted back. Meaning?

Lou's response: She's mute. Not pursuing.

I'll be damned. His mind leaped back to the incident at the Aeroméxico flight and Sacramento airport. He couldn't remember Douchebaguette arguing out loud with the flight attendants. She'd squeaked, not screamed, when Domingo had assaulted her partner in crime. Her job was to eyeball Girl Boss. Nobody needed her voice. The drug cartel knew how to choose pawns. Who the hell would suspect a nonspeaking young woman? Or insist on interrogating her? Even Lou couldn't be bothered. Douche Couple no longer posed a threat. To the drug cartel, they were as handy as paper napkins and not meant to be reused.

He texted Lou. Tessa meeting Julian & Alice. I'm on scene. Summoning Jim Havant.

From Lou: Get blueprint ASAP.

Lou Harold had a one-track mind. Next, Domingo texted the location to Lou's colleague.

He tucked his phone in his pocket and scanned his surroundings. The houses and buildings on Bridge Street glowed, but there were no lights in the park.

Since he'd flown on a private plane, he'd been able to bring the tools of his trade: a Glock, a flashlight, and zip ties for restraining assholes. He tucked the gun in his waistband, at the back under his shirt, and stuffed the other items in the pockets of his cargo pants. He climbed out of the car.

The evening breeze from the river kicked up and prickled his skin. The trill of crickets filled the night. He turned on the flashlight. His long-sleeved polo shirt would have to do—his jacket was in his duffel bag.

Numerous thoughts floated in his mind as he walked toward the bluff. What if the cartel wanted to harm Alice but Julian had actually saved her? What if the cartel wanted to harm *both* Julian and Alice? Was that the reason Julian had waited hours before seeing Tessa? Someone could have been pointing a gun at his head when he'd called Tessa. There were so many possible scenarios.

There it was—the sign he needed. He pointed the light at it. **American River Parkway, Fair Oaks Bluff.** He didn't have to cross the bridge. The plaque warned against drinking alcohol and bringing glass bottles into the park. Dogs must always be on a leash.

He squatted on the ground, set the flashlight down, and pulled out his phone. Its screen glowed. He checked the GPS map and gazed up ahead. It seemed like the sign marked the beginning of a dirt trail leading to the bluff. Another quick glance at the tracking app—Tessa remained in the same spot.

A crunching noise made him pause. He shoved his phone in his pocket, got up, and swept his surroundings with the flashlight. Nobody around, but maybe a nocturnal animal had made the noise.

He trained the flashlight's beam down on the ground, lest Julian detect him. Even with the downward light, darkness swallowed him up. He climbed up the steep path gingerly. He didn't want to trip and break a bone.

The tree branches rustled. The flowing river gave off a low shush. Why had Julian chosen to meet here? It was pitch dark at the moment, but he imagined a gorgeous view of the river in the afternoon. Maybe from Historic Folsom, where Alice had made the phone call, she and Julian had proceeded here. Alice would like the water, and she loved watching birds. The weather was perfect. If they'd arrived here in the afternoon to enjoy the view, it made sense that they'd decided to stay put.

Suddenly, a loud screech followed by a shrill cry—Alice's voice.

Fuck! Domingo scrambled up the hill. Every fiber of his body had moved into a state of ultra-alertness. Any kind of trouble transformed him into a fighting machine. *Julian, you bastard, I'm coming for you.*

CHAPTER 32

Domingo crested the bluff and turned off the flashlight as soon as he heard Julian's voice. The world suddenly plunged into darkness, but he couldn't risk being spotted. He crouched behind a tree, panting from the uphill climb.

"Are you really going to just stand there, babe? There's so much I want to tell you." Julian's voice rang out in the stillness of the night. He and Alice sat by a weird-looking tree that leaned out toward the river. On Julian's right, a flashlight lay on the ground, producing a wedge of glare in the direction of Tessa, who was about five feet away.

A high-pitched ruckus erupted from the river. Alice shrieked again.

"That's just the geese." Julian rubbed her shoulder.

That explained the scream Domingo heard a few minutes ago. He inched forward to get a better view.

Julian and Alice sat under the leaning tree. They both faced the river; their legs dangled over the cliff! One false move and they could fall about sixty or seventy feet down to the river. How come Alice wasn't freaking out as she sat on the precipice? Maybe it was Lover Boy's knack for making a girl feel safe. Perhaps the cover of the night helped too. It hid the immense gap between where they sat and the rocky riverbank below.

Tessa, on the other hand, was well aware of the danger or she wouldn't be standing a good distance from them. She was carrying a tote bag in her right hand and a flashlight in her left. Her purse hung from her right shoulder.

Both Alice and Julian were facing the river. Domingo couldn't see Alice's face, but she wore a jacket and jeans. At least she was warm.

"Julian, let's continue this talk at home. Can we go home now?" Tessa aimed her flashlight at the weird-looking tree.

Holy crap. Half the tree's massive roots were exposed and hung from the ridge. The tree looked like it was about to jump off the bluff.

"Can you please help Alice get up and let her come to me?" Tessa pointed her flashlight at Alice's walker and scanned the landscape beyond the leaning tree.

Domingo could make out other trees, ghostlike in the silvery dark. No other people around.

"I doubt you'll talk to me again after this." Julian moved his free hand back and forth, gesturing *come here.*

Tessa shook her head. "I'll stay here." She was wearing the same outfit she wore at home: a sweater, leggings, and ankle boots.

The wind whistled. The sound of crickets grew louder.

"Are you cold?" asked Julian. "You want my jacket?"

Domingo wondered if a gun was tucked underneath Julian's leather jacket. He hoped he wouldn't have to use his Glock.

"No, thanks. I'm fine." Tessa set down her things and plopped onto the dirt.

"You asked me if I meant to leave you behind in the desert," said Julian. "Remember asking me that?"

"It was a silly question. Just forget it, okay?"

"Well, I'm going to come clean now." He glanced at her with a dull smile. "When I first heard your dad's car horn blaring, I knew there must be an accident. I wanted to steal whatever I could, but the coyote showed up. And after I chased it away, you came out of the blue. *You* got in my way too." He kept his gaze straight ahead across the river. "I thought of just . . . you know . . . getting rid of you. A little girl—how hard can it be? Mamaita's safety depended on my success as Oldie's scout. And you were going to screw up my mission."

"So why didn't you get rid of me?" Tessa's voice cracked. "Why didn't you kill me when you had the chance?"

"Because you cried."

"What?"

He gave her a somber smile. "You cried so hard, and you held me so tight. You wouldn't let go. I couldn't bear to hurt you."

Alice squirmed.

"Julian, you're upsetting my sister."

"I told Alice how you dumped me in Mexico City. That was cold of you."

Tessa drew her knees up in front of her. "Leave her out of this."

"You know what Tio told me?"

"I don't want to hear it. Please let Alice come to me."

Julian kept talking, his voice dropping to a mumble. Domingo could barely hear it, but he picked up two words—*marry* and *kill*. Could it be that Tio had told Julian *Either you marry Tessa, or you kill her*? Julian had been so impatient to talk to Tessa on the phone but had then waited until nighttime to see her. Was it because he was going to kill her? Domingo fingered the gun in his waistband.

"I don't care about Tio," snapped Tessa.

Alice began to sob, which prompted Julian to whisper to her. That told Domingo he was right about Tio's sinister advice to Julian. Why else would Alice cry?

Tessa got up. "Please let my sister come to me now. I have the Frida Kahlo picture. This is what you want, right?" She extended the tote bag.

Domingo remembered the framed reprint of a Frida Kahlo self-portrait, Julian's gift to Tessa in Mexico City. Why was she returning it to him?

Julian didn't even glance at Tessa. After calming down Alice, he faced the dense darkness across the river. Domingo scooted to his right, peering down below. It was too dark, but he could hear the water.

"Julian, let Alice come to me," pleaded Tessa, her hand with the tote bag still extended.

At last, Julian pushed himself up, picked up his flashlight, and faced her. He smirked. "Are we doing the exchange now?"

Exchange? Domingo's thoughts hurtled in all directions. Had Julian kidnapped Alice to get the picture back from Tessa? Why? It was just a museum souvenir. It couldn't have cost more than one hundred bucks. What was the picture's hidden value? The very word *hidden* brought clarity to his senses and cleared all the fuzz in his mind. The tunnel blueprint, which was on a piece of paper, must be hidden behind the picture. Tessa had been keeping it safe for her ex-boyfriend without knowing it. And when Tessa refused to see Julian or even answer his texts and phone calls, he was forced to take the extreme measure of kidnapping Alice. Now Alice's safety depended on the blueprint.

Julian's back was to Alice, but the poor woman would never be able to move fast enough around him to escape. Should Domingo let the exchange take place and hope for the best? Would Julian keep his end of the bargain and let Alice go?

A terrible scenario flashed in Domingo's head. Alice was only one shove away from a fatal fall. Tessa wasn't too far from a similar fate. Julian could take the blueprint and push both sisters down the cliff. His heart bottomed out, but only for a moment. He stuck the flashlight in his jeans pocket and crawled to his left without a noise. He would move around Tessa, past Julian, and behind the bizarro tree, closer to Alice.

"Remove the picture from the bag and hand it to me," commanded Julian. Although he'd sounded firm, Domingo couldn't help but notice how Lover Boy's shoulders drooped. He extended his left hand while his other clutched the flashlight.

Tessa took several steps forward.

"Not too close. Stop right there," warned Julian. He took a step back himself, like someone afraid to cross enemy territory—or someone trying to control his emotions.

Only a month ago, Julian and Tessa had been so in love and entwined with each other, like they were wired together on the same circuit. Domingo could only imagine how much Julian missed Tessa and vice versa.

"Give me the picture." Julian's tone had dropped a notch, as though his resolution was fizzling out.

"No. Let Alice go first." Tessa shone her flashlight at him.

He squinted. "Put that fucking flashlight down and do exactly as I tell you!" He dragged his hand down his face. "Christ, Tessa . . . Do you think this is easy for me? Babe, don't make me yell at you."

Tessa set the light down and removed the framed picture from the tote bag. "Here, take it."

Domingo crept ahead.

Julian set his flashlight down so both his and Tessa's flashlights were on the ground; their beams cut the otherwise dimly lit night.

"I'm going to step forward." Julian held out his arm. "Don't move, okay?"

Domingo had reached the weird-looking tree without being detected. He exhaled a sigh of relief.

Tessa leaned forward to hand Julian the picture. A distance of about two feet kept them apart.

"Did I tell you the DEA ransacked my office and Tio's house? They made it appear like a burglary, but I know better. I'm glad I'd anticipated their move. You've been the best keeper of my blueprint. I'm sorry I had to do it . . . but thank you just the same."

Julian put the picture down and fidgeted with his flashlight. Only then did Domingo realize that Lover Boy's light came with a headband—a forehead lamp, which he shone on the picture.

Of course, Julian would have to make sure the blueprint was there. How long would it take him to dismantle the frame, remove the Frida Kahlo picture, and retrieve the blueprint? Sixty seconds? Longer? Either way, Domingo couldn't wait.

He crawled forward to get closer. He would grab Alice with both hands and pull her away from the precipice. He would kick Lover Boy's ass, no problemo. Here we go. *One, two—*

A blow to the back of Domingo's head sent him face down on the ground. His skull had been hit so hard that a popping sound rang out in his head.

Someone kicked him in the side, making him groan and roll onto his back. *What the fuck?* A flashlight shone on him.

"Who is this *hijo de puta*?" growled a man.

Now Domingo could see his attacker. Patricio Senior, a.k.a. Patty, was standing over him with a gun, while the son, Little Patty, was guarding Tessa. Julian grabbed Alice's arm with one hand while his other hand clutched the picture. His forehead lamp shone brightly.

Where did the Patricios come from? They'd been lying in wait, apparently. Father and son were both armed. So this was the reason Julian wanted the meeting to take place at night. Maybe he had to wait for the goons. Plus, he needed the cover of darkness.

Domingo started to get up, but Patty pointed the gun at him with one hand and the flashlight with his other hand. "Stay, stay!" The bastard sounded like he was commanding a dog.

Domingo's anger frothed, but he held back. He managed to sit up.

"Sunday, you should have minded your own business," Julian needled. "You're making this twice as hard for me and the sisters." He'd stepped forward, dragging Alice with him. Now everybody was facing Julian and Alice, who both stood with their backs to the cliff and the river.

"*This* is my business," Domingo hissed. "You have the picture. Let the sisters go. If you need a hostage as insurance, I'll stay. I'm all yours." He glanced up at Patty, with his perpetually startled rooster eyes, and translated what he'd just said in Spanish.

Patty bared his teeth. In Spanish, he told Domingo to place his gun or any other weapon on the ground slowly. His freaking light was blinding Domingo. He raised his palm to shade his eyes, and that was when the idea hit him.

"All right, man. Take it easy." Domingo did as he was told, setting his Glock before him.

Tito Mando had instilled in him that he need not rely on a weapon to win. Focus, speed, and timing were more important in times like this. His uncle had never even taught him how to fire a gun. It was Joe Medina who had tutored Domingo at the shooting range. An ex-cop like Joe believed in the power of a gun. Domingo considered a firearm an insurance and a bonus but never depended on it.

He locked eyes with Tessa. She was still holding the tote bag, while her purse hung over her shoulder. Her flashlight was at her feet. Little Patty was right behind her with a pistol.

Domingo waggled his eyebrows just once. *Be prepared to run.* She flashed her eyes—yes. He fingered his flashlight, pulling it a little so it was sticking out of his cargo pants pocket.

"Kick the gun toward me," commanded Julian, training his headlamp on Domingo. "Don't get fucking cute with me."

Again, Domingo obeyed.

Julian picked up the Glock and hurled it toward the bluff.

Son of a bitch! Five hundred bucks of Domingo's hard-earned money wasted. He took a deep breath to compose himself.

Patty spoke to Julian in Spanish, then Little Patty joined in. The three of them exploded in rat-a-tat Spanish. Patty reprimanded Julian for his slowness and ineptitude, for being smitten with the gringa. If Patty and his son hadn't been here, Domingo would have beaten him. He castigated Julian for being a henpecked boyfriend. They could have taken the blueprint by breaking into Tessa's house, even if it meant shooting the heiress and the bodyguard. But no, Julian had been too damn nice to do it.

Julian called the Patricios idiots who owed their jobs to Tio. He threatened to get them fired. Little Patty only wanted to finish this tedious job and haul ass. *Rapido*, hurry, he'd said more than once.

Patty told them both to shut up. He turned to Domingo, and in Spanish, he ordered him to put his hands up and turn around, with his back toward the river. Patty swayed the flashlight in his left hand when he commanded, "*Ahora.*"

Domingo pivoted around while Julian and Alice moved so their positions had been reversed. The cliff and the river were behind Domingo. Everyone else was facing him.

Patty, only about three feet from Domingo, waved the gun in a gesture meaning *backward.*

Domingo heeded. His face grew clammy as his adrenaline surged. The motherfucker was going to push him down the ravine without touching him. Make it appear like a suicide or an accidental fall. *Like hell.* He pulled the flashlight from his pocket and shone it squarely in Patty's eyeballs, momentarily blinding him.

He rushed at the man, toppling him down. Patty dropped the light.

"*Mierda!*" yelled Little Patty. Tessa had stomped full force on his foot before running away with her flashlight.

While Patty was sprawled, Domingo straddled his chest and struck his wrist with a swift karate chop to disarm him. Domingo had neutralized Patty and snatched up the bastard's gun in a matter of milliseconds. He pistol-whipped the ugly mug.

Alice screamed, stopping Domingo dead in his tracks. He jerked his head toward her, catching sight of Julian lunging at Little Patty. Lover Boy had let go of Alice and the picture to stop Little Patty from chasing Tessa. The two men traded jabs, their heads close together like rams locking horns.

In the few seconds of Domingo's distraction, Patty Senior headbutted him weakly in the chest, followed by flailing punches in his face. The man, still hurting from being pistol-whipped, fought like a drunk. Domingo drove the heel of his left palm into Patty's face and brought down the gun's butt to his head. Not once but three times. The last one finally knocked the wind out of Patty's sails. Blood dribbled from his scalp to his face.

Adrenaline hummed in Domingo's head. He turned Patty over, took out a couple of zip ties, and restrained his hands and feet. He seized the man's gun, a Beretta with an eight-round magazine for nine-millimeter bullets. He tucked it in his pocket for safekeeping until he could surrender it to the cops.

Julian had just pummeled the shit out of Little Patty. He was panting, staggering toward Alice. His headlamp was on the ground. "Are you okay?" He touched her arm.

As much as Domingo hated Julian's guts, he had to give it to Lover Boy for choosing to protect Alice and Tessa from his own cronies.

Three flashlights lay on the ground, their beams shining sideways.

Domingo picked up his own flashlight. On his right, just a few feet away, was the prize—the Frida Kahlo picture hiding the tunnel blueprint. He raised his gaze, his eyes falling on Julian, who had just noticed the same thing. Domingo's pulse jumped.

Julian's face lit up the way a cut power line sparked. His life depended on the blueprint.

Domingo dove for the picture at the same time as Julian. They ended up entangled, Julian on top of him, but he managed to kick the picture, which landed near the cliff's edge.

Julian flipped over and began crawling, elbows first, toward the picture. Domingo, still down, grabbed Julian's legs and pulled him back. He tried to shake off Domingo, kicking and swinging his arms like a fish out of water.

In the background, Alice yelped.

Domingo held on to Julian, pinning him down with his body. They rolled together in a struggle, closer to the picture—and the precipice and the certainty of a free fall. The dread in Domingo's gut bloomed, making him vulnerable for a split second, and Julian managed to get on top of him and reared back to thrust a fist into Domingo's face.

The blow stung, but he took it and allowed Julian to throw another punch and another. Let the fucker think he was winning as he braced himself for his next move. *Now!* He blocked Julian's next punch with his forearm.

Julian's face registered surprise, just before Domingo's counterpunch nicked Julian's chin. It hadn't hurt Julian, but it made him tilt his head back, and Domingo grabbed Julian's neck with both hands, squeezing his throat tight until his eyes popped and his mouth opened.

Julian's arms flailed, a useless attempt to hit Domingo, who was pressing his hands with such force he would surely break his thumbs.

Tessa snuck into view behind Julian with a flashlight in her hand. She raised her arm and struck Julian's head with it.

Julian fell like a cut tree on top of Domingo, loosening his stranglehold. Domingo found himself trapped inside Julian's bear hug, which could smother the life out of him. Julian was taller and bigger.

Everything he'd ever learned about fighting from the bottom position came back to him as he wrenched away, using his elbows to create a gap big enough to slacken Julian's embrace. He drove the crown of his skull against the side of Julian's neck and his shoulder toward his chest to open his guard. Then he brought his knees together to slam the man's gut. He broke free. Now he rolled sideways, from shoulder blade to shoulder blade, and ended up on all fours, panting, only a few feet from Julian, who was also on his hands and knees.

Domingo had almost killed Julian with his bare hands. If Tessa had arrived even a second later, he would have continued to tighten his grip around Julian's neck for the inevitable result. The thought chilled his heart.

Julian made a wheezing sound as he touched his throat, as though to make sure it was still there.

They faced each other, both crouching in a stalemate. Julian was about a foot away from the drop-off.

"Stop it!" Tessa's voice boomed. She was on her knees beside Alice, who sat on the ground. "I called the cops. It's over, Julian."

Julian blinked and sat up, his eyes on Tessa. "It was over for me since the day I met you. Tio warned me the rich little white girl would be the end of me."

Domingo jumped to his feet and snatched up the Frida Kahlo picture.

Julian also rose.

Domingo drew Patty's gun and aimed it at Julian. "Don't move!"

Julian didn't even glance at Domingo. He was talking to Tessa alone. "When my white parents abandoned me, Mexicans cared for me. Raul and Maria Beltran are my parents. I *am* their son, and like them, I *am* Mexican—if not by the color of my skin, then in mind, heart, and soul." Julian's eyes blazed, wide and beautiful and wounded.

Tessa stood up, wrapped her arms around herself, her hair billowing in the breeze, her flashlight shining sideways. This was the stuff that had melted her heart and made her fall head over heels with Lover Boy.

"You're a white man with a brown heart. Do you know how ironic that sounds?" Domingo aimed the Beretta at Julian's chest. "Thousands of Mexicans risk their lives crossing the border illegally to taste a crumb of the American dream, but here you are—a privileged white male—pretending to be a Mexican."

"Sunday, please put that gun down," said Tessa.

Domingo's face stung. His upper lip was busted, and he spat blood. At least his fingers were intact, though raw. He set the weapon on the ground but held on to the picture.

"I don't expect anybody to understand how I feel." He waved dismissively at Domingo. Then he turned once again to Tessa. "When I sleep, I dream of you in Spanish. And when I wake up in the morning, I think of you in Spanish. This is who I am. I lied about many things, but I never lied when I said I love you."

"Wow, you're smooth." Domingo raised the picture. "All for this, right?"

In an instant, Julian's expression turned fierce. Not that it would stop Domingo from pushing the guy's buttons. "I can accept that you identify as a Mexican. But why are you working for a drug cartel?" Domingo shifted in place. "Building a high-tech underground tunnel for a cartel is entirely different from pretending to be a Mexican. The drugs you'll be smuggling into the US will kill people and destroy millions of lives. I can't accept that."

"I don't want to work for the fucking cartel! Can't you see I'm doing this for Tio? He *believes* in me!" Julian jabbed his forefinger at Domingo. "Where would I be without Tio or Papi and Mamaita? What would I be without the Mexicans who took pity on me, huh?"

"Tio believes in you like an investor waiting to cash out," countered Domingo. "When the cartel crashes, he's going to sell you out fast, like any panic-stricken investor. Tio doesn't care about you. You know how I know this? Because he made sure you willingly cut off ties with the two people in the world who love you unconditionally—Raul and Maria Beltran." He raised the picture. "Give this up, Julian. Choose your parents over Tio. Choose the woman who's loved you since she was a little girl over the cartel. Cooperate with the DEA. It's not too late."

"Shut up!" Julian rubbed his eye with his knuckle, which made Domingo wonder if he was crying. "You don't know a damn thing about me."

Tessa stepped forward with the flashlight in her hand. "Julian, I want to talk. But first, can you please move away from the edge. Come to me." She extended her free hand.

Julian coughed as he pawed at his windpipe. He wiped the dirt off his face with the back of his hand. To Tessa, he said, "You really want to talk?"

"Yes." She pointed her flashlight down on the ground. Her free hand remained outstretched, waiting. "You're not alone. We're in this together. Whatever troubles you have, we'll find a way out. I'll always be at your side."

Julian neither touched Tessa's hand nor stepped away from the ridge. He hung his head. "Sometimes I wish I could simply disappear from the face of the earth."

"Please don't say that." She took another step forward.

A rustling emanated from the dark, behind Domingo.

"DEA! Everyone, freeze!"

They all glanced at the newcomer—a muscular Black man. DEA Special Agent Jim Havant had arrived, his gun drawn.

An enormous hush descended. The air bristled with tension. Domingo glanced at Tessa, then Julian. *They love each other,* came the thought, as sure as his heart galloped. And it saddened him.

A tremendous honking erupted, followed by the wild flapping of wings—the geese in the river. Domingo got a jolt.

Alice shrieked, which made Tessa turn toward her sister.

At the same time, Julian twisted his head back, startled by the cacophony of noises.

When Tessa shifted her attention back to Julian, she warned, "Watch out, Julian!"

Too late. His left foot slid back—a small step in a split of a second. And then, he was gone.

"Juliaaan!" She rushed to the ledge, Domingo and Havant on her heels.

Domingo and Tessa knelt down, palms flat on the ground, and peeked below. The craggy rocks and the foliage sprouting from the side of the bluff looked like an ancient catacomb—massive, forbidding, and silent.

"Julian!" Tessa was sobbing, shoulders heaving.

Havant was barking on his phone, presumably talking to a 911 dispatcher. He was giving directions to the bluff and describing Julian's fall.

A stiff wind whipped the trees. It blew Domingo's hair and brought gooseflesh to his skin. He got up, his senses sharp as fangs. The sense of relief would come much later, much slower.

Havant turned around and got busy restraining Little Patty with real handcuffs made of steel. The agent single-handedly moved the

Patricios side by side. The two had regained consciousness, judging by the explosion of Spanish cusswords.

Domingo picked up the Frida Kahlo picture and shambled toward Alice. "Are you okay?"

"Yes." Alice was slumped on the ground. There was nothing she could sit on. She swiped her hand under her nose. "I want . . . want to . . . go . . . home."

He bent down to look into her face. "Okay. I'll go get your sister." He plodded back to the edge of the cliff where Tessa was. His adrenaline had dissolved into utter exhaustion, and he stopped for a beat to take in his environment.

The high elevation offered a full vista of the blanket of pinprick stars. At any other time, this could have been a beautiful night. But instead, a man was dead—no way Julian could have survived the fall—and a young woman's heart was shattered.

Tessa sat hunched on the ground, as though the weight of the world had just dropped onto her shoulders.

"I'm sorry for your loss." Domingo touched her back.

Julian might not have deserved her love, but Domingo respected her grief just the same. He understood what it meant to love someone for as long as Tessa had loved Julian. He himself had yet to recover from his ancient love for Monica Reed.

She gazed up at him, sniffling and wiping her tears with her fingers. "I didn't get a chance to tell him that I wanted to marry him after all. I meant it when I told him I'd stand by him. I can't believe it—one moment he was facing me, the next moment he wasn't anymore. When my parents died, I realized life was short. But I never thought it would take only a millisecond for me to lose the man I loved."

"It was terrible that you saw Julian fall, but he was falling long before tonight," said Domingo.

She pressed the heels of her hands against her eyes, trying to stop her tears.

Domingo once asked Cheryl what Tessa's weakness was, and they both agreed it was Julian Alondra. Even Tessa's therapist had called Julian her "addiction." Julian might have been Tessa's weakness, but it didn't mean she was weak. She'd searched for Julian, found him, and loved him for what he was, though it had meant pain and risk. In Domingo's book, that was strength.

A loud squawk made both of them turn to the river, but it was too dark to see anything. The honking and flapping grew intense as though the geese were at war.

"You're too close to the edge." He extended his hand. "Come on, Alice is waiting."

Tessa latched on to his hand, and he helped her get up.

They loped toward Alice, who fell inside Tessa's arms. Tessa hugged her sister tightly, assuring her that everything would be all right. Grammy and Susie were waiting for them at home.

Up above, lights flickered, accompanied by the thwack-thwack-thwack sound of a helicopter. They all gazed up. A police siren wailed nearby. More law enforcement people.

Domingo picked up the Frida Kahlo picture and Julian's headlamp. This was the longest day of his life and still going. Fatigue washed over him, but he forced himself to act.

He wore the headlamp, shone it on the picture, and finally removed the blueprint hidden behind Frida Kahlo's selfie.

CHAPTER 33

Thanksgiving Day

You Ain't Dora the Explorer

I don't have kids, but I've heard of the Nickelodeon show Dora the Explorer, *about the little Latina who loves adventures. Don't believe any coyote who says you can be a grown-up version of Dora. The sales pitch goes something like this.*

Coyote: *Would you like to go to the great US of A?*

You: *Yeah, but I can't afford your fee.*

Coyote: *My offer's completely free! You just have to carry a backpack for my boss.*

You: *A backpack?*

Coyote: *La mochila, like in* Dora the Explorer. *You got kids? Ask them. They love Backpack, Dora's special buddy.*

You: *What's in the backpack?*

Coyote: *Nothing to worry about.*

You: *What would I do exactly?*

Coyote: *Very easy. I'll tell you where to go and when. I'll give you water, food, and the backpack. My cousin, Hernan, will be your team leader. There will be about twenty of you,* mochileros *and* mochileras, *in your team. It will be a great desert adventure!*

You: *Will Hernan take care of us? How old is he?*

***Coyote:** He's fifteen, but very mature for his age. Of course he'll take care of you. So we got a deal?*

In this dialogue, you have to read between the lines. Here's what you need to understand. The backpack will be filled with heroin, meth, or fentanyl, or all three. Hernan, the teenage migrant smuggler, will most certainly NOT take care of you. He will show you the way across the desert, but you have to do all the dangerous work.

You'll carry the illegal substance, stay alive throughout the grueling trek, and not get caught by Border Patrol or shot to death by American vigilantes. That, my friend, isn't an adventure but a death wish. And you ain't a grown-up Dora the Explorer but Dora the Illegal Crosser, whose ass will get hauled off to an immigration detention center at best or whose head will get decapitated by the cartel at worst. So if you get an offer from a coyote, you have only one thing to do. In the words of Nancy Reagan—JUST SAY NO.

◆ ◆ ◆

Domingo had just finished writing a page of his book when it was time to eat again. Thanksgiving Day at Charito's house meant an eating marathon that began at noon and stopped only when everyone dropped from exhaustion or indigestion or both. That could be any time between six o'clock in the evening and midnight.

Charito, Mamang's goddaughter, was two years younger than Domingo. She was the daughter Mamang could only wish for—a physical therapist happily married to a fellow Filipino physical therapist. The clincher: Charito's precocious nine-year-old daughter always reminded Mamang of the grandchildren Domingo had failed to provide for her so far.

Domingo and Mamang had been spending every Turkey Day at Charito's house for ten years now. Each Thanksgiving celebration showcased everything his mother wished Domingo had: a career that didn't involve chasing criminals, and a spouse and a child.

Today, however, he tried not to dwell on his mother's "Charito envy." At least Mamang was healthy and able to spend this weekend outside Vista Nursing and Rehabilitation Center. In addition to hosting the daylong food-a-thon, Charito planned to take Mamang shopping at an outlet mall in New Jersey tomorrow and watch a Rockettes show at Radio City on Saturday. God bless Charito for assuming the tasks that Domingo was simply not up to.

It was only three thirty in the afternoon. Time for coffee, pumpkin pie, rice cakes, leche flan, and other diabetes-inducing desserts. While everyone ate and watched football on TV in the living room, Domingo slinked to the stoop at the front of the house to call Tessa and Alice. The gray November sky blanketed a cold afternoon. The sharp breeze felt like a slap on his face.

They'd agreed in advance to video call through Zoom so they could all see each other despite a distance of twenty-eight hundred miles between Folsom, California, and Brooklyn, New York. It was only twelve thirty in the afternoon in California. Tessa and Alice were using a laptop, while Domingo was on his smartphone.

The sisters' faces were close together, filling the phone screen. "We haven't eaten yet. We're waiting for our cousins," said Tessa. "Grammy hired a caterer. I mean, there are eighteen of us right now, and three more are coming. It's too much work for her. How about you . . . How's your Thanksgiving?"

"It's the best kind—I'm a guest, and all I did was bring a bottle of cabernet. I get to eat lunch, dinner, and all the desserts I want until I drop. It's the very definition of freeloading."

The sisters chuckled. Tessa and Domingo exchanged news about their jobs for the next few minutes.

"How are you, Alice? Do you still like the hammock?" asked Domingo.

She nodded a big yes, her neck wobbling.

The last time Domingo had spoken to Alice alone, on the same night Julian had died, she'd said that Julian had showed up in Grammy's front yard while Susie was indoors making lunch. Julian had arrived without the Patricios. He'd invited her to drive to Historic Folsom for some frozen yogurt. When Alice asked to call Tessa so they could all go together, Lover Boy had simply scooped Alice up from the hammock and put her in a white car. He'd also grabbed Alice's walker and left a note for Tessa in the hammock. "Your sister will join us later," he'd assured Alice.

Alice had realized that she'd been kidnapped. She'd known enough not to make a fuss, lest Julian got mad at her. She'd left her cell phone in her room, but the antique phone in Beverly's shop in Historic Folsom had given her hope.

Julian had sipped coffee, and Alice had eaten a cup of pistachio yogurt at the yogurt shop. All she could think of was the accessible antique phone next door. It had been important to stay close to Beverly's shop, so after yogurt, she'd asked Julian if she could have a sandwich at the deli on the other side of Beverly's store. Julian had gladly taken her there.

When Julian had used the restroom at the deli, Alice had finally gone to Beverly's shop to call Domingo. She'd memorized his phone number, bless her heart. She'd been about to call 911 when Julian had caught her in the act. She hadn't lied when she'd denied calling the cops.

It had been a leisurely outing until the Patricios had showed up later that afternoon. Julian and Alice had even visited a pet store to see the puppies and the cockatiels. They'd hung out at the Fair Oaks Bluff to watch the sunset. Alice had used her walker until they got to the bluff, where Julian had simply carried her like a princess. He'd been sweet to her as always. Just as Domingo had theorized, Julian hadn't made any attempt to hide Alice.

But then the Patricios had arrived at the bluff, and they'd argued quite a bit with Julian. Alice had felt relieved when Julian finally called Tessa to do the exchange—the Frida Kahlo picture for Alice.

Tessa brushed the hair from Alice's eyeglasses. "We were just outside, watching the hummingbirds and enjoying the hammock."

Alice wore her hair short. As for Tessa, something had changed. It was as though a rosebud had blossomed into a diamond. She was as stunning as ever, but no longer fragile—more like a gem that could cut glass. Yep, she'd grown harder from her heartbreak. He couldn't fathom her love or obsession or whatever it was. She might as well be a widow at the age of twenty-seven. She had assumed the role of a bereaved wife, from the filing of Julian's death certificate to burying him and taking care of his possessions.

Lou Harold had surmised that Julian's choice of Fair Oaks Bluff—at night when any intervention would have been impossible—attested to Julian's plan to end his life, perhaps as a last resort if he failed to retrieve the blueprint. Tessa had rejected this theory flat out.

The memory of Julian's last few minutes burned in Domingo's brain. Julian had jerked his head toward the explosive geese noise. It had been the crucial moment: He'd glanced back when his brain had commanded the foot to step in the same direction as his gaze—the millisecond he'd stepped back onto nothing. The same principle applied to driving. A driver steered the wheel in the same direction as his gaze. That was why it was best to keep one's eyes on the road.

The Patricios had been arrested on the spot by DEA Special Agent Havant and the cops, who had come ten minutes after Havant had arrived. The father and son had been charged with illegal possession of the firearms they'd carried that night. A charge of transporting narcotics in the past had also been added since.

The authorities had found Julian's body within an hour of their search at the bluff. Had it been a suicide or an accidental fall? It might have been somewhere in between. Julian had been ready to die, judging by his lack of fear of the precipice, but he'd also hoped for redemption.

Lou had based his suicide theory on Julian's last words: *"Sometimes I wish I could simply disappear from the face of the earth."* But Lou hadn't seen Julian's tender expression when he uttered those words or heard the rueful lilt in his voice. Julian's tremendous affection for Tessa had been evident from his gaze alone.

Domingo didn't mention any of these thoughts. "Tessa, I never had the chance to say thanks before I left, so thank you for saving me."

"What do you mean?" She narrowed those green eyes. "I'm the one who owes you a great deal."

"If you hadn't stepped in . . . well, who knows where I would be today?" What he meant to say was, if Tessa hadn't struck Julian with the flashlight while Domingo was strangling him, he would be a bona fide murderer today, comrade in arms of the BTK Strangler and the Hillside Strangler. His motive would be scrutinized in court for months of protracted litigation. It had been pure instinct for survival, the closest he'd ever gotten to killing someone with his bare hands.

Alice nudged Tessa, or maybe she was just swaying her head, but her movement stopped the conversation. They waited for her to chime in.

"Tes . . . Tessa . . . prevented you . . . from . . . strang . . . gling . . . Joo . . . lian."

"Yep. Thank you for saving me."

"Oh my God." Tessa palmed her forehead. "That night was surreal. Alice and I are in therapy. We both need to learn some coping skills."

Alice nodded. "I miss him."

"Me too." Tessa touched her sister's arm. "His absence hurts so much."

So there was no avoiding this dicey subject. Despite everything Julian had done, the sisters still adored him. They were hanging on to the best parts of his memory—the chivalry, the charm, and the doting quality underneath the shady dealings and all the lies.

"How was Julian's funeral?" he finally asked.

"It went smoothly. A dozen of my relatives came. Mr. and Mrs. Beltran really wanted to come, but my lawyer advised against it. ICE is itching to round up undocumented immigrants. I buried Julian in Ravine, instead of here in Folsom, so they can visit his grave whenever they can, preferably when ICE isn't around. My lawyer's working on transferring Julian's assets to the Beltrans. It's going to be tricky because of their status, but I know it's what Julian would have wanted."

Alice rested her head on Tessa's shoulder. Was she going to cry?

"I'm sorry I couldn't attend the funeral," he said.

"I understand." Tessa put her arm around her sister's shoulders. "You've gone above and beyond what was expected of you. Any news from Lou?"

"I talked to him three days ago. At last, he was able to confiscate Julian's computer in Mexico City. He was fighting red tape from both sides of the border. Now that he's got the computer, he's going to nail down Tio and work his way up the cartel hierarchy."

That fateful night of Julian's death, Domingo had handed the blueprint—a technical drawing on white paper with blue lines—to Agent Havant. Julian normally used CAD software for his work, but he'd diverted to old-fashioned paper to dupe whoever had been on his trail. The blueprint was a big deal. Obtaining it had upended the drug cartel's secret-tunnel project. The bad guys would have to start from scratch, if at all.

Alice cast her gaze down. All the negative talk about Julian was probably depressing her.

"Hey, Alice. I have a new joke. Wanna hear it?" he asked.

She trained her gaze at the webcam.

"Knock, knock," he began.

"Who . . . who's . . . there?"

"Lou Harold."

Alice beamed her lopsided smile. Lou had thanked Tessa and Alice in person a few days after he got the blueprint, so Alice knew him. "Lou . . . Har . . . old . . . who?"

"Long, loose hair and old—yes, it's Lou Harold!"

They all chuckled.

Domingo pressed his forefinger to his lips. "That's our secret, okay? Or Lou's gonna kick my ass."

In the background, the sound of a knock on the door. Tessa glanced over her shoulder. "I think we have to go now. It's time to eat turkey."

"Okay. It's really nice to catch up with you both."

"Same here."

They exchanged a "Happy Thanksgiving" wish and said their goodbyes. After Domingo hung up, hooting and laughter erupted inside Charito's house. He glanced at the door, but he wasn't ready to rejoin Mamang and the others. He tucked his phone in his jacket pocket, then rubbed his hands to stave off a chill. He enjoyed sitting on the stoop as he watched people, his favorite pastime.

A group of Orthodox Jews in distinct-looking black trousers, jackets, and hats were walking on the sidewalk. Across the street, an old lady shuffled with her Yorkie, which was barking at the men in black. Cars streamed by at twenty miles per hour in this residential area.

A flock of chirruping birds made him gaze up. Tepid sunlight struggled to pierce the darkening sky. What a pity about Tessa and Julian. They could have been soulmates. He blamed their tragic love story on poor timing. The couple had reconnected too late, long after Julian had already committed himself to Tio and the cartel. Julian's fierce loyalty had molded his life and caused his death.

All this philosophizing brought to mind a famous quote from *The Dark Knight*. Lover Boy hadn't been the man Girl Boss deserved. He'd been the hero she wanted. A lame-ass paraphrase, but true. Now that he'd succumbed to introversion, he couldn't help but see Monica in his head, her sad image as persistent as his regret. What a lonely thing, to possess a river of love that couldn't flow. But if all rivers eventually found their way to the ocean, there was hope for him yet. Maybe he would accept Elena's invitation to speak to her students on career day. Maybe he would ask her out after that.

A plump pigeon landed a few feet away from him. It was cooing and chilling out on the paved sidewalk, something the happy hummingbirds and beautiful scrub jays in Alice's front yard would never do. Those California birds hung out on well-stocked feeders and leafy trees, not bare pavements.

The bluish-gray pigeon waddled all the way to the middle of the street. A true New Yorker, this bird. At home on blacktops or in your face, and not afraid of traffic. When a car zipped by, the pigeon burst into flight. Yep, just like any New Yorker with the keenest sense of self-preservation. Just like him too.

Prevailing over Julian and his demons—the whiteness he'd denounced and the brownness he'd craved—was no badge of honor. It was sheer survival.

Domingo's conscience was clear, and yet he sometimes woke up in the wee hours with guilt clogging his throat. Could he have prevented Julian's death? Sure, if the man hadn't chosen a cliff as a meeting place. If only Julian had chosen love over loyalty, Tessa over Tio, the present over the past. Domingo would never understand some things in life. Julian Alondra, a.k.a. Jules Alexander, was one of those things.

His butt was freezing. Time to go inside. He got up. When he gazed up one more time, the clouds parted. The sun glimmered for a glorious moment before the day surrendered to dusk.

ACKNOWLEDGMENTS

For immigrants, identity is inherently intertwined with a sense of belongingness. The more they feel accepted in their new country, the stronger their sense of identity. For some, dropping the old social identity is a price they pay willingly for a chance to forge a new, more acceptable identity in their new country.

I wrote the character of Julian Alondra to explore the notions of self and identity, in particular the concept of transracial identity. The word *transracial* originally referred to transracial adoption of a child whose race is different from the child's adoptive family. It's often used to describe children of color adopted by white families.

The word took on a new meaning when the news about Rachel Dolezal broke in 2015. Dolezal was born white but identified as Black, lived as a Black woman, and became the president of the NAACP's Spokane (Washington) chapter.

In 2017, a white man from Florida named Ja Du also made news. He identified as Filipino and wanted to change his gender. He said he was drawn to Filipino culture early in life.

I wrote the first draft of this novel in 2016. The public debate on transracial identity hasn't changed since then. The questions remain the same. Is transracial identity real or a con? Is it a psychological disorder? Is it cultural appropriation? Are transracials running away from their white privilege by refusing to accept it? I have no answers to these questions, but I hope this novel sparked your curiosity.

This book would still be sitting in my computer today if not for the help of two extraordinary women I'm blessed to know—my literary agent, Maria Napolitano of KT Literary, and my editor, Chantelle Aimée Osman. I'm grateful beyond telling.

All my thanks to Megha Parekh, editorial director, for ensuring a smooth transition and maintaining the momentum after Chantelle left.

I also extend my deepest gratitude to the following:

- Charlotte Herscher, Amazon Publishing developmental editor. Like a great surgeon, you have a light and nimble touch but an astounding impact. I feel very lucky to work with you.
- Corinne DeMaagd, friend, author, and editor. It's my privilege and pleasure that you're always the first to read my manuscripts.
- Ploy Siripant. This book's theme is not the easiest to translate visually—hats off for a remarkable book cover!
- Jenna Justice, copyeditor. Please know that your work has made mine a lot more efficient and effective. I'm very grateful.
- Miranda Gardner, Amazon Publishing production manager. Given my previous experience with small presses, I can honestly say that having you on my team is a privilege and luxury.
- Rachel McClure, proofreader. Thank you for being my last line of defense.
- Elsa Klingensmith, cultural research reader. I learned so much from your thoughtful insights, and for that I'm grateful.
- Andrew George and Allyson Cullinan. As a former PR and marketing person myself, I appreciate your work more than I can express.
- Crime Writers of Color, especially the founders Kellye Garrett, Gigi Pandian, and Walter Mosley. Thank you for creating a most welcoming and supportive writing community.

As always, special thanks to my family—Vince and Nina—for the inspiration, love, and support. I can't do this without you.

ABOUT THE AUTHOR

Cindy Fazzi is a Filipino American writer and former Associated Press reporter who has worked as a journalist in the Philippines, Taiwan, and the United States. The first book in the Domingo the Bounty Hunter series, *Danger No Problem* (formerly titled *Multo*), was a finalist in the Best Literary category of the 2024 Silver Falchion Award. Her historical novel, *My MacArthur*, was published by Sand Hill Review Press in 2018. Her short stories have appeared in *TOUGH*, *Snake Nation Review*, *Copperfield Review Quarterly*, and *SNReview*. She's also written articles for the Daily Beast, *Electric Literature*, *Publishers Weekly*, and *Writer's Digest*. To learn more, visit the author's website at www.cindyfazzi.com.